DEVIL DRAGON
A MONSTER NOVEL
BY
DEBORAH SHELDON

SEVERED PRESS
HOBART TASMANIA

DEVIL DRAGON

ISBN: 978-1-925493-97-9

FOR ALLEN AND HARRY

PROLOGUE

The giant lizard, splay-legged and heavy, plodded through the eucalypt forest. After waking in its burrow that morning, it had smelled prey on the breeze: something alive, warm and sizeable. The lizard had been hunting for about half an hour. Despite hunger pangs, it walked slowly, conserving energy for the kill.

In the glades, the summer sun took the chill from the air. The forest came to life. Birds started to warble and chirp. Small mammals skittered through the undergrowth. A wallaby checked its course and bolted. The lizard ignored these distractions. Its slender forked tongue, gliding in and out, delivered scent molecules to the twin passages of its septum, allowing the lizard to pinpoint the prey's location with the exactitude of radar.

Near, very near.

The lizard broke into a trot. The long body undulated from side to side. Much as a freestyle swimmer moves each arm, the lizard swung each leg in a wide arc, keeping its talons clear of the ground. Its tongue tasted the air every two to three seconds, homing in, the information allowing nonstop course adjustments.

The eucalypts, wattles, native cherry trees and weeds suddenly ended at a fence. And on the other side of the wire, close enough to touch, stood the lizard's next meal: an Angus heifer. The young cow was grazing on grasses that had escaped the national park and taken root in the paddock. The lizard halted, but not soon enough. Startled at the noise of movement beside her, the heifer flinched, lifted her head and stared into the forest.

The lizard froze.

It kept its body impossibly still, without breath, as still as a tree trunk. Skin and scales blended against the greens, greys and browns of the landscape. The heifer continued to watch the forest, her ears turning this way and that.

Nothing stirred.

Reassured, she kept eating.

Cockatoos screeched through the wide hoop of sky. The farmhouse and barns lay on a faraway hilltop. In the distance, the rest of the herd fed on hay arranged at intervals across the uneven slopes and valleys of the paddock. Cabbage moths and bees zigzagged. The lizard dismissed it all; everything but the heifer.

She was a type of prey it had eaten before, larger than a pig or deer, capable of satisfying hunger for a few days. The lizard calculated the attack.

The heifer, standing almost parallel to the fence, would spot any charge with enough time to run. And a kicking hoof might cause injury. The best way to attack live prey was from the rear. Soundlessly, slowly, the lizard retreated. It circled back through the trees and edged again toward the wire fence.

It lowered its belly to the ground. With gradual shuffles of its feet, the lizard approached the fence. The heifer ate, unaware. The lizard could hear her munching on weeds; hear the occasional swish of her tail against her rump as she swatted flies. She emanated a strong, hot scent of meat. The lizard's mouth watered. It raised its head and lifted its body on both front legs. The heifer's hide shivered, dislodging a raft of flies that immediately landed again.

Lower lids rolled up to protect the lizard's eyes. It opened its mouth, put its front legs on the uppermost wire, and leaned over the fence. Saliva drooled from its scissor-like teeth. A heavy slop of dribble hit the heifer's back. Alarmed, she lifted her head. In the same instant, the lizard clamped down on her pelvis.

The heifer bellowed. Various bones snapped. Blood gushed into the lizard's gullet, exciting it, urging it to bite harder. The heifer weighed 200kg, but the lizard lifted her rear legs with ease and shook her while its jaws came together to pulverise skin, muscle, gristle and bone into paste.

Then her spine broke.

With a gasping snort, the heifer went limp. The lizard placed her on the ground but held on, waiting. Prey often faked the extent of injuries, hoping for a chance to get away. The heifer didn't move. Instead, she panted and bawled.

Frightened by her panicked noises, cattle ran toward the farmhouse and barns.

A minute passed. The lizard did not let go. Blood pumped across the grass. The heifer stopped bawling. Now she could only pant with her mouth hanging open. When she finally dropped her head, the lizard relaxed its grip.

Time to eat.

The jaws bit between the heifer's legs at the tender parts, and began to systematically tug, tug and tug at the hide until it sheared free. The lizard swallowed the chunk of hide and took another bite. Tug, tug, tug. Meat came away in a sheet. With a swipe of its foot, the lizard broke the meat from the body and gulped it down, snapping its jaws. Blood foamed at the heifer's nostrils and mouth. The lizard worried its snout into her body and pulled out organs. The heifer let out soft, distressed grunts. The lizard kept ripping and swallowing.

***

On the other side of the farm, old Noel Baines sat on his idling quad-bike, frowning at a broken wire on the fence, wondering if that dickhead of a son-in-law had remembered to buy the reel of barbed wire. The appearance of cattle galloping over the rise made Noel kick his quad-bike into gear. He spat into the dirt.

Those damn feral dogs.

Or was it pigs this time?

The Baines's family farm lay next to a national park full of feral animals. Attacks on his cattle were commonplace. Noel rode across the hilly terrain of the paddock as fast as he dared.

And then he saw it.

For a few moments, he looked at the monster but couldn't believe his eyes. He actually blinked, hard. When he looked again, the monster was still there. He grappled for his .22. The rifle fell from the quad-bike. He ran over it. Fucking hell, why was he still on the throttle? He was closer to the monster than he'd ever want to get. Noel jammed the brakes. They squealed in protest.

Reacting to the noise, the monster lifted its head from the heifer's carcass and looked straight at him. Noel hadn't gone to church since childhood, but he crossed himself—*Holy Mary, mother of God, pray for us sinners, now and at the hour of our death*—and executed a clumsy U-turn.

He kept checking over his shoulder as he rode pell-mell toward the Robinson farm next door. Kept checking long after the monster was out of sight. Kept checking even when he was safe inside the Robinson kitchen, Megan pressing a glass of whisky into his trembling hand despite the early hour. Noel couldn't tear his gaze away from the windows.

The Robinsons believed him. That was all that mattered. They believed him. He'd seen the impossible and somebody believed him.

"We ought to ring the coppers, the shooting club, any bastard with a gun," Jamie said. He had started loading the rifles as soon as Noel, stammering, had finished describing the monster. Now, Jamie lined up the firearms on the kitchen table. "Everyone in town has to know about this monster," he said. "What if it tries to eat people?"

Megan wound her hair into a hasty ponytail. "Quit flapping your gums. Let's just go kill that motherfucker."

"Okay," Noel said. "Give me a second."

He closed his eyes and drained the whisky. Neat, it burned his throat. The glass clattered against his false teeth. He couldn't stop shaking. Since that first sight of the monster, Noel's flesh goose-bumped continuously, as if fingernails were raking down an endless blackboard, on and on and on.

"Noel, are you right?" Megan said.

He opened his eyes. "Yeah, I'm right."

"Then come on."

Megan pushed a Remington 700 across the table. Noel took hold of the stock. His palm felt sweaty. When he got to his feet, he had to steady himself against the chair. Black dots swam in his vision.

1

"Here he is now," the pub owner said, and pointed.

Dr. Erin Harris turned her head. Across the room, Noel Baines stood at the open double-doors of the pub, hands on his hips, squinting, looking about for her. Erin took a moment to observe. The scattering of lunch-time patrons had stopped to stare at him, too. A few whispered together. Some grinned; others sniggered. What Noel Baines had told Erin yesterday on the phone appeared to be true: since the local paper had published his story, most of the townsfolk thought him crazy, a doddering fool.

On the contrary, the old farmer seemed robust and agile, much younger than his seventy-one years. He wore the uniform typical around here of most men and women: jeans, boots, long-sleeved button-down shirt, bush hat. Erin regretted her summer dress and sandals; she should have worn jeans. Standing up from the bar stool, she took a few steps and waved. Noel Baines tightened his mouth into a line, removed his hat and nodded at her. When he sat at the nearest empty table, he put his back to the other patrons.

Erin approached, touched the chair opposite him. "May I?"

Like a gentleman, he half-rose as she sat down. She extended her hand. Noel Baines hesitated before gripping her fingertips for a brief second, and letting go.

"Thank you for meeting with me, Mr. Baines," she said.

"Call me Noel."

"Yes, of course. Noel, I appreciate your time."

Noel called to the pub owner, "Dave, a pot. And a glass of whatever the lady's having."

"Mineral water, please," Erin added.

Noel fidgeted with the brim of his hat. Erin waited. Placing the hat over the cruet set, Noel said, "So you're the doctor from the university."

"That's right. Erin Harris."

"Hell's bells, I remember your name, I'm not a complete idiot."

She had intended to tape this conversation, but for the moment decided to keep the digital recorder in her handbag. "As soon as I saw your interview in the local paper, I knew you were telling the truth."

"I figured no one outside of town bothered to read that rag."

Erin smiled. "I do Google searches every morning on my particular topics of interest. Your interview came up. That's why I called you. As a scientist, I can investigate your story."

He shrugged. "So you know about lizards."

"Actually, I know a lot of things about reptiles in general."

"You're some kind of zookeeper?"

"No. I lecture in evolutionary biology, but herpetology is my chosen field; in reptiles, though, not amphibians. Frogs don't appeal. I study reptile evolution."

Noel raised his eyes and waved a dismissive hand.

Okay, Erin had a reasonable handle on him by now: proud, barely literate, probably a high-school dropout, suspicious of city people, white-collar professionals in particular.

"I believe your story," she said.

"I'm starting to doubt it myself."

"You saw that lizard with your own eyes."

He shot her a wounded glance. "People talk around here. Some reckon I must've been blotto at the time."

"Of course you weren't."

"No bloody way. You know how dangerous it is to ride a quad-bike, even sober?"

She hesitated. "To ride a what?"

"A quad-bike. You really don't know what that is? Well, it's kind of like a motorcycle but with four wheels. Bloody handy on a farm, but it's got a high centre of gravity and a narrow wheelbase. That makes it unstable and prone to tipping if the ground isn't dead level. If your quad-bike rolls over you, kiss your arse goodbye. Well, shit, all my paddocks have an incline. Why would I get on the grog before getting on my quad-bike?"

"You wouldn't." She smiled. "Noel, you don't have to convince me."

He sighed, gave a begrudging nod.

"That's why I wanted to meet up," she continued. "I study evolution. I'm interested in how reptiles have changed over thousands and millions of years; why some species survived, why others died out."

Noel sniffed. "Excuse my saying so, but you look more like a lady for ballet and poetry and whatnot."

Erin had experienced this countless times before: the prejudice against her from academics and lay-people alike on account of her slight frame, glasses and pale skin. She knew plenty of field herpetologists—the roughest, drunkest and most outdoorsy scientists she'd ever met—who liked to rib her for being "precious", but she considered herself a geneticist first and a lecturer second, one who had a reasonable amount of hands-on experience with reptiles, including tiger snakes, death adders and saltwater crocodiles.

She said, "I've studied Australian reptiles for a long time."

"Uh-huh," Noel said. "Only from books, I'll bet."

God, if she only had a dollar....

She regretted looking so young, almost teenaged, despite being thirty-four. The average person, like Noel Baines, typically assumed that safety in the presence of a deadly creature relied on brawn. Not so: it boiled down to knowing the inbuilt behaviours and activity patterns of an animal, the set and unvarying weaknesses and strengths determined by its DNA. From theoretical knowledge alone, Erin was certain she could overcome or outwit just about every known creature in the three orders of Australian reptiles—Testudines, Squamata and Crocodilia— however she preferred a simpler answer for her detractors.

"Occasionally," she said "the easiest way to verify an animal's diet is to manually search through their faeces. I do that all the time."

"Aw, get out." Noel frowned, smiled. "You put your hands in shit?"

"It's why I don't bite my nails."

Her standard joke. They both laughed.

The pub owner, Dave, came over with the pot of beer and glass of mineral water. "Anything else?" he said, placing the drinks on the table.

Noel shook his head. Uh-oh, Erin thought, it's past noon; he doesn't intend to stay for lunch. Noel handed Dave a note, told him to keep the change. As soon as Dave left, Erin said, "Tell me what happened."

Noel became withdrawn, sullen. "I told you already on the phone."

"A brief account. I'd like to hear the full details."

He took a long drink of beer, wiped the froth off his lip with the back of a gnarled hand. "I'm willing to talk to you for one reason only."

"Okay. Name it."

"One hundred and twenty years ago, the Baines family helped build this town. My great-grandparents set up one of the first cattle farms in the area. I've been working cattle here on this same farm ever since I was knee-high to a grasshopper." Noel stopped, swallowed the catch in his voice.

"I understand," Erin said.

"No, you don't. For the past thirty-six years, I've officiated at the Shire's annual Boxing Day rodeo. The committee passed me over this time." He took a quick drink. "You need to prove me right."

"And I will."

"You sure about that?"

"I promise. Just tell me what you saw, in as much detail as you can."

Noel huffed through closed teeth, briefly shut his eyes. Gripping both hands around his beer glass, he stared down at his drink and said, "It was last Friday morning, around seven-thirty. I was out checking the fences, like I do every week. My farm backs onto the national park. If you don't know, the park's got a big problem with feral animals—goat, deer, pig, horse, dog, fox—any pest you can name, this park is teeming with it. Some of these animals bust my fences to get at my grass and feed, or attack my stock. Happens on a regular basis."

"And you were checking your fences."

"That's right."

"And what did you see?"

Noel frowned, began to fidget with his beer glass, turning it around and around on the tabletop. "I've complained to the Shire Council about the feral animals God knows how many times, but they don't give a stuff. If the council won't allow hunting in the park, then farmers like me, whose land backs onto it, should be entitled to a tax break." Noel looked up at her. "You know how much money these ferals cost me every single month?"

Hurry up with your goddamned story, Erin thought, eager to hear only about the lizard. Instead, she said, "Oh no, that must be so frustrating."

"Too right, mate. My youngest daughter still lives at the homestead, and she's pregnant, so she's not much chop around the place anymore and neither is her husband, my dickhead son-in-law. If I don't fix the fences myself I've got to pay one of the hands and with beef prices as low as they are, I don't have much leeway."

"Of course not." Erin fidgeted in her chair. "So you were checking the fences."

He nodded. "And a bunch of my cattle came running over, all spooked. I figured it was dogs. So I drove to the back paddock to look. And when I came over the rise..." Noel licked his lips. "Like I told you before, my paddocks are pretty hilly."

"Yes, I remember."

"I didn't see anything until I came over the rise."

"So you came over the rise...and then what?"

"Yep," he said, and stared at her. "I saw it."

Erin leaned forward. "Saw what?"

"By the fence." Noel rubbed a hand across his stubbled chin, gazed out the window. "A bloody great big lizard attacking one of my heifers."

Erin's heart thrummed against her ribs, the hairs rising on her arms. "Tell me what it looked like."

"A bloody huge bastard. I could see right away by the spacing of the fence posts that it was about eight metres long from nose to tail. From the height of the posts, it stood about a metre at the shoulder, even higher when it lifted its neck." Noel shook his head, as if trying to clear it. "The monster was eating my heifer, but pecking, like how a chicken pecks at grains. Each time, it took out a chunk the size of a bloody watermelon."

"Had the lizard broken through the fence?"

"No. It was big enough to climb the fence and lean over."

"Did the lizard see you?"

"Not at first. I stopped the quad-bike. The brakes always squeal. That's when the monster looked at me." Noel rubbed at his forehead. "It had empty eyes, black as night. Dead eyes."

"Then what happened?"

"Hah! I nearly shit my pants."

"But did the lizard do anything different after seeing you?"

"No. It went back to eating. I got the bejesus out of there, and rode at full throttle to the Robinson farm next door."

"They're the neighbours you told me about on the phone?"

"Yeah, they run the horse stud. On the side, they hunt in the park and sell the deer and goat meat to interested parties, including myself. It's illegal hunting—poaching, by the exact letter of the law—so I'd be grateful if you kept your trap shut about that. Anyway, the Robinsons have a lot of firepower on account of their particular hobby. I rustled them up. The three of us went to my back paddock on our quad-bikes with rifles and ammo. Too late, as it turned out. The lizard was gone."

"But the Robinsons believe you?"

"Yep. And they'd be the only ones in town to do so."

Noel stared into his beer, his chin quivering. Erin wanted to touch his hand but resisted the impulse. Compassion would almost certainly irritate him. Instead, she gave him a few moments. To pass the time, she sipped at her mineral water.

At last, he said, "I know it sounds crazy."

"Not to me. Can you describe the lizard?"

"Like I told you already, a big bastard."

"What did the shape of its head look like?"

Noel looked up, raised his eyebrows. "The shape of its head?"

She nodded.

He managed to chuckle. "Well, exactly like the head of a giant bloody lizard."

Softly, softly, she reminded herself. "Triangular like a blue-tongue?" she said. "Long and thin like a crocodile?" She had to be careful. It was important not to lead the witness. "Blunt with a beak, like a turtle?"

The old man sighed, dropped his shoulders. After a gulp of beer, he said, "It looked like a dinosaur, that's what."

Under the table, Erin laced her fingers together and squeezed hard. Arranging her face into a smile, she said, "You know, there are so many different kinds of dinosaurs. I'm really not sure what you mean."

Noel pursed his lips. "A big forehead and a snout like a skinny T-Rex. And it had a tongue, a long forked tongue like a snake that it kept flapping about."

Holy shit.

Erin had to use every ounce of self-control to sit quietly and still. Her blood whipped through her veins. Adrenaline and cortisol fired up her muscles, raced her thoughts, and tamped her lungs.

"I think I know what it is," she whispered.

"Without even seeing it?"

"*Varanus priscus*, commonly known as Megalania, a relative of the Komodo dragon from the Pleistocene era which ended about twelve thousand years ago," she said, breathless. "Some Australian animals were gigantic versions of present day species. Kangaroos triple the weight and size, and wombats as big as baby hippos."

Noel laughed. "Are you bullshitting me?"

She shook her head. "It was the age of Megafauna, huge beasts like something out of a nightmare. Ducks the size of emus, the precursor of the emu three metres tall and weighing over half a tonne. And then the apex predators, chief among them *Varanus priscus,* your monster: a huge Komodo dragon."

Noel regarded her, drained his glass. "Look, you're the expert, but we don't have Komodos in Australia. Not outside of zoos, anyway."

"Yes, you're right," Erin said, lightheaded. "The Komodo dragon is only found on certain Indonesian islands, thanks to the rise of sea-level after the last glacial period, which turned Australia into an island and cut off the free movement of Pleistocene animals...."

"I don't know the hell what you're talking about."

"*Varanus priscus* was thought to be extinct. Over the past century, there have been rare sightings of it throughout south-eastern Australia, but no photographs, nothing confirmed. At least not yet."

Varanus priscus: she knew the classification by heart— Animalia *Chordata, Reptilia, Squamata, Platynota, Varanoidea, Varanidae*—and could still remember the first time she'd ever seen a picture of the beast, when she'd been about twelve years old....

At the time, she had already owned a couple of terrapins— Buster and Atlas—that she kept in a glass aquarium by her bedside. Her bookshelves were filled with various tomes on crocodiles and lizards. Year after year, her parents had flat-out refused, under any circumstances, to allow her a pet snake. This had seemed particularly ridiculous, considering that Erin's father had been an assistant curator of an animal park, and had known that many varieties of snake were not only without venom but docile, easily handled. Suffering from a cold or flu, while idly flipping through a dog-eared dinosaur book in the waiting room of a doctor's surgery, Erin had seen a two-page colour spread of the *Varanus priscus*. She remembered catching her breath. According to the text, only scattered fossil remains had ever been found, so the artist had used his or her imagination: the colossal lizard, grey-scaled, with torn, bloody flesh hanging from its jaws, standing over a felled Diprotodon....

Noel said, "Dr. Harris, are you all right?"

Erin blinked. "I'm sorry?"

"You look like you're about to faint."

"No, I'm fine."

"I'll get you a whisky."

"You know what I need?" she said. "To see the remains of that cow. Please tell me you kept the animal's remains."

"I did this time."

Erin sat back in her chair. "Your cattle have been attacked before?"

"Yeah, two other times this year. Those corpses I burned and then buried."

"When can you show me the remains of this latest cow?"

"This afternoon. I've kept it under a tarp in one of my barns. The vet wanted a squiz, thanks to the story in the local paper." Noel checked his watch. "Meet me at my homestead at about two o'clock. I've got to make lunch for my daughter. My son-in-law can't cook to save his life, so I've taken over kitchen duties. Chicken liver is good for a growing baby, so I've heard."

"What?"

"My daughter is pregnant, remember? Seven months gone. She needs iron."

"For sure," Erin said, and laughed a little wildly. "See you at two o'clock."

"You know my address?"

"I know it."

Noel stood up. "Take the last dirt road out of town and follow it towards the ranges until it stops at a gate. Drive on in, but shut the gate behind you, mind. I don't want any of my cattle wandering off."

He grabbed his hat, tipped it towards her before putting it on, and walked out. She watched through the window as he strode across the car park and got into his ute.

After he'd driven away, she continued to stare at the bluish-green haze of the ranges that lay on the horizon. The idea that there could be only one giant lizard in the park was implausible. Out there somewhere, hiding in those 30,000 hectares of national park, feeding off the plentiful supply of native, feral and farm animals, would be at least one small population of lizards. She would find evidence. When she did, she would dub the species *Harris's dragon* to the world's media. The moniker would stick. And if the lizard turned out to be a new species entirely, then the scientific community would definitely name it after her: the *Varanus harrisii*. Either way, her name would go down in history.

Just the thought of achieving such an accolade sent a shiver down her back.

2

Erin stayed at the pub and ordered lunch.

While she waited, she flipped through the information about the national park that she'd printed from the university servers. The park, big enough to support a range of eco-systems, included wet and dry eucalypt forests, and even patches of rainforest. It sounded like the perfect environment for *Varanus priscus*.

Then again, data on the lizard was scarce.

During the past couple of centuries, just a few bones had been found. A palaeontologist had reconstructed a skeleton for the Melbourne Museum using more than a few educated guesses to fill in the blanks. Some scientists, including Erin, used the skeleton to classify the lizard as the direct relative of the Komodo dragon. Cryptozoologists, untrained enthusiasts who believe in Bigfoot, the Loch Ness Monster and chupacabras, didn't care either way and just called it the Devil dragon.

Erin's mobile phone sounded. She rummaged through her handbag. It was Dr. Russ Walker-Smith, clinical pathologist, head of the Biomedical Research Centre at the university. Erin hesitated, almost didn't accept the call, then figured it'd be easier if she just got this awkward conversation over and done with. Russ Walker-Smith was a good friend, yes, but he could be a royal pain in the arse at times. And this would definitely be one of those times.

"Hi, Russ, how are you?" she said, rubbing the back of her neck.

"Don't tell me you've gone to that shitty little town."

"Okay, I won't."

Russ paused. "After everything we discussed, you went ahead and ignored my advice. Why would I lie to you? Lead you down a dead-end garden path?"

"It's okay," she said. "I've spoken to the farmer at length, on the phone and just now in person. He's a credible witness, I'm sure of it."

"A man in his seventies? When you met him, was he wearing spectacles?"

"He can see perfectly well." Erin said. "Christ, will you please listen to me?"

"Maybe he takes hallucinogens on a daily basis. Maybe he's got dementia."

"Noel Baines is coherent."

"Maybe he wants his fifteen minutes of fame. And has it occurred to you that his story about a giant lizard could be a calculated lie? What if he's doing this to drum up business to stave off bankruptcy? This could be a publicity stunt."

"I think he's telling the truth."

"You've wanted to prove the existence of this animal for so long..." Russ said, and then he stopped with a sharp intake of breath.

Erin felt a hot flush in her cheeks. "You think I'd bend facts to fit a theory?"

"Lord, that's not what I meant, and you know it."

"That's pretty insulting, Russ. I would never fudge data."

"The university needs to make cuts in the New Year. Just don't give them a reason to let your contract lapse, that's all I'm trying to say."

"Oh, relax. No one's going to care if I investigate cryptofauna on my own time. Not when I'm still fulfilling my contract and getting studies published."

"No, you're wrong. The Dean is striving for scientific credibility, world-class ranking. The requirement for credibility extends to all staff. He'll let you go."

"Let me go?" She laughed. "If I find this lizard, I'll put the university on the goddamned map. Russ, consider this: the Komodo dragon was thought to be a myth until 1910 when Hensbroek brought back a specimen."

"That's not an equivalent example. The planet is a global village now. Every inch of it can be mapped from outer space. We've run out of frontiers."

"Not true," Erin said. "Last December, a new species of goanna was found in the Kimberleys, remember? The Dampier Peninsula goanna, *Varanus sparnus*, believed to be extinct for millions of years. A bunch of environmental consultants happened to stumble across it. They weren't even looking for it."

Russ sighed, exasperated. "Yes, but how much does the little bugger weigh, twelve grams? That's the equivalent of, what, three teaspoons of butter?"

"So?"

"So *Varanus sparnus* is incredibly small, a hand-span from nose to tail. It's easy to overlook. You're talking about a lizard that's larger than the average adult crocodile. It's impossible. How could creatures that size live in modern Australia for all these years without detection?"

Erin rolled her eyes. "You're actually asking me that newbie question? Wow, because our population is clustered around the coastline. We've got millions upon millions of hectares of unexplored land. Anything could be out there."

Russ made a tutting sound. "Yes, but what about forest surveys?"

"What about them? They don't cover every inch of a park or forest."

"Let's be logical. If your giant lizard exists, don't you think at least one camera trap somewhere would have taken a photograph by now?"

"Ah, Christ," Erin said and rubbed at her temples. "You talk as if the whole goddamned continent is covered in thermal cameras. Look, discount the modern eyewitness accounts if you like, but you can't ignore the Aboriginal rock paintings."

"Oh, please, not the 'Mungoon Galli' myth."

"Listen to me, Russ. Yes, officially *Varanus priscus* is listed as extinct for twelve thousand years, but the rock art near Sydney shows warriors fighting giant lizards. Those paintings are only three thousand years old."

"According to some scientists. Not all."

Erin gazed out the window at the ranges, clenched her phone and said nothing.

After a time, Russ said, "Come home."

"No."

"I can't hold off the university."

Erin sat bolt upright. "You've told the faculty about my trip?"

"No, Lord no, but Erin, be realistic. How long can you hide the fact that you're searching for an extinct, dinosaur-sized lizard? What if Farmer Joe blabs to the press? I can see the headline: *Evolutionary biologist believes crock of shit, crucifies career.*"

She contemplated hanging up.

Finally, Russ said, "Erin, how long do you intend to stay in Turdsville?"

"Actually, it's a very charming little town."

"Oh, please."

"Only seven hours away by car. You should check it out."

The silence went on and on. Erin felt a tremble of anxiety. Her scientific reputation was everything, her job the bedrock of her life. No husband, no kids, no hobbies, dead parents, extended family members on the other side of the continent, her circle of friends consisting entirely of academics from the university....

"Don't miss your lectures," Russ said at last, low and flat. "The Dean is watching. Not specifically you, of course, but all of us. Budget cuts, Erin. Don't forget the budget cuts. Your last paper was about the variation of banding in coral snakes. Not exactly earth-shattering. Just come home."

Movement caught her eye. Dave, the pub owner, was approaching with a plate, her Thai beef salad. "Russ, I've got to go," she said. "I'll be back by Monday, I swear."

"Come back now."

"It's only Thursday. I'll call you Sunday night."

He didn't answer.

"Look," she continued, "I appreciate your concern, honestly, but I know what I'm doing. Trust me. I have to do this."

Russ said, "Even though your credibility is at stake?"

She disconnected the call, her heart pounding.

***

Erin gagged. The smell reached down her throat, tried to evert her stomach.

"Yeah, it stinks to high heaven," Noel said. "Wait there."

The barn doorway was wide enough for a tractor. Erin stepped back, turned her face, and sucked in fresh summer air, laden with the scent of hay. Then the stench began to waft out from the barn. Excrement was a familiar, disgusting odour—the stool from carnivores particularly vile—but this, the smell of rotting flesh? She gagged again. Christ almighty, the corpse must be riddled with maggots.

"All right," Noel called. "If you want, here it is."

Erin wished she had something to hold over her nose. However, she wasn't the type to carry handkerchiefs. Her summer dress was too well-fitted for any slack in the bodice. She dropped her hands from her face. In the cool, dim shadows of the barn, Noel stood with his fists on his hips, back straight as a rod.

Goddamn it.

Erin squared her shoulders and entered the barn. The smell intensified. She tried to pretend that it didn't exist. Blowflies buzzed around her. The barn held all sorts of farming equipment that Erin didn't recognise. She approached Noel.

"Well, there it is," he said, gesturing with one arm. "My half-eaten heifer."

The stink was almost unbearable. Was Noel immune to it? Carefully, slowly, Erin slid her gaze from Noel's face toward the mess on the ground. She had seen a lot of nature's carnage during her professional career—half-digested prey cut from the guts of snakes or crocodiles—but this heifer was something else. Only one-third of it remained: head, chest, a single front leg.

Oh, Jesus.

And blowflies, maggots. So many blowflies, so many maggots.

"You okay, Dr. Harris?" Noel said.

"Thank you, I'm fine."

The heifer, bloating and turning black, had a few rib bones remaining, then nothing but a dark red slop of entrails, crawling with insects. The Thai beef salad gurgled in Erin's throat. She swallowed hard. Then she took out her mobile phone and took a few snaps.

She said, "The vet saw this?"

"Yep," Noel said. "Can't say I agree with her findings."

"Which were?"

"That my heifer got took by wild dogs." He spat into the dirt.

Erin groped through her handbag, found the box of a half-dozen test-tubes. She said to Noel, "We need to take a few samples."

"Of what?"

"The tissue around the bite marks. I want to check for venom. Most scientists agree the *Varanus priscus* would have had venomous saliva, much like the Komodo dragon." Erin took a few paces toward Noel. "Do you have a knife?" she said.

From the shadow-wall of tools, Noel selected a machete. "Like this?"

"No, something smaller. A pair of scissors?"

"What about secateurs?"

"That'll be fine."

The flies buzzed. Erin's stomach turned over again. She fought hard to blot out the memory of her Thai beef salad to keep herself from vomiting. God, the corpse reeked; nearly one week old, its liquefied tissues ran into the ground in a dark glop, thick as molasses, the mummifying flesh crawling and roiling with maggots.

God*damn* it.

Erin put the test-tubes on the nearest bench. She popped the lids. From her handbag, she took the black marker pen. Noel approached.

"Are you feeling okay?" he said gently. "Dr. Harris?"

She turned to face the heifer. The animal's wounds were serrated, cut clean with tooth marks, much like the marks one might expect from a great white shark.

"I need samples of flesh taken from the bites," she said. "Once I put the samples into the test tubes, I'll courier them straight to the university."

"How much do you need?" Noel said.

"A sliver from various points: the dewlap, brisket, elbow, withers, chest floor, a slice from the innards. The lab will check for poisons. Hand me the secateurs."

Noel gave a sad smile and shook his head. "Let me do it."

"I'm a scientist," Erin said. "I'm not afraid of dead things."

"No shit," Noel said. Brandishing the secateurs, he bent over the heifer's corpse, lifted its remaining foreleg. "Allow me, Dr. Harris. Get your test-tubes ready."

***

Erin drove into town. At the post office, she sent the samples to Dr. Russ Walker-Smith by courier, same-day delivery guaranteed. Out on the footpath, she called Russ, but only reached his voicemail. He'd be in class by now, treading the boards back and forth, portly and bespectacled, his chubby face dimpling like that of a baby, his students transmogrified by his articulate and persuasive way of talking. Russ would have made an excellent politician. *The building blocks of life and death are more important than any social whims,* he'd say to her whenever she openly admired his skill for rhetoric. Dear old Russ.

"Six test-tubes containing samples from the heifer are coming to you today by courier," she said to his voicemail. "I'd like your lab to check for Komodo dragon saliva and anticoagulants, toxic proteins, Komodo-specific mouth bacteria. Put a rush on it, would you? The sooner, the better. Thanks, Russ. I'm counting on you."

She hung up. Across the road stood a building marked VET in giant blue letters across its roof. Looking both ways, Erin walked over.

A bell jangled when she opened the door. The waiting room was empty and had a clean antiseptic smell. Wide-eyed, a spotty teenaged boy looked up from behind the counter as if startled to see anybody.

"Uh, hello?" he said.

"I'd like to see Tania O'Farrell."

"You have an appointment?"

"No, sorry, I don't," Erin said. She fished a business card from her handbag. "Tell her I'm Dr. Erin Harris, lecturer in evolutionary biology from the state university. Tell her it's urgent that I see her straight away."

The boy took the card and gaped at it. Then he pushed open the door behind him that led to the rest of the premises and yelled, "Tania, you got a walk-in."

"Give me a minute," a harsh female voice yelled back.

The boy said to Erin, "No worries, she won't be long."

"Thank you."

Erin leaned against the high counter and glanced around. The waiting room featured old and faded posters of rabbits, cats, birds. Stacked in neat rows on the counter was a range of pamphlets: "A guide to leptospirosis in cattle, sheep, pigs and horses," "Vaccinations are important," "Health tips for alpacas." A framed picture of cattle breeds hung on a wall. Erin checked her watch.

The door behind the counter opened. The vet, Tania O'Farrell, was stocky, perhaps in her sixties, with rings under her eyes, and grey, unwashed hair raked into a ponytail. She had her sleeves rolled, and was vigorously drying her hands on a towel.

"Yes, dear?" she said. "What do you need?"

Before Erin could reply, the boy held up Erin's business card, which Tania squinted at down her nose.

"A lecturer from the university, hey?" Tania said. "Goodness gracious, we don't get many city academics around here. But I can guess why you've come."

"You can?"

"Noel Baines and his big lizard."

The boy laughed, and then clapped his hand over his mouth. Shooting an apologetic look at both women, he mumbled, "Sorry."

"It's okay, Luke. Most people in town think it's a funny story." Tania flipped the towel over her shoulder and smiled. "But you don't agree, Dr. Harris?"

Erin blushed. "I'd like to have a copy of your report, that's all."

"My report of what?"

"The attack on Noel's heifer."

"Oh, that." Tania shrugged. "I didn't type one up."

"Sorry?"

"I know the sign of wild dogs. A pack pulled down the cow. End of story."

"What about the size of the bite marks?"

"What about them?"

"Each one was at least fifty centimetres across. There's not a dog on this earth with jaws that wide."

"It's a nibble pattern; a number of dogs feeding side by side." When Erin didn't reply, Tania tipped her head and said, "Are you trying to pull my leg?"

Erin felt uncomfortable. The boy, Luke, was staring at her with his eyebrows raised and his grinning mouth hanging open. Indicating the door behind the counter, she said, "Tania, can we talk somewhere in private?"

"No time. I've got a lame horse to put down."

"But the bite pattern—"

"Oh, shush, let me explain that," Tania said, putting her hands on her hips. "I take it you're familiar with the decay process? Flesh shrinks and hardens. Given enough time, a mouse bite starts to look like the work of a Rottweiler."

"I'm aware of that phenomenon. But I've seen the heifer's remains."

"Well, I'll be stuffed," Tania said. "You honestly think a big lizard did it?"

Luke snickered.

"That's enough," she said to him, as if chastising, but she was smiling.

Emboldened, the boy said, "Noel's lizard is about as real as a unicorn."

"Noel Baines seemed a credible witness to me," Erin said.

"Everyone reckons the old bugger was drunk," Luke added, as if he hadn't heard. "He must've been, right? Drunk or going senile. He's been weird since his wife died, that's no mistake. My dad reckons that old Mr. Baines is going off his rocker."

"Don't be disrespectful." Tania took the towel from her shoulder and gave it to Luke. "Now I'm off to the Gilbert's farm," she said, opening the door behind the counter that led to the rest of the premises. "Call me the minute you hear from the pharma rep.

Anything else, just send me a text. I'll be back in about, oh, half an hour."

"Wait a minute," Erin said.

Tania turned with her hand still on the door knob. "What is it, dear?"

"So you're just going to ignore the facts?"

"The facts?"

"Of the heifer and what Noel saw."

With a frown, Tania crossed her reddened, chapped arms over her chest. "All right, child, let me tell you the facts as I see them. When I first started here, we had three vets at the practice. One retired, the other left to have a baby. I've been the Shire's only vet for some eight years now. I work fifteen, eighteen hours a day. You're lucky to have caught me at the office at all. Now I don't know about you, but I certainly don't have the time to gallivant around investigating crazy stories."

Erin smiled. "I understand. Thanks for your time."

"Uh-huh." Tania skewed an eye. "How long have you had your qualifications?"

"Over ten years."

"And despite that training, that scientific viewpoint you're supposed to have, you believe in cryptozoology?"

"What's that?" Luke said.

"The study of make-believe monsters," Tania said.

"Like bunyips?" The boy rolled his eyes. "Holy moly."

Erin looked away, took a moment to keep her temper in check. "I'd be grateful for your professional opinion on this case."

"Which I gave you already: wild dogs. Now, dear, please don't take this the wrong way, but someone with your training ought to show a bit more common sense."

Erin didn't know what to say. Tania kept looking at her with steady, unblinking green eyes.

Blushing, Erin gave a quick nod. "Well, thank you for seeing me."

"That's fine, dear. Now go on back to your university."

Cheeks burning, Erin left hurriedly, the bell jangling as the front door closed behind her. She could hear the boy's laughter from the street.

3

The second story of the pub was divided in half: the front section with the balcony formed the bistro and *a la carte* restaurant; the back section, the rooms for rent. Erin had booked the only room with an en suite. Admittedly, you couldn't open the bathroom door without hitting the toilet, and the shower was the size of an upright coffin, but at least the accommodation offered privacy.

As a favour, Dave, the pub owner, allowed room service for her that night: a chicken parmigiana. Erin sat on her lumpy double-bed and picked at the meal without much interest. The television was the old type with a cathode tube, upgraded with a digital set-top box. Listlessly, Erin thumbed through the channels on the remote. Apart from blurred national stations, the TV had a single pin-sharp channel that seemed low-budget, amateurish, and preoccupied with local issues like olive markets, corn mould, new breeds of wheat. Erin sighed and turned off the TV.

I'm a fool, she thought.

A stupid gamble: her reputation versus a single, unsubstantiated sighting of a monster lizard. Maybe Russ was correct. The farmer had orchestrated a publicity stunt. Or perhaps the vet had the right angle: a mistaken autopsy result. Either way, if the university found out about this trip, she might be seen as a kook.

What if the Dean decided to let her contract lapse? Then what?

If she couldn't get a position as a lecturer in evolutionary biology or herpetology at another institute—a long shot in itself— the remaining options didn't appeal. She could apply for work at a government agency such as the Department of Primary Industries, or go for a position as an ecological consultant in the private sector or an animal care specialist at a zoo; she could even start her own business and get paid by the hour to bring reptiles to a child's party. The parmigiana caught in her throat. No, she didn't want to ever give up teaching. The university life had her heart.

She reached into her handbag and checked her mobile. Nothing yet from Russ. Outside the single window, night began to fall. Erin pulled the shade. Having eaten as much of the parmigiana as her churning stomach would allow, she left the plate outside her door. The shower dribbled lukewarm. She welcomed the ablution anyway.

Later, as she lay on the bed staring at the ceiling, listening to the murmur and chatter of patrons that rose through the floorboards, the old memory came back. *You'll never be better than me*, her embittered father had said when Erin's first scientific paper had been accepted for publication. *Watch me,* she'd replied, hurt and angered. Her dad had once been the assistant curator at a small animal park before getting sacked and turning to gin for solace. As a kid, she'd looked up to him. His job had seemed so important: supervising the junior staff in feeding the animals and mucking out the cages.

Well, the old man was dead now. Shot himself in the head during a drinking binge. And Mother was dead, too, after a brief struggle with ovarian cancer. Erin hunkered beneath the worn sheet and closed her eyes. Despite the risks, she couldn't back out now. She wanted to make a name for herself. The hardwiring of her personality wouldn't allow things to be any other way.

***

The pub's bistro served breakfast. While waiting for her bacon sandwich and cappuccino, Erin sat at one of the tables by the window and flipped through her manila file on *Varanus priscus*. She hesitated over the photograph of the full-scale skeleton prowling down a set of stairs at the Melbourne Museum. As always, the skull drew her gaze. Those large, serrated fangs that pointed inward were the kicker. Once *Varanus priscus* closed its jaws, the angle of those teeth prevented the prey from wriggling free.

"Dr. Harris?"

Startled, Erin looked up, slapped the manila file closed. A slim, bearded man in his fifties or thereabouts stood by her table, holding out his right hand. He wore a short-sleeved khaki shirt and matching shorts. A park ranger, she surmised. Recovering, Erin shook with him.

"I'm Gregory Lee," he said.

"Park ranger?"

"Yep, that's me. The senior ranger, as a matter of fact." He smiled and tugged at his lapel, bringing her attention to the logo embroidered there. "Uniform gives it away, I guess. Dr. Harris, it's a pleasure. Sorry to be so forward. Tania O'Farrell rang me last night and told me you were in town. I figured you might be staying here and Dave confirmed it. Hopefully, you don't mind me barging in like this."

Damn, did everyone know about her visit? Who would be the next to show up, a journalist from the local newspaper? Russ Walker-Smith's mock headline came to mind: *Evolutionary biologist believes crock of shit, crucifies career.* Just the thought of it hollowed out Erin's guts. She put on a smile and said, "No doubt Tania, the vet, described me as crazy."

"Ah, something along those lines," Gregory said, chuckling, his speech a nasal, country drawl. "Don't take any notice. Old Tania tends to be grouchy, but she's a great vet, that's for sure. We couldn't do without her."

"So she told me." Erin regarded him for a time. "Why did you want to meet?"

He raised his eyebrows. "Are you kidding?"

"No, I'm not."

"The chance to meet a scientist with your qualifications? It's an honour."

"Uh, thank you."

He continued to beam at her. Was he playing it straight? Erin couldn't tell. She was habituated to university people, the majority of them science nerds—let's face it—too cloistered or socially inept to be duplicitous. Having spent her adulthood within tertiary institutions, Erin knew she didn't have a bullshit-radar. Gregory Lee, a golly-gosh park ranger. Or not? Perhaps he and Tania had enjoyed a good laugh at Erin's expense, and now he wanted to see the loonie with his own eyes.

Smiling, he indicated the seat opposite her and said, "Can I sit?"

"Oh, yes, of course."

As soon as he did, he cleared his throat and said, "I hear you're after Noel's lizard. The national press ignored the article that ran in our newspaper last week. Did Noel contact you direct?"

"No. I just happen to have an interest in *Varanus priscus*."

He laughed. "You have an interest in a what-now?"

"The animal that attacked Noel's heifer: a relative of the Komodo dragon."

"Heck, you really suppose poor old Noel is telling the truth?"

Erin considered. "Put it this way," she said at last. "I don't believe he was drunk at the time of the sighting and I don't believe he is mentally deficient or in the habit of lying."

"You reckon there might be a real monster?"

Erin shrugged.

Gregory paused, nodded. "Apart from your visit, the item in the local rag gave us something else that the farmers around here value: a few more hunters in the park. They're not supposed to be there, of course, but since we can't keep them out, I quietly point them in the right direction so they don't shoot each other. You see, we have a problem with pest animals. It's a terrible scourge."

"So I understand."

"To be frank, we can't cope with the scale of pests. They either out-compete the native wildlife for resources or prey on them for food. We're losing our native species hand-over-fist. The pigs alone cause erosion and soil loss, which destroys our plants. Every year it gets worse."

"And hunting helps?" she said.

"Sure, it does, to a degree. Anything's better than nothing." Gregory stared at her carefully. "Hunting is legal in some national parks, but not in others such as ours."

"Why not in yours?"

He leaned in conspiratorially. "From one professional to another, I'll be honest: we're suffering under Greenie left-wing policies. The current state government won't allow hunting on account of unfounded concerns like environmental damage, animal cruelty, scaring off picnickers, and the like. When city people think 'hunter', they imagine an amateur or a drunken hooligan, some half-wit firing off rounds from the back of a ute. But most hunters aren't like that at all."

Actually, this was precisely how Erin imagined hunters to be. But, she said, "So what are they really like?"

"Most of them consider themselves environmentalists, protecting the habitat and native wildlife." He sighed. "But politicians need votes. Right now, I'm paid to keep hunters, even licensed ones, out of the park. Whether or not I think it's a good thing doesn't factor into the equation."

"I'm sorry to hear that."

"But the support of a learned person such as yourself.... Well, you can imagine how an educated opinion might sway things."

No, he was wrong; Erin was nobody. Her opinion would mean shit unless she could produce conclusive evidence of *Varanus priscus* to the world. Erin looked away. Beyond the pub's window, the cloudless summer day raised a heat-haze from the eucalyptus trees peppering the ranges. The hills filled the horizon, left to right, front to back, on a scale that lifted the hair on Erin's arms.

"Noel Baines saw an animal that can be best described as prehistoric," she said.

Gregory said, "Yeah, that's what I heard."

"I've organised for some tests on the cow. If the evidence pans out, I'm hoping you might lead me into the park. On an expedition, if you like. I want to hunt and kill a lizard. I can pay you."

Gregory winced. "Dr. Harris, on my own authority, I can't allow any sort of private or scientific incursion for something like that."

"Why not?"

"Chain of command, I'm afraid. You see, I'm on the bottom rung." He smiled. "If you wish to go through the proper channels, you'll need to fill out forms. I can send you the URLs for each one if you like. There are plenty of them. Your request might take months to get through the system."

"But I only have this weekend."

She must have looked crestfallen, because he reached out and patted the back of her hand. "You know," he continued, "if I were you, Dr. Harris, I wouldn't even ask me about any kind of expedition into the park. If you did, I might have to report your intentions to my boss. I wouldn't want to put you in a bind."

Bewildered, she stared at his beaming face. He winked at her.

"All right," she said. "Well, it's a good thing that I didn't ask."

"Yes, a damned good thing."

Shit. Erin glanced out the window again. The ranges went on and on, a seemingly endless wilderness. She'd never camped in the bush. In childhood, she'd occasionally slept in the backyard, zippered inside a pop-tent. Dad, despite being an assistant curator at an animal park, had rarely allowed her to stay there overnight, even though the Moonlight Tour had been a solid money-earner. As an adult, most of Erin's "field" expeditions had occurred at zoos, wildlife shelters, aquariums, places that had Wi-Fi....

"Let me ask you something," she said, and stared at Gregory intently. "Is it possible, in your opinion, that giant lizards could live unnoticed in your park?"

He chewed on his cheek.

"Off the record," she said.

Gregory looked away, rubbed his nose.

"Tell me," Erin said. "Listen, we're just chatting. Help me out here."

He ran his hand across his beard. "I've heard things."

"What sort of things?"

"I don't know. Odd things, way off in the distance. Noises like a big cat, a growl. Maybe a lion." He shrugged. "The park is larger than quite a few countries. There are a handful of roads going in or out, a few dirt tracks. The interior of the park is rugged. I doubt some of it's ever been seen by a single person."

"No intrepid bushwalkers or bird watchers?"

He laughed and waved as if she'd made a joke.

"What about wildlife surveys?" she continued. "Baited camera traps?"

"Oh, we've got a few cameras around the fringes of the park, sure."

"So you're saying that giant lizards are possible?"

"Well, it's a funny old planet we live on. Strange things happen all the time. I reckon nothing could surprise me, not even a giant lizard."

There was a thick scar along Gregory's left forearm from elbow to wrist, cross-hatched with dozens of thin scars as if whoever placed those stitches hadn't taken too much care. He probably had plenty more scars, plenty of frightening experiences in the park. She wondered if he carried a gun while on duty.

"One more thing," Erin said, "from one professional to another."

At that, he sat up straighter, and squared his shoulders. "Okay, Dr. Harris."

"Assume that Noel's giant lizard is real. Why now? The park is thirty thousand hectares, packed with food. Give me one plausible reason why the lizard would need to visit the edge of town."

Laughing, Gregory opened his eyes wide. "You didn't hear about the fires?"

Erin paused, shook her head.

"Man," he said, "you city folk really do live inside a bubble."

"What?"

"Last year, we had the bushfires, remember?"

Erin cast her mind back. The previous Christmas, she'd noticed the occasional reference to a fire on a TV news bulletin, mentions of unfamiliar towns, unknown places. She had eaten her toast and flipped the remote to the next channel.

"Sorry," she said. "Fill me in."

"The fire burnt out about thirteen thousand hectares in the southwestern areas of the park. Any animals that didn't perish got driven further north."

Animals including *Varanus priscus*.

Erin said, "If I went into the park, would you stop me?"

He spread his arms and grinned. "The park's open to everyone, nine until five, seven days a week. Don't forget your sunscreen, sunhat and water."

They shared a smile. Perhaps they understood each other.

***

Erin was in her room, checking emails on her laptop, when Russ Walker-Smith called.

"I've got your test results," he said. "They required moving heaven and earth."

"And?" She clenched the mobile phone. "Tell me."

"To start with, you owe me a big favour. Do you realise how many jobs I skipped to put yours on top of the pile? Admittedly, they were simple tests but we had to run them several times to verify results. Every member of the staff is miffed."

"I'll treat you to dinner, wine included. Tell me."

"Okay. You know how I hate to eat humble pie? Guess what? I'm eating it."

She stood up. "What's the analysis?"

"We tested every piece of heifer. Naturally, we had plenty of putrefaction bacteria, particularly anaerobic strains from the digestive tract; standard, really."

"Any saliva?"

"Yes, as you'd expect from a half-eaten animal. But we also found what I believe you're looking for, hence, my humble pie reference."

Erin held her breath. "Meaning?"

"Meaning we found septic pathogens in the saliva."

"What kind of pathogens?"

"Plenty," Russ said, "but particularly *E. coli*, strains of *Staphylococcus*, traces of *Providencia*, *Proteus morgani*, *Proteus mirabilis*, *Pasteurella multocida*. All of them virulent, covering the Petri dishes within hours. We found evidence of anti-coagulants too, although we can't be absolutely certain, given the decayed state of the samples."

"Oh my God...."

"Feel free to say 'I told you so', but really, gloating isn't necessary."

The blood drained toward Erin's feet. She sat heavily on the bed. Experts were divided on some aspects of Komodo dragon biology, but most agreed that it harboured a cocktail of bacteria within its saliva—a cocktail identical to the one Russ had just listed. The Komodo usually ate carrion; sometimes, it hunted by ambush. With one bite, it could infect its prey and then stalk the hapless animal at leisure, waiting for blood poisoning to set in.

"But listen to this," Russ continued. "The icing on the cake, so to speak, the evidence you've been waiting for, is that we found traces of a venomous toxin."

She couldn't speak. The breath locked in her throat.

Russ said, "Are you still there?"

"What?"

"I thought you'd fainted."

"No, I'm here," Erin said and swallowed hard. "Jesus Christ."

"You can say that again."

She said, "It fits the profile of the wild Komodo dragon."

"Apparently, yes, at first glance, but we need more tests."

"Noel Baines was right. Goddamn it, he saw the *Varanus priscus*." Nauseated, Erin stood up, crossed to the bathroom, leaned over the sink for a moment, panting.

"Erin?"

Finally, she said, "There's a population of living *Varanus priscus* somewhere in this park."

"Perhaps not," Russ said. "Yes, there's at least one animal that shares a similar profile of venom and saliva pathogens to the Komodo. Perhaps there are two or more animals that, combined, make up the profile. But that's all we know at this point."

"Oh, don't split hairs."

"Let me remind you: as scientists, that's precisely what we're supposed to do."

A wave of giddiness swept over her again. Erin left the en suite, sat on the bed. For a time, she stared at the pattern in the carpet, a hodgepodge of colourful rectangles and triangles in a stiff, cheap nap. She had to get a grip on herself.

"Erin? Are you there?"

"Yes, for Christ's sake, stop asking me that."

"You keep going silent."

"I'm trying to figure out what to do."

"That's easy," Russ said. "Come back to the university. You've got your evidence. We'll go to the Dean for a grant to bankroll a survey of the park."

The ranger, Gregory Lee, and his friendly warning came to mind: *Your request might take months to get through the system.* She couldn't afford to wait. If word got out that a population of giant and undescribed reptiles prowled this park, the stampede of worldwide scientists might trample her. No, *Varanus priscus* belonged to her, nobody else. One of the lizards would be found and the species renamed *Harris's dragon* or it wouldn't be found at all.

4

"Erin," Russ said. "We'll approach the Dean together. Come back today."

She swapped the phone to her other ear, got up from the bed and began to pace the room. "I told you. Monday morning, I'll be there for my first lecture."

Russ said, "But what are you intending to do?"

"I'm not sure. I have to get into that park. The ranger's hands are tied, the vet thinks I'm nuts." She bit on a fingernail. "Noel Baines has a couple of hunter friends I might be able to hire for the weekend, given the right price."

"Hunters? Oh, please no. You mean drunken roo-spotters?"

"Licensed hunters care about the environment," she said, feeling like a hypocrite.

"God, you sound like a bumper sticker."

"These friends of Noel's know the park. They can take me to the interior."

Russ laughed in surprise. "On a camping trip? You?"

"Oh, shut up."

"Let me ask you one question: in living memory, have you ever defecated anywhere other than into a plumbed toilet?"

"That's your response? I could be making the discovery of the century, and you want to make jokes about shit?"

"Don't go into that park."

"You told me not to investigate this sighting. But I was right, wasn't I?"

She heard his noisy exhalation. "Listen," he said, "if there's an unknown animal in that park, you need a proper search party. That takes money. Drive back to the city. We'll front the Dean together. We'll put forward your findings."

Her eyes fluttered shut. She could see Russ at his desk; button-down shirt, neatly pressed trousers. He would be playing computer solitaire. Whenever he talked on his office landline, he'd run through successive hands until the conversation ended. Russ Walker-Smith couldn't bear to do one thing at a time. Once, he'd confessed that he would only brush his teeth while in the shower waiting to rinse the conditioner from his hair.

"Please," Russ whispered. "Think about what you're getting yourself into."

"Like I told you," Erin said, "I'll be at work Monday. Thanks, I've got to go."

She hung up. A moment passed wherein she acknowledged the adrenaline, cortisols, excitement and fear. Then she thumbed through the numbers listed in her mobile phone and selected one. The ring-tone sounded. She waited, trembling.

The phone picked up. "Yep?"

"Noel Baines? It's Erin Harris. Where are you? I must see you right away."

***

Behind Noel's homestead and barns lay a huge swathe of land, a paddock as large as two or three football ovals, in Erin's estimation. They rode out on the quad-bike. The vehicle looked exactly like Noel had described—a four-wheeled motorcycle—but there wasn't much room for a pillion passenger on the seat. Unless she wanted to press herself tight against Noel's back, which she didn't, she had to mostly sit on the flat storage rack. Her hands rested lightly, reluctantly, on Noel's hips. There was nowhere to put her feet, so she held them out, fearful of catching them under the wheels.

The trip from the barn to the back fence of the farthest paddock took about fifteen careful minutes, since Noel took each incline and dip at walking speed. For this, she was grateful. The quad-bike felt twitchy, ready to tip. Why weren't they wearing helmets? She kept involuntarily tightening her grip on the old man's hips.

"Relax," he called back to her once. "I won't roll us over."

She took a breath, forced herself to relax, to concentrate on the scenery. At this time of year, the paddocks were brown and dry. The vehicle made a racket. Even so, the cattle acted as if the noisy quad-bike didn't exist. Each animal kept its head down to chew on hay. The air smelled of dirt, shit and dust. Erin closed her eyes.

At last, the quad-bike slowed, came to a stop. The motor cut out. Erin opened her eyes as Noel climbed off.

"Here we are, Dr. Harris," he said and offered his hand.

She took it, slid awkwardly from the quad-bike. Standing up, her legs felt like jelly. Far behind them, the homestead and barns looked like tiny red bricks. Ahead, beyond the fence, lay a thick line of eucalypts.

Noel adjusted his hat, indicated the ground at his feet and said, "Right here."

"This is where you saw the lizard attack your heifer?" Erin looked left, looked right; contemplated the long and unvarying line of posts and wire. "Are you sure?"

"It might seem all the same to you, but I know each part of my land like I know my wife's face, God rest her," Noel said. He stomped one foot, pulled it back through the dirt, raising a tiny dust-devil in the breeze. "It happened in this very spot."

Erin squatted. The ground did hold evidence of dried blood. She rubbed the grains between her fingers. If only she'd brought more test tubes.

"Can I climb over your fence?" she said.

"I don't know, Dr. Harris." Noel smiled with the corners of his mouth turned down, in the manner of someone not used to laughing. "Can you?"

"I mean, is it electrified?"

"Not unless you see any insulators."

"I'm not a country person," she said. "You'll have to explain things to me sometimes, if you don't mind. Honestly, I'm not trying to be cute."

Noel fussed with his hat. God, she'd offended him. She waited.

At last, he said, "I've no electrified fences. I don't believe in them."

He stepped on the bottom three lines of barbed wire and lifted the top three, offering her a narrow space to slip through.

"Thank you," she said.

The barbs snagged her clothes and snicked the skin along her arms, but she said nothing. On the other side, the forest stood thick, trees side-by-side, a multitude of shrubs waist-high, leaf litter ankle-deep. She could hear the call of unseen birds, the rustle of unseen animals. It felt like another world.

"What now?" Noel said.

She turned. He was right next to her.

"Do you know how to track?" she said.

"Nope. What are you looking for?"

"I'm not sure. Broken tree limbs, evidence of a large beast passing through."

"A herd of feral pigs or deer makes a wide trail," he said. "We can't go far into the bush without a compass. Spin around twice and you're lost."

Erin gazed about. "Are you aware of a sunny spot close by?"

"I might be. Why?"

"The Komodo dragon is cold-blooded. To speed digestion, it lies down in sunny spots after eating. Otherwise, the food tends to rot in its guts."

Noel compressed his lips, swiped the perspiration from under his hat-brim with one finger. "This way," he said.

He strode off. Hampered by her flimsy sandals, Erin stumbled after him, trying to keep his blue jeans and checked shirt in sight. Were they travelling too far into the forest? Everywhere looked the same. The heat made her sweat. She had left her mobile phone in her bag, which was sitting on Noel's kitchen table. The canopy threw a deep shadow. She looked back. The fence was gone. Oh Christ, would they get lost?

"Noel?" she called, and ran ahead a few steps, panicked. "Noel, wait."

She came into a clearing and pulled up, almost running into the old man.

"Is that what you're looking for?" Noel said.

At first, she didn't know what he meant. She took a few hesitant steps into the clearing. A handful of trees, perhaps struck by lightning, had fallen away, leaving a bright circle of sunlit grass. In the middle of the grass lay a huge lump of some kind of excreta.

Erin removed her glasses, polished them on her blouse, one lens at a time. Then she put her glasses back on and advanced. Dear God. The lump, as she got closer, revealed itself to be a putrefying amalgamation of organic matter caked within some kind of white paste. Blowflies buzzed around it. She had seen a similar kind of regurgitate before. Once again, she wished for test-tubes.

"What is that?" Noel said from behind her. "Be careful, Dr. Harris."

Ignoring him, Erin neared the hellish mash to within a few feet. The stink was awful. She found a stout, long stick and approached the organic mass.

"What are you doing?" Noel said, sounding alarmed.

She thrust the end of the stick into the mass with force, and used it to spread out the material, poking and prodding. The material fell away, revealing bugs, clots of slag. Within the mass, she uncovered bones, hooves, hide. It looked like a cow that had been turned inside out.

"Would you say these remains are from an Angus heifer?" she said.

"Oh, sweet Virgin Mary," Noel muttered.

"Are they from an Angus heifer, in your opinion?"

"Yep," he said, beside her now. He took off his hat and hit it across his thigh as if to remove dust. "That's one of mine, I'll wager."

Erin hurled away the stick. Why hadn't she brought her phone? She couldn't even take a photograph. Noel slowly approached the mass. Pale, he pressed his boot into the slough and jerked back as if stung.

He turned to her. "What the bloody hell is it?"

"A gastric pellet."

"Huh?"

Erin took a deep breath, wiped her hands over her sweating face. "When a Komodo dragon eats, it consumes the whole animal. Later, it vomits all the matter that it can't digest: keratin products, mostly, like horns and hair. The vomit is called a gastric pellet."

"You mean the lizard chucked up my heifer?"

"Only the parts it couldn't digest."

"That son of a bitch cost me a thousand bucks."

Erin bent over, began to look carefully in the area around the pellet.

"What are you doing now?" Noel said.

"After a Komodo regurgitates a gastric pellet, it wipes and scrubs its mouth against the ground or low-lying bushes."

"Like it's trying to get rid of the spew taste?"

"Well, that's the theory."

Noel made a small sound of disgust. Next time she looked at him, he was on the other side of the glade with his head bent, searching the ground. She felt a rush of appreciation for his care, his interest, before reminding herself that Noel Baines only wanted to find some way to kill the lizard that had cost him another thousand dollars.

And then she found the unmistakeable sign.

Deep ruts that ploughed the forest floor in a repetitive pattern, as if a bogged car had spun its wheels in the mud, leaf litter either thrown aside or ground into the earth. The sight kicked her in the guts. "Here," she called, voice cracking.

Noel walked over. "You're sure?"

"Sure as I can be. That's where it cleaned its mouth."

"The giant lizard?"

"Some people call it the Devil dragon," she said.

"I suppose you believe me now." His face seemed collapsed, eyes wet.

"I've believed you all along." Embarrassed for him, she turned her gaze to the trees; each one just like the other. The fear of being lost came over her again. "Let's go back."

"Whatever you say, Dr. Harris." He turned and started walking.

Erin fell in behind. "I'm sorry about your heifer," she said.

"Thanks. You mightn't understand, but I want to kill that lizard."

"Me too," she said.

"Huh?" Noel stopped, turned, and regarded her with a frown. "I thought you were some kind of animal activist. You know, like a vegan or a Greenie."

"No, I'm a scientist."

How to explain? Eye-witness accounts, photos, films: all worthless compared to a specimen, alive or dead. In 1912, Lieutenant van Steyn van Hensbroek of the Dutch colonial administration in Java had brought back to civilisation a dead Komodo dragon. Its corpse had proved the reptile's existence. Without similar concrete and irrefutable evidence, curiosities like Bigfoot, the Loch Ness Monster, Chupacapra—and living *Varanus priscus*—would remain nothing more than tales, spooky stories told around a fire at school camps to give children the creeps.

"I need someone to lead me into this park," she said.

Noel stopped, jerked a thumb behind him. "You want to go in there?"

"Yes. What about your friends?"

"What friends?"

"The ones who live next door to you: the horse-stud couple; the hunters."

The old man looked her up and down.

For a moment, she felt foolish in her blousy top and Capri pants. She'd packed like a city person for a summer holiday. "I've got experience with reptiles," she said. "I've worked with five-metre saltwater crocodiles, six-metre scrub pythons. Look, I may be small, but I know what I'm doing. I want nothing more than to kill that lizard."

"You don't want to trap it alive?"

She shook her head. "Impossible. No one can trap an eight-metre carnivore like the sort you described. The animal is too big, the terrain too rugged."

"You want to kill it?"

"That would be the best option."

He nodded and smiled grimly. "Well, okay. I'll introduce you to my neighbours, Jamie and Megan Robinson. Nobody knows the inside of the park like they do. Just keep your mouth shut about them being hunters. Don't tell another living soul about the Robinsons, promise?"

"I promise." Russ didn't count, she thought. Russ never gossiped.

Noel nodded. "Fair enough. Let's go back to the quad-bike."

***

Noel's kitchen was typical of a country homestead: a huge space with countertops and cupboards on all sides, and a scrubbed wooden table dead-centre that could seat eight without any chance of knocking elbows. Sitting at the table, Erin listened to the one-sided phone conversation between Noel and Jamie Robinson. It seemed Robinson suspected Erin of masquerading as a university lecturer, and that she was actually some kind of government official trying to arrest him for illegal hunting. Erin sipped at her glass of water and watched Noel pace the kitchen. Limited by the cord of the wall-mounted telephone, he could only go a few steps in any direction.

"No worries," he said at last. "See you soon."

He hung up and sat near her at the table.

"You think they'll go for it?" she said.

"I reckon. Jamie thought I was leading him into a trap, silly bugger, but you'd have got the gist of that. Jamie and Megan are heading over now."

"Do they still believe your story?"

He shrugged. "They haven't told me otherwise."

The sound of shuffling footsteps turned Erin's gaze towards the hallway. A tall, sickly-looking woman, heavily pregnant, came into the kitchen and went straight to the refrigerator.

"How are you feeling?" Noel said.

"Like crap." She opened the fridge, took out a carton of orange juice.

"Kylie, here's the scientist I told you about."

"Uh-huh," Kylie said, pouring a drink without looking around.

"Dr. Harris, this is my daughter. As you can see, she's feeling a little poorly."

"Poorly?" Kylie returned the carton to the fridge and glanced at Erin. "If I can keep this drink down, it'll be a miracle."

"I'm sorry to hear that," Erin said.

Kylie began shuffling from the kitchen, glass of juice in hand.

"Where's the son-in-law at?" Noel said.

"Checking the cattle like you told him."

Noel consulted his watch. "Are you expecting him anytime soon?"

"Dunno," she called back from the hallway, and was gone.

Noel shook his head. "Lazy bastard. He's on my best horse and still dawdles all day long. If he's not back soon, I'll have to repair that irrigation pipe myself."

"You don't have anyone else to help?"

"Kylie used to be my right-hand man." Noel scratched his head. "They say the first baby is always the worst."

"Yes, that's right," Erin said, although she had no idea. Most of her friends at the university were at least twenty years older than her, and any children they had were fully-grown. The exception, of course, was Russ Walker-Smith, single with no kids at forty-two. She said, "You don't have any hired hands?"

Noel looked sideways at her as if she were kidding. "Yeah, but shit; only as contractors. I'm not made of money."

"You must like raising cattle."

"Like it?" He seemed perplexed. "What do you mean? It's my living."

"Dad," Kylie yelled from somewhere in the house. "I threw up again."

He shot an apologetic look at Erin, stood, took a bucket and mop from one corner of the kitchen, and hurried off down the hallway. Erin hunted through her bag and found her mobile. Russ answered on the second ring.

"Hey, it's me," she said. "I found the gastric pellet."

"Which is?"

"The regurgitation of keratin products: hooves, skin."

"Good Lord," Russ said. "Send me the picture."

"I didn't take one. I forgot my phone. But I'm going out there again this weekend. Noel thinks the next-door neighbours are willing guides."

"The hunter-bogans? Oh, why can't you come back and get a grant?"

The kitchen door to the yard opened, creaking on its hinges and startling Erin. A tall, thickset man with a dark mullet looked about, saw Erin, and gave her a broad smile.

"I'll call you later," Erin said, and hung up.

The man took a few shy steps into the kitchen. Aged about forty, he wore boots, faded shorts and a singlet; his exposed skin a deep brown as if he'd lived every day of his life outdoors, which he probably had. The man's eyes were a light, almost luminous shade of blue.

"Hey, I'm Jamie Robinson," he said. "You know, from next door?"

"Erin Harris. Thanks so much for coming."

She stood up, approached and held out her hand. Jamie stared at it for a moment, as if confused. Then he took it slowly. His hand was about the size of an oven mitt. The screen door creaked open again. A stocky and capable-looking woman strode into the kitchen, her blonde hair held in a low ponytail. Jamie dropped Erin's hand immediately. Erin offered the woman her hand. It was accepted without hesitation. The woman's palm felt callused. Oh God, how Erin regretted wearing the lavender blouse and Capri pants.

"Megan Robinson," the woman said. "Noel reckons you need our help."

"I sure do. Pleased to meet you, I'm Erin Harris."

Megan let go of Erin's hand, stepped back. "You're a lizard expert."

"Well, I'm a university academic who lectures in evolutionary biology, but I specialise in herpetology."

Jamie chuckled, and then looked from one woman to the other. "What? Come on, it's funny. It sounds like herpes."

Ignoring her husband, Megan said, "Where's Noel?"

Erin gestured towards the hallway. "Uh, I think his daughter just vomited."

"Again?" Megan crossed the kitchen, sat down at the table. "They need to change doctors. Morning sickness shouldn't last that long."

"You have children yourself?" Erin said, taking a seat.

"Yeah, two sons: one twenty-three, the other nineteen."

"Wow, really?" Erin smiled. "You look too young to have children that old."

Megan's grin showed white teeth and dimples. "We got started early." She glared at Jamie, and said, "What are you waiting for, a written invitation?"

Jamie pulled out a chair.

5

"Noel, we're here," Megan shouted. "Come out, you son of a bitch."

"I'll be there in a minute," Noel shouted back.

The three of them regarded each other around the table for an awkward amount of time. Jamie lit a cigarette. Still nobody spoke. The pressure to make small-talk, it seemed, rested on Erin. She said, "Noel tells me you run a horse stud."

"Yep," Megan said. "We've been running for only a few years, so there's a way to go yet before we're established and start making any money."

"Do you breed a lot of horses?"

"Enough to keep us busy."

"Oh?" Erin said, not sure of what else to offer.

Megan, however, seemed to take slight offence. "Hey, it's a shitload of work. There's paperwork coming out our arses. We have to group each horse into families, keep note of the mother and daughter, guarantee a certificate for the foundation mare. And that's just for starters. And sales are slow. It's hard to break even sometimes."

Erin didn't know how to reply. She nodded and said, "Sounds hectic."

The conversation ground to a halt.

Jamie shook his head, raked one giant hand through his mullet. "Jeez Louise, so you reckon Noel's dinosaur is real?"

"Yes, I do," Erin said.

"Shit, hey? That's the kind of weird shit that stops you in your tracks."

"It's actually a reptile, not a dinosaur," Erin said. "It's called *Varanus priscus*."

He laughed. "Fucken 'anus' what?"

"The Devil dragon. And I'm willing to pay both of you to lead me into the park to hunt one of those animals."

The couple stared at Erin, exchanged a glance between them.

"How much are we talking?" Megan said.

"I don't know. I guess we'll negotiate."

Noel entered the kitchen with the bucket and mop. Putting it down in one corner, he said, "You've introduced yourselves?"

"We're talking money now," Jamie said.

Noel took a seat. "Then talk to me. I'm picking up the tab."

"Wait a minute," Erin said. "No, this is my expedition."

"And it's me losing cattle, one thousand bucks a pop." He leaned his elbows on the table, and fixed the Robinsons with a direct, unblinking stare. "I'll pay one thousand dollars for your work over the weekend."

"But, no, hang on—"

Raising his voice, Noel said, "Dr. Harris, this is our expedition, yours and mine, not yours alone. I'm coming with you. It'll be a team of four: us and the Robinsons. And I'm paying. I won't take any arguing, you get me?"

Jamie thumped his palm on the table. "The four of us are gonna hunt a dinosaur this weekend? Shit, we'll need a couple of slabs."

"Of beer?" Erin said. "But there are firearms. You don't drink and hunt?"

"There's no other way to do it," Jamie said, and laughed, blue eyes shining.

***

Erin paused in the doorway of the disposals store, feeling stupid.

Megan said, "Have you at least got a sleeping bag?"

"No."

"Any equipment for camping? Anything at all? A can of insect repellent?"

"Not a single thing. I came here to do an interview, not go bush."

Megan offered a gracious, pitying look. "Wait by the counter. Jamie and I will collect the stuff. At your cost, you understand. We're not paying for any of this."

"Naturally," Erin said. "Does the store accept cards? Or only cash?"

"Sure, it accepts cards. You think we're the Back of Bourke?"

Yes, thought Erin, I do, but she bit her tongue. Megan and Jamie brushed past her and disappeared into the depths of the store. Erin looked about. Tents, camping and cooking equipment, work-wear, fishing rods and reels, military supplies like camouflage jackets and helmets, and an extravaganza of stuff that Erin had never seen before filled the shop. She approached the sales counter. Beneath the glass-top lay a shelf filled with head-mounted torches, retractable batons, Swiss Army knives.

"Can I help you?" the staff member said, a teenage girl with a stud in her nose and a streak of blue in her hair.

"No, I don't think so."

The girl lifted her eyebrows.

"I've got people choosing items for me," Erin said. "I'm to wait here."

The girl nodded as if this were an everyday occurrence. "No worries," she said. "Give us a yell if you want help. You're off into the park?"

"I'm sorry?"

"You're camping in the park? We get most of our visitors in autumn and spring. Summer's a little hot for most tourists." The girl roamed her gaze over Erin's face and bare arms, pale as dough. "Gosh, you'd better buy a shitload of sunscreen."

"Great suggestion. Now why don't you show me those Swiss Army knives?"

***

The shopping trip cost Erin close to seven-hundred dollars for equipment that she would most likely never use again. They returned to Noel's homestead. Megan and Jamie spread out the items across the kitchen table.

"Looks like you went the whole hog," Noel said.

"We had to," Megan said. "She didn't bring anything useful at all."

Erin felt herself blush. "For the last time, my intention was simply to interview people, not go on an expedition."

"Anyway, let's go through it." Megan pointed at different items. "Here's your tent: one-man, lightweight for plenty of ventilation, pretty easy to erect. We'll help you if you can't figure it out. There's your sleeping bag and air mattress—just roll up some clothes for a pillow; it's easier and uses less space. Backpack, first aid kit, compass, torch and spare batteries, a pot and cooking utensils, insect repellent, sunscreen, bottles for water."

"What about clothes?" Noel said. "We can't have her flouncing through the bush like a hippie."

Erin blushed again. "I've got trousers, socks, hiking boots, sleeved t-shirts and a waterproof jacket, all in camouflage green." Hesitantly, she picked up the shopping bags that sat near her chair, wondering if she should haul out the clothing as evidence.

"What about a hat?" Noel said.

"And one of those, too," Erin said. "Brimmed, Legionnaire-style."

Jamie said, "We'll bring the cooker, food, rubbish bags, rifles and ammo."

Noel reached into his back pocket and took out a sheaf of notes. "Here you go," he said, putting it on the table, "one grand."

Jamie picked up the money. "You want to give us the whole lot now?"

"Why, you'd rather get it in dribs and drabs?"

Jamie said, "But we might not even find your dinosaur. What then?"

"If it's there, we'll find it," Erin said.

They all turned to her.

"*Varanus priscus*—Devil dragon—is related to the Komodo dragon of Indonesia," she said, "so I can make educated guesses on its diet and behaviour."

"Guesses like what?" Megan said, crossing her arms.

Erin sat up in her chair. "It's a carnivore that mostly eats carrion, although it stalks live animals, too. Tests on the Komodo show that it can smell a dead or dying animal from about ten kilometres away, depending on wind conditions. Because of its greater size, I assume the Devil dragon has a better sense of smell than that."

Megan and Jamie regarded each other.

"The park is about three-hundred square kilometres," Megan said. "We'll be looking for a needle in a haystack."

"Not necessarily," Erin said. "The Devil dragon might be territorial. And we already know that the perimeter of Noel's back fence is within the lizard's current territory. So we'll lay a few baits and lure it."

"Lure it how?" Noel said.

All three of them gazed at her expectantly. For the first time all day, Erin felt sure of herself.

"It's cold-blooded," she began. "In summer, its number one concern is to prevent overheating. In very hot weather, it has only two periods of peak activity per day: early in the morning, and late in the afternoon. That's when it hunts. On cooler days, it might hunt all day, if it can stay in the shade. One meal of, say, a single goat might take the Devil dragon about a day or so to digest. Like all carnivores, it has a short intestinal tract. Whatever it can't digest, it vomits."

Megan wrinkled her nose. "Yuck. That's disgusting."

"You don't know the half of it," Noel said. "Me and Dr. Harris found a pile of its spew this morning."

The Robinsons regarded each other with mirrored expressions of distaste.

"All right, you old bastard, I'll bite," Jamie said. "How'd it look?"

"Like a turd from the Devil's own arse: hooves, skin, insects and some kind of slime that had dried into a huge bloody clot."

"Jeez, sorry I asked."

"Let's forget the gastric pellet for now," Erin said. "I want to tell you about the Devil dragon's habits. When it's not hunting, it focuses on temperature regulation: either basking or seeking shade. If necessary, it'll dig a hole in the ground. Hunting a live animal is hot work. That's why it prefers carrion."

Noel said, "How do you explain the beast attacking my heifer?"

"An opportunistic kill. The heifer was likely right next to the fence."

"You don't think she would run at the sight of a lizard that size?"

"I doubt she saw it at all," Erin said. "The Devil dragon is an ambush hunter. It would have approached slowly and quietly, and attacked from the rear."

Jamie shook his head and lit a cigarette.

"The teeth are serrated," Erin continued, "curved posteriorly, sharp at the tip and broad at the base like the teeth of a great white shark: perfect for holding onto prey. All it needs is one bite. The Devil dragon would have shaken and crushed the heifer until she stopped moving, much like the eating pattern of a great white."

Rocking back in his chair, Jamie dangled the smoke between his lips so that he could show both open palms. "What the actual fuck?" he said, looking from his wife to Noel and back again. "Are youse hearing the same shit as me, or what?"

"Yeah, we're hearing it," Megan said.

Jamie took a quick draw on his cigarette. "How big is this dinosaur, anyway?"

"Reptile," Erin said. "Its size is a contentious issue."

"Come again?"

"Palaeontologists don't know for sure, but Noel estimated it to be at least eight metres from nose to tail tip. That sounds about right to me."

"Eight metres?" Jamie's gaze again darted around the table. "That's nearly twice as long as our Land Rover."

"Quit yabbering, boy, and let Dr. Harris speak."

Jamie sat back and rolled his cigarette tip against the ashtray, knocking off the burnt tobacco, focusing too much on the task. He looked frightened. So did Megan and Noel. All of their faces had the same pinched and serious cast.

Erin said, "My guess is that the Devil dragon eats larger animals, such as Noel's heifer, in portions. Smaller animals would be devoured whole, headfirst."

Megan compressed her lips. "Like how a snake eats?"

"Yes, exactly like a snake."

Jamie elbowed his wife and smiled. In response, she closed her eyes and pinched at the bridge of her nose for a moment.

"She's got a thing about snakes," Noel said.

"Look, snakes don't bother me unless they're eating," Megan said. "The way they unhinge their bloody jaws gives me the creeps. It's not normal."

Jamie added, "If we're watching a doco on telly and there's a snake about to eat a rat or whatever, she's gotta leave the room."

Noel and the Robinsons shared a nervous laugh.

"Then you're not going to like the Devil dragon."

The laughter stopped.

"The Komodo is known to repeatedly ram a tree to force oversized prey down its gullet," Erin continued. "I'd expect the Devil dragon to do the same. And by the way, there's probably more than one lizard."

Noel's eyes popped. "More than one?"

"Of course. It would be extremely rare if you had witnessed the very last of a species. All animals exist as members of a population."

"What if they attack us at once?" Megan said.

Erin shook her head. "The Komodo is a solitary creature that never travels in a pack. I would expect the Devil dragon to be the same. To avoid unnecessary fighting, each individual would stay within its own territory. We'll be hunting the one that lives near Noel's back fence."

Everybody looked stunned; no one spoke. Jamie stubbed out his cigarette and lit another. Megan stared down at the table. Time passed. Noel, as if growing agitated, began tugging at his ear and shifting around in his chair.

"Well?" he said at last. "What do you reckon?"

Jamie rubbed his chin. "A lizard the size of a four-berth caravan? I dunno."

Noel lifted his jaw. "You saying you want more money?"

"Don't get your knickers in a knot, old man," Megan said. "We agreed to the hunt, and that's that." She turned to Erin. "How do we bait this thing?"

"We'll catch a few goats," Noel suggested, "stake them by my back fence and hope the bastard comes back."

Erin shook her head. "Absolutely not. Under no circumstances should we try to lead the Devil dragon close to town. Ideally, I'd like to be inside the park with at least a five kilometre buffer zone between us and any picnic areas or hiking tracks."

"Okay," Jamie said. "Anything else you need?"

"If I could pick and choose, I'd ask for a flat, open area within a few kilometres of Noel's property that has about fifty metres of clear sight in all directions."

Jamie nudged Megan. She nodded. Obviously, they had a spot in mind.

Megan said, "If you drive the main road into the park, head southwest on a particular fire-trail and bush bash for a while, there's a clearing that overlooks the escarpment. That'd be our best bet."

"Okay," Jamie said, "so we get to this clearing and then what?"

"We set up camp dead centre," Erin continued. "We slaughter four deer and hang one carcass in a tree at each point on the compass. Then we watch and wait. The aroma of so much carrion in one spot should prove irresistible. You keep your rifles at the ready."

For a moment, the three of them didn't move, or even seem to breathe.

"Oh, fucken *what*?" Jamie said at last, and laughing, slapped his forehead into his open palm. "I need a beer."

Noel stood up. "I reckon we all do." He went to the fridge, gave a can to each of them, and kept one for himself.

Erin didn't usually drink beer, but for the sake of camaraderie, she opened hers and took a sip. It tasted fizzy and bitter, as awful as the last time she'd tried it. She glanced around the table. Noel and the Robinsons appeared sombre, perhaps overwhelmed. Jamie butted out a smoke and lit another. A minute or so passed while they drank in silence. Erin could hear a couple of magpies warbling from the backyard. Finally, she said, "We don't have to do this if you don't want."

Noel frowned at her. "I'm in."

"Us too," Jamie said.

Erin felt a rush of gratitude, a tingling of excitement—or perhaps fear. She looked at Megan. "How powerful are your rifles?"

"What do you need?"

"I don't know much about firearms. But the Devil dragon would most likely be thick-skinned like a crocodile, covered in organic chain mail. No one knows for sure. I'm taking an educated guess. Does that help?"

The Robinsons looked at each other. Jamie shrugged and nodded as if to say, *Go ahead and tell her*.

Megan said, "We're both licensed. We're legally allowed to use semi-automatic rifles. Places up north hire us to hunt feral boar from a chopper."

Erin sat back in her chair. "You shoot pigs from an actual helicopter?"

"All the time," Megan said matter-of-factly, but there was a ghost of a smile at her lips, a proud lift to her chin.

"But not in this particular park," Noel said. "There's no hunting allowed."

"Putting that fact aside," Megan continued, "we've got a lot of firearms at our disposal. We're able to consider the animal, the terrain, the weather."

Jamie turned to his wife and said, "We're going to need semi-autos for quick back-up shots. And mushroom slugs."

Erin said, "Mushroom slugs?"

"Hollow-points," he said. "The bullet is the bit at the end of the cartridge, right? If you shoot an animal with a regular bullet, it'll probably go straight through and out the other side. Unless you hit the bugger right in the head or chest, it might still be able to run away. But if you make a little hole in the bullet, then it kind of explodes once it hits the target and makes a big mess of the animal's guts. Nothing's gonna walk away from damage like that."

Oh my God. But Erin just smiled and nodded.

Noel said, "You got many hollow-points at home?"

"Nah," Megan said, "but it won't take long. We've got a custom press."

"I'd like to leave as soon as possible," Erin said. "I have to be back at work Monday morning."

Jamie said, "Then we'll go tomorrow. What time do we want to get started?"

"It depends on the weather," Erin said. "Does anyone know the forecast?"

"Low forties," Jamie said. "A stinker."

"Then I would guess the lizard's peak activity times would be about ten in the morning and five in the afternoon."

Noel glanced at the Robinsons. "How long do you reckon to shoot the deer?"

Megan tapped at her lips with a forefinger and stared at the ceiling, as if calculating. "Well, let's see, the red and fallow should be at the creeks by sunrise. We can split up, take one creek each. If you don't care too much about size, with a bit of luck we could get four of them inside two hours, easy."

"Easy as having a shit." Jamie crushed his cigarette into the ashtray. "Does it have to be deer?"

"No," Erin said. "Any kind of meat will do."

"What about pig or goat?"

"That should be fine, as long as the carcasses are big enough."

"Got it," Megan said. "To be on the safe side, give us about four hours to hunt, shoot and hang; a couple of hours to drive and set up camp."

"Okay," Noel said, "So, Dr. Harris, allowing for some leeway, we'll pick you up outside the hotel at three-thirty a.m. on the dot."

"Fine," she said. Everything felt surreal. Under the table, she interlocked her fingers and squeezed her hands to the point of pain. No, she wasn't dreaming. This was really happening.

Noel raised his beer can. "Cheers. To us, and to our Devil dragon."

While Erin and Jamie raised their drinks, Megan pulled a sullen face and kept her arms crossed. Her attitude took the air out of them, especially Jamie, who lost his grin and stared down at the table.

"Got a bee in your bonnet, Missy?" Noel said.

"Yeah: in a way."

"Care to share with the rest of us?"

"We're going into the park without a camping permit or any documentation," Megan said. "Do you understand, Erin?"

"Of course I do."

Megan continued, "We're doing this without hunting permits, public liability insurance or guide licences. If something goes wrong, we don't call for help. We deal with it ourselves. That's important. I want to make this clear. If we get sprung hunting in the park, me and Jamie are in a shitload of strife. If anyone blabs about our monster hunt and the authorities find out we took firearms into the park, the same shitload of strife. Understand?"

Noel exhaled. "Look, the four of us are on the same team."

"Sure we are." Megan cut her eyes at Erin. "I'm just being thorough."

Erin leaned across the table. "Listen to me. When we kill a Devil dragon, we're going to shout it from the rooftops."

"Screw that. We'll lose our hunting licences."

"No. We won't have any trouble. On the contrary, we'll be bringing to civilisation the greatest zoological find in a hundred years or more. I'm talking front page news around the globe, bigger than the discovery of the *Coelacanth* in 1938."

Jamie pulled a face. "The discovery of what?"

"A fish everyone thought to be extinct for sixty-five million years until fishermen in South Africa caught one that was very much alive."

Noel clamped a hand on her shoulder. It felt like solidarity.

"Maybe finding the Devil dragon will be more important than that," she said, spurred. "It might be up there with the discovery of *Archaeopteryx*, a dinosaur with feathers: the missing link that bolstered Darwin's theory of evolution." Erin's hammering heart made her stop, take a breath. When she spoke, her voice shook. "We'll be famous. All four of us: rich and famous. Rich beyond your wildest dreams."

Jamie gasped. "No shit?"

"No shit. Look, new species are found all the time—insects and fish, in particular—and no one but experts gives a damn. A new butterfly, and the public thinks, *oh, how boring, so the spots on its wings are pink instead of red.* But how do you think the world is going to react when we show off an eight-metre long monster? A huge, living beast, a creature straight out of a Hollywood special-effects movie?"

Jamie laughed. "People are gonna lose their shit over it."

"You bet they are," she said.

Of course, *Varanus priscus* would be renamed *Harris's dragon.* She would never share that glory. But the others could have their interviews on TV talk-shows, two-page magazine spreads, book deals: their fifteen minutes.

"There's nothing to worry about," she continued. "Once we find and kill one of these lizards, we'll all be living the high life. Trust me."

6

After a dinner of salad and an obscene amount of wine—perhaps half a bottle if one added up the three glasses—Erin retired to her hotel room and called Russ Walker-Smith.

"I'm investigating the park," she said, "before sunrise."

As she told him about the hunting expedition, she became increasingly aware of how insane it sounded. And besides all that, *Varanus priscus* had last roamed southeastern Australia some 12,000 years ago. What the hell did she know about the creature? What did anybody know? Maybe it didn't behave like a Komodo. Maybe her every assumption could be wrong. The reconstruction of its skeleton that ranged down the Melbourne Museum steps was more guesswork than fact, after all....

"Russ?" she said. "Is baiting with carrion a dumb idea?"

"I'm in two minds. On the one hand, your idea is sound from a practical point of view. But if this reptile exists and is actually in the park, then the idea is exceptionally dumb because it is dangerous."

She lay back on the bed, stared up at the stippled, yellowed paint on the ceiling. "Just in case, a copy of my will is in the top-right drawer of my desk at the office. I've left everything to the university."

"Are you serious?" Russ said. "Don't be maudlin."

She'd meant it as a joke, but now that she'd articulated her fear, a chill began to crawl along her spine. "I have a couple of presents for you, by the way. In my flat, on my dressing table, there's a keychain with a biohazard emblem."

"This isn't funny. You're worrying me. Is that your intention? To worry me?"

"And on my wardrobe's top shelf," she continued, "wrapped in plain paper, there's a poster reprint of Ernst Haeckel's engravings of diatom formations. I was going to frame it for your birthday."

"Lord. Tell me you're joking or I'll hang up."

The silence stretched on. She could hear Russ breathing. She closed her eyes. The bed swayed a little beneath her. Oh, too much wine.

Finally, she said, "You like me, Russ. Don't you?"

"Like you? What a ridiculous question."

"Tell me why you like me."

"I'm sorry?"

She sighed. "What is it that you like about me?"

"I don't know; everything."

"That's not an answer."

He paused. "Uh, well, you're attractive, smart, incisive.... How's that?"

"So, if you met someone who was equally as attractive, smart and incisive," she said, hearing the edge in her own voice, "you'd like her just the same?"

"I've made my feelings clear over the time we've worked together." After a while, he said, "You sound terribly drunk. Are you?"

"Yes. And soon, I'm going into the park. My alarm is set for three a.m."

"Come back instead. We'll get a grant and launch a proper expedition."

"No, there's no time. I can't share this discovery with anybody. It has to be called *Harris's dragon*, okay? Remember that: *Harris's dragon*."

"You're so bloody stubborn."

"Maybe that's something else you like about me." The bed slewed beneath her. "I have to sleep now. Forget this whole conversation. Scout's honour, I'll give you the keychain and the Haeckel print on your birthday. Just fake a look of surprise." She smiled, closed her eyes. Hot tears slid into her hairline. "Okay, I'll call you Sunday night, and see you first thing Monday morning."

She disconnected and switched off her phone in case Russ tried to call back.

Turning on her side, she regarded the bags of camouflage clothing sitting on the floor nearby. Khaki was a colour she avoided. It made her look positively jaundiced. On impulse, she got up, put on the hiking boots, and stomped around the room for a couple of minutes. The boots hurt her toes. Great, she'd develop blisters in record time, be limping within hours, appear even more foolish to her country born-and-bred companions. She unlaced the boots and kicked them off.

Her eyes pricked with fresh tears.

Oh, screw it.

Nerves, she decided, and nothing more. She was out of her comfort zone. Erin always took weeks—sometimes months—to methodically prepare for a research project. Spontaneity wasn't her strong suit. And guns? Shit, no. Camping? She didn't even like picnics. The possibility of confronting the *Varanus priscus* itself, one of the most ferocious apex predators Australia had ever known? And conversely, the possibility of not confronting it; finding out that the lizard didn't exist after all.... Erin groaned. No wonder she'd gotten drunk. Slumping onto the bed, she put her face in her hands. Dad's words came to mind: *You'll never be better than me*. The memory caused Erin to straighten up.

"Watch me," she said out loud.

She considered the scars criss-crossing her hands. Over the years, countless lizards, snakes and turtles had bitten her. Once, the snap of a baby saltwater crocodile had left a tooth embedded in her knuckle. And the very first time she had helped manhandle a big croc, the staff of the wildlife sanctuary had asked her to take charge of its jaws and she'd done it despite the terror, thanks to knowing what to do.

No more pissing and moaning.

She was scared. So what? As a trained scientist with years of experience, both theoretical and in the field, she could and would lead this expedition successfully, no matter what happened, no matter what scared her.

***

In summer, a city retains most of its daytime temperature overnight. Not so in a country town, apparently. Perhaps the lack of high-rise buildings, concrete and bitumen impedes heat absorption; Erin didn't know. Waiting on the footpath outside the hotel, she shivered, feeling preposterous in camouflage gear and boots. Her watch read 3.34 a.m. Noel and the Robinsons were late.

She tried to hunker deeper into her jacket, pushing her fists into the pockets, wishing for gloves. Why hadn't they told her to buy gloves? Overhead, the stars gleamed bright as flashbulbs in the clear black sky. There were no sounds apart from the faraway trilling of cicadas. After five hours of sleep, Erin felt drunk yet hungover: a horrible combination of wooziness, queasiness and headache. Oh, why had she consumed so much wine? Some water might help. Her rucksack held two full bottles. However, it lay between her feet. If she bent down, she might topple over or throw up.

Damn, she was cold.

Perhaps underestimating the night-time temperature of a small town was the least of her worries. This whole expedition was crazy. Then last night's phone call with Russ. Had she said anything silly? In all likelihood, everything she'd said had been silly. Vaguely, she remembered talking about his birthday presents. *You like me, Russ. Don't you?* Wincing, she contemplated ringing him. She checked her watch again: 3.36 a.m. Like every other sane person, he'd be asleep right now. And where the hell were Noel and the Robinsons?

The distant sound of a tractor caught her attention. The rumbling gradually came nearer. *This is it.* She looked about. A four-wheel drive turned onto the street. City roads may be crammed with four-wheel drives, but she'd never seen a vehicle quite like this before. It looked like a monster truck. The cabin sat up high on enormous nobbled tyres. The lights along the roof-rack must be for kangaroo spotting. Erin's nervous system gave a little kick.

She raised one hand to shield her eyes from the headlights. The vehicle pulled up next to her, jostling from the slow, heavy chug of its diesel engine. Megan sat behind the wheel, Jamie in the passenger seat. Noel leaned across the back seat to open the door. Hoisting her rucksack, Erin wondered how to get in. The height of the cabin made the back seat level with her chest. Would she have to clamber in headfirst?

"Take hold of this," Noel said, pointing upward at the grab-handle, "and use the step." He pointed down at the running board. "First, give me your luggage."

She handed him her rucksack and managed to awkwardly climb into the cabin. The open door leaned out a lot further than those on her sedan, and she had trouble closing it without falling out. At last, she sat back and fastened her seatbelt, panting a little from her exertions.

Megan turned and with a raised eyebrow, said, "You right?"

Blushing, Erin nodded.

Megan put the car into gear. They soon left the hotel behind. Erin watched it disappear with a pang of regret. For the next two nights, she'd be sleeping on the ground and going to the toilet behind bushes.

After a few turns, they left the town. There were no more streetlights. Erin gazed out the side window. Silhouettes of trees and shrubs swept past in the darkness. She took off her glasses and polished them on the hem of her t-shirt. The warmth of the cabin relaxed her, made her eyelids droop. How much time to get to wherever they were going? Perhaps she could doze.

"You been to the park before?" Jamie said, turning in his seat to glance at her.

"No."

"How come? Not enough reptiles in it?"

"I'm not a field herpetologist," she said. "I spend most of my time in a classroom teaching evolutionary biology."

"What's that?"

She put her glasses back on. "Well, I suppose the central idea is that every living thing, from the blue whale to the pygmy shrew, shares a common ancestor. Evolutionary biology is concerned with the history of all life on earth."

"Shit, hey?" he said.

"What about wrestling a crocodile?" Megan said. "Ever done it?"

"I teach, so I'm usually behind a lectern. Twice a year, I conduct a small research study with my students, but only in controlled environments, like zoos or wildlife sanctuaries. Sometimes we conduct pilot studies using museum collections. Pure field herpetology is a different discipline altogether."

"But you're into lizards, right?" Megan said.

"Yes, I prefer lizards, but I study Australian reptiles and amphibians, which are good subjects when it comes to the study of modification through descent. That's one of my core interests: small-scale evolutionary adaptations. My last field study focused on changes in gene frequency from one generation to the next within a single population of amphibians; a particular species of frog, to be exact."

Utter silence. Damn, she'd slipped into lecturer-mode.

Then Jamie began laughing. He turned in his seat to grin at her, his luminous blue eyes shining in the dim light. "Fucken *what*? Were you talking English?"

Erin scowled. Fleeting memories of high school made her momentarily long for the safety of the university staff room, dubbed "Nerd Haven" by the faculty staff.

"Pay no mind, Dr. Harris," Noel said. "Some of us have brains, others don't."

Jamie gave another laugh. "Hey, old bugger, want to walk to the campsite?"

"And some of us have manners, too."

Megan said, "So, how's your daughter going to manage while you're gone?"

"Oh, I've got my sister dropping in with food," Noel said, "morning and night."

"That cranky battle-axe? Why didn't you ask Mavis?"

"She's got enough on her plate. Didn't you hear? Jack's having an operation."

"Another one?" Jamie said. "What's wrong with the bastard now?"

"His back problems again?" Megan said. "Don't get me started."

Sighing, Erin leaned back into the headrest and closed her eyes.

***

The quiet woke her up. The engine had stopped.

Patting at her hand, Noel said, "We're here."

But where was "here" exactly? Erin scrubbed at her eyes. It was still night-time. Fumbling, opening the car door, she clutched the grab handle and slid down, down, down from the vehicle until her boots touched dirt. She checked her watch: almost five o'clock. A false dawn brightened the horizon. Noel and Megan were already outside and watching Jamie climb a ladder to the roof rack.

Erin needed to pee. She looked about. The four-wheel drive was parked in the middle of an empty plain ringed with faraway trees: the exact kind of spot, Erin realised, that she had requested. *Fifty metres clear in all directions....* Standing on the vehicle's roof, Jamie began throwing down bags, alternately, to Megan and Noel, who placed them on the ground. Everyone seemed to know what to do without any kind of discussion.

Approaching Megan, Erin whispered, "I have to go to the toilet."

"Then go."

Erin hesitated.

Megan caught a bag, dropped it, put her hands on her hips. "Wait a sec, Jamie," she said, then faced Erin. "Look, it's easy. Pick a tree. Check for creatures before you squat. You don't want to get bit on your lady parts. Hey, Jamie, where's the dunny paper? She's gotta go."

Erin blushed. Jamie turned this way and that, looking over the remaining bags. Then he unzipped one and tossed a roll of toilet paper at Erin, which she caught.

"You need a trowel?" he said.

"A trowel?"

Megan smiled patiently. "Number one or number two?"

"Uh...number one."

"No trowel." Megan slapped Erin on the back. "When you're done, push the paper into the dirt, okay? It helps to rot it down faster."

"One more thing," Jamie said. "See that over there?"

She looked where he was pointing. The clearing, in fact, wasn't ringed with trees all the way around. On one side loomed the vault of sky above a lip of bare dirt.

"That's an escarpment, right?" he said. "We're off the beaten track. There's no fencing, and trust me, it's a fucken long way down. Stay away from the edge."

"Okay," she said. "I will."

Wandering off alone seemed crazy. Was it safe? Erin dawdled toward the trees. It took a slow couple of minutes. Would she encounter wild animals? A *Varanus priscus*? She kept looking back. Noel and the Robinsons continued to unpack. None of them bothered to keep an eye on her. Their *laissez-faire* attitude made her feel bolder. She gazed around. The open area was flat, a little rocky, mostly soil. Here and there lay exposed tree roots. The Robinsons had picked the perfect spot. But why the localised deforestation? Perhaps a fire had once run through here and, for whatever reason, the area had never recovered.

When she got behind a stand of trees, she realised that her small backpack, the one that held her torch and headlamp, lay in the car. Damn. She'd have to be more organised from now on. In lieu of sighting the ground, she stamped on it for a good minute. Then she unzipped, hesitated. Standing stock-still, she listened to the night, trying to identify any sounds that might suggest danger. Nothing except crickets, the occasional twitter from a hidden bird.... Quickly, she dropped her pants. As she urinated, the widening puddle made her shift her feet until she almost tipped over. Shouldn't soil absorb liquid? She put a hand against the nearest tree for balance. A line of ants ran over her fingers and she shook them off, almost losing her balance again. Shit. If only she had a can of insect spray.

Goddamn, how she hated the outdoors.

By the time she got back, she'd calmed down. Noel and the Robinsons had almost finished setting up camp. The tents were erected. A large rectangular awning ran perpendicular from the car's roof-rack to a couple of poles, with Jamie opening up canvas chairs beneath it, while Noel and Megan unpacked the stove. Erin placed the toilet roll on one of the eskies. No one so much as glanced at her.

"Can I do anything?" she finally said.

"I don't know." Noel said. "Can you?"

"Forget it. I'll leave it to the experts."

From her larger rucksack, she took out the backpack. Climbing into the car, she opened the backpack and examined its contents: high definition camcorder with optical zoom, spare battery and additional memory card; compact digital mega-zoom still camera, spare battery and extra memory card; mobile phone with various charger cords—everything in perfect working order. Then, of course, the items that the Robinsons had picked out for her at the disposals store: compass, binoculars, first aid kit, torch, headlamp, butane lighter, sunscreen, insect repellent, water bottle, a couple of high-energy snack bars. She lifted the backpack by one strap: hefty as all hell. Was she expected to lug this thing around? The expedition was meant to focus around the campsite. That's what she had envisioned, anyway. Did Noel and the Robinsons have other ideas? She wanted to ask, but they were still hard at work. Instead, she took out her mobile to send a text to Russ. He deserved an update—or perhaps an apology after her drunken call last night.

No signal. Her heart gave a flutter.

"Sorry, Dr. Harris." Noel stood at the open door. "We're cut off out here."

"Then I'd like to use the satellite phone, if I may."

"Satellite phone?" Jamie stuck his head in the doorway. "Jeez, do you know how expensive those things are?"

"We're hunting illegally," came Megan's stern voice from somewhere behind the vehicle. "Nobody needs to know where we are."

"But what if we need help?"

Megan appeared in the doorway. "Remember what I told you? If we need help, we deal with it ourselves."

"And in an emergency? If we need to be evacuated?"

Megan smiled, opened her arms wide. "Then tough shit."

Erin didn't know how to respond. A broken bone, a dead car battery, getting lost, mauled by wild animals: why didn't the Robinsons have an emergency plan?

"It's coming up on sunrise," Jamie said. "We'd better get hunting. Brekkie will have to wait 'til we get back. Erin, you coming with me?"

The thought shocked her. "To shoot a deer?"

"Nah." He winked. "To shoot two of them. Hey, no worries, it'll be fun."

Erin bit her lip. Her first impulse was to refuse. Then again, what about her drunken resolve of last night? *Watch me, Dad.* She put her mobile into the backpack and climbed down from the car. Jamie already had some kind of rifle slung by a strap over his shoulder. Erin had never seen any kind of firearm up close. Likewise, she'd never seen an animal being shot. Yes, with a tranquiliser gun, of course, but with a real gun? Shot dead?

"Better grab your backpack," Megan said. "You might need it."

7

After trekking over uneven ground and dodging tree branches for some half-hour, Erin hurt all over, particularly her boot-shod feet. God, her blisters must be bleeding. If she were at home, she might be showering by now, or preparing a bowl of puffed quinoa for breakfast.

"Are we walking in a circle?" she said.

Jamie glanced back, frowning. "Shush."

"Fine," she hissed. "But it seems to me we're walking in a goddamned circle."

"That's to keep the breeze in our faces, right? Otherwise the deer can smell us downwind. Don't get your knickers in a knot. We're almost at the creek."

"How can you tell?" she said. "Everywhere looks the same. Exactly the same."

"Yeah, but nah. Me and the missus sometimes hunt in this spot. Big creeks are where the deer hang out. So for fuck's sake, woman, be quiet."

He kept walking. Fuming, Erin followed. Occasionally, he stopped to note the immediate surroundings. She finally realised he was looking for and finding signs—scrapes in the tree bark, spoor, broken branches—and felt embarrassed at her outburst.

"Mind what I told you," he said. "Look where you're stepping."

"I'm being as careful as possible."

"Then don't make so much noise."

She exhaled through her teeth. "It's your fault for asking me to come with you. I could have stayed at camp."

"Yeah? And who's going to carry the second deer?"

"Oh, that's just great. Now you tell me. How much does a deer weigh? More than a case of wine, I'll bet."

Jamie stopped abruptly. She ran into him, mashing her nose into his backpack. Then he lifted one forefinger, slowly, in a gesture that froze her to the spot. He lowered himself to his haunches. Behind him, Erin did the same. He unslung the rifle. She peeped over his wide shoulder.

Nothing: just trees, trees and more trees.

The first light had tinted the landscape an eerie palette of cold yellowish-grey. She'd been focusing on keeping Jamie's backpack in her line of sight during this whole trek and hadn't noticed the beginnings of sunrise.

"What is it?" she whispered. "A deer? Where?"

He didn't reply. Instead, he took the earplugs hanging about his neck by a cord and put them in, one at a time. For some reason, at the disposal store the Robinsons had bought her earmuffs instead of plugs. What, did they assume she wasn't capable of inserting plugs? How ridiculous. They insisted upon treating her like a child. Then Jamie tapped at one of his ears, as if signalling her, but Erin was too busy fuming to acknowledge him.

Jamie lifted the rifle, putting the stock against his body. A leisurely, metallic one-two sound; he must be loading, getting ready to fire. His head lowered. She guessed he was putting his eye to the scope. A jolt of excitement coursed through her. Where was the deer? She couldn't see it. Despite herself, she huddled closer. The landscape seemed identical in every direction. Eucalypts, shrubs, granite outcrops. What could he see that she couldn't?

He stood up.

Erin was still rising from a crouch when the shot rang out, sharp as a whip crack. Already unbalanced, the shock of the sudden noise toppled her into the dirt. Jamie turned, took out the earplugs and smiled at her.

"One down, one to go," he said, and held out his hand. She took it. He pulled her to her feet in an instant. "You right?" he added. "Aw, silly duffer. No earmuffs?"

"I forgot to put them on."

"Forget too many times, you'll go deaf."

He gripped the walkie-talkie clipped to his belt and thumbed a button twice.

"What are you doing?" Erin said.

Jamie winked. "Just told the missus that we got a clean kill, and we're okay."

Two responding clicks sounded almost immediately.

"That's her buzzing back to let me know she got the message." He laughed. "We're first cab off the rank. Hah, she'll be so pissed off. That woman's got a competitive streak a mile wide."

Erin nodded. Her ears rang. Jamie slung the rifle over his shoulder and hurried down the steep embankment, slowing himself here and there by grabbing at tree trunks. Erin followed as fast as she could. Somehow, Jamie had the knack of negotiating at once both the rocky, uneven ground and the branches at head-height without tripping or losing an eye. Erin had to take the terrain at a much slower pace. The blue-check of his flannel shirt almost disappeared into the trees and then he stopped.

At last, she caught up to him, panting. The creek was about three-metres wide and ran quickly around fallen branches and rocks in its bed. The water looked fresh and inviting, the air smelt clean. For a moment, Erin almost understood the appeal of camping. Almost.

"Come and have a look at this little beauty," Jamie said.

He was on his haunches next to the body of the fallen deer. Erin squatted nearby. If she wasn't mistaken, this was a fallow deer, *Dama dama*, a young buck, its furry antlers a couple of underdeveloped spikes, coat a deep chestnut mottled with white spots. The deer lay on its side. The open eye glistened like a wet, black marble, and Jamie touched it.

"If it doesn't blink," he said, "it's dead." He pointed at the blood on its chest. "See that? How it looks pinkish with some froth? That means I hit a lung, killed the bugger straight out. That's what you want. You aim for the upper shoulder. Hit anywhere else, you've got to track the poor bastard to finish the job, and all the while he's running from you, he's suffering."

In the chilly air, the heat from the animal rose as if from a low fire. Erin reached out, touched the deer's belly. She had never touched a deer. The fur was stiff, wiry. Somehow, she had expected the fur to feel soft, like that of a cat, and the realisation made her feel uncomfortably foolish. *What the hell am I doing here?* For a moment, her office at the university came to mind: the spotless desk, the tiers of file-holders, three-drawer metal cabinet. Most people decorated their spaces with photographs, knick-knacks, and pot plants. Not Erin. Despite occupying it for many years, her office always looked as if it had been set up a few minutes ago. *Spartan,* her colleagues called it. If only she were back there now.

"Is he big enough?" Jamie said, lifting the deer's head by the snout as if to inspect it. "Will the Devil dragon go for him?"

In all honesty, she didn't know. Instead, she said, "I'm sure this deer is fine."

A distant shot boomed and echoed. Two clicks sounded on Jamie's walkie-talkie, which he returned. Megan and Noel had bagged their first kill. The breeze nipped at Erin's nose and ears. She wished she were home, reading the paper over a coffee.

"Okey dokey," Jamie said, and hung his rifle and backpack on a nearby branch. "Let's get started."

"On what?"

"Field dressing this little bugger. You're not squeamish, are you?"

She recalled her reaction upon viewing the remains of Noel's heifer. Yes, she was squeamish, that's for sure. Despite dissection being a necessary evil when one is a biologist, her stomach never got used to it. Instead, she said, "Squeamish? Not particularly."

"Good, because shit's about to get messy."

He took a knife from the scabbard on his belt and cut the deer's throat in one stroke.

***

"This is ridiculous," Erin said. "Wouldn't it be easier if you shot the second deer yourself? The others have probably finished their hunt and returned to camp."

"Pipe down and concentrate."

Erin could hardly hear him through the earmuffs. She huffed out an exasperated breath, lifted the rifle again and sighted down the scope.

"Not like that," Jamie said. "You'll end up a pirate."

"I'm sorry?"

"Blind with a patch. If you pull the trigger now, the recoil from the scope will punch those fucken spectacles and your eyeball right out the back of your fucken head. Yeah? Put the recoil pad to your shoulder, like I told you."

She obeyed, or, at least, thought she did.

"Not against your collarbone, dummy," Jamie said. "You'll break that, too."

He manhandled the stock to rest against the meat of her front deltoid. Erin could feel her cheeks burning. She wasn't used to feeling stupid. Her students looked up to her. In any conversation with her peers, she held her own.

"Now open your feet," he said, demonstrating. "One foot in back, with your weight on your front foot, like a fighter, see? You've got to brace for the kick."

"Fine," she said, and did as she was told.

"The magazine holds four rounds. There's a round in the chamber. Put the crosshairs on the mark in the tree. Hold her steady."

"May I shoot now?"

"That depends. Have you got the mark in your crosshairs?"

"My arms are getting tired."

Jamie made a tutting sound. "Shit, I hope you teach as good as you whinge."

She gritted her teeth and pulled the trigger. The shot sounded loud through the earmuffs, the stock punched her shoulder as hard as a fist and the rifle jerked violently in her hands as if it had come to life. The sheer power of the firearm amped her pulse. *Holy shit.* She felt like whooping. But when she looked around at Jamie, he had his arms folded at his chest and his lips pursed.

"Well, that was shithouse," he said. "Try again."

Humiliated, she dragged off the earmuffs and held out the rifle.

He shook his head. "Eject the shell and reload, like I showed you."

"I don't see the point."

"The point is practice, so you can shoot a deer. And you can't shoot a deer if you don't know how to use that Remington. Now, go ahead and reload."

"Oh, for Christ's sake, just shoot a deer yourself."

He dropped his arms and stepped closer, his expression stony. Involuntarily, she took a step back. Despite his dopey face, twinkly blue eyes and joke of a mullet hairstyle, Jamie was a big man. His sudden intrusion into her personal space felt intimidating.

"If your Devil dragon turns up," he said, "we'll need all hands on deck."

"Are you serious? I wasn't planning on shooting the lizard myself."

"So what was your plan? Tea and scones while the rest of us do the work?"

But she had engaged *them* as the hunters. However, it would seem churlish to throw that fact at him. Erin adjusted her earmuffs, lifted the rifle, and used the bolt to eject the shell and reload. Jamie nodded and stepped back. Putting the stock to her shoulder and squinting down the scope, Erin contemplated the "X" Jamie had carved into the tree trunk some 15 metres away. How might the scales of *Varanus priscus* look in these crosshairs? Round, triangular, hexagonal, square? Would they juxtapose like the dermal plates of a crocodile? She pulled the trigger, reflexively blinking at the critical moment. The power of the shot reverberated through her whole body.

She lowered the rifle, gasping.

Jamie rubbed his chin, shrugged, and said, "At least you hit the tree this time. Go on, give it another go."

***

"Don't hold your breath," Jamie said, close to her ear. "Before you take the shot, take a few breaths through your mouth, slow and steady. It'll stop you from shaking."

The vision within the scope had black edges. That meant she was too close. Erin moved her head back slightly. But the deer had gone. She looked up from the scope, trying to see the animal with her naked eyes.

"To the right," Jamie said. "Use the scope. Look towards the right."

Erin put her eye back to the scope and shifted the rifle. Saw the deer. Just its back leg and tail. The fur was a reddish-brown with light spots. Of course, this must be a red deer, *Cervus elaphus*. The tunnel view through the scope began to quiver. Sweat slicked Erin's palms. She had her finger on the trigger shield, as Jamie had instructed, but her finger stuttered against it. Her entire body had turned into a pulse beat.

"I can't do it," she said. "I can't keep the gun still."

"It's a rifle, not a gun. And yeah, you can. Breathe. Relax. In a while, he's going to turn around and have a drink from the creek. For now, he's checking things out, figuring if it's safe."

Erin's shoulder muscles started to burn. The rifle felt heavier with every passing second. The deer stepped delicately along the bank of the creek, its slender legs full of muscle and tendon. Sweat gathered along Erin's hairline.

"It's okay," Jamie said. "Keep breathing."

Erin had never killed a free, wild creature. She had pithed lab toads, euthanized lab rats, put injured animals out of their misery with injections of pentobarbital. This wasn't the same. Not even close.

She needed to wipe the sweat from her eyes, but she couldn't let go of the rifle. The deer turned around. Its moist nostrils winked at the air. Could the animal smell them? Were they downwind or upwind? Erin didn't know. Her long pants and long-sleeved top blocked out the breeze. The deer stepped one elegant leg and then another toward the fast-flowing creek. Erin's heart rate kicked up. The deer lowered its head to the water. Erin noted the antlers: two single, unbranched antlers that curved to face each other. This was a juvenile, she realised. During her shooting lesson, Jamie had referred to juvenile red deer as "brockets".

"Put the crosshairs on the shoulder," Jamie said, "at the base of the neck."

The vision within the scope wobbled harder. Then, Erin became aware of Jamie coming up behind her, gently, softly, pressing his body against hers as he supported her trigger arm with one hand, took the weight of the rifle in the other. She could feel the heat coming off him. She closed her eyes momentarily.

"Base of the neck," Jamie said. "Aim for the base of the neck. Put your finger on the trigger."

She did as she was told. Her heart slammed against her ribs.

"Got it?" Jamie said.

"Got it."

"Squeeze the trigger, nice and slow."

The scope's magnification showed the individual hairs on the brocket's body. They reminded her of the bristles in a paintbrush. Erin blanked her mind and curled her forefinger. The rifle slammed into her shoulder. Jamie held steady, not just the rifle, but Erin's body as she lurched backward.

Then he was gone, sprinting off with the rifle in hand, leaving Erin to stumble onto her behind. She yanked off the earmuffs.

"You got him," Jamie shouted as he moved toward the creek. "Fucken hell, you got him clean, I reckon."

Running a sleeve over her face, Erin mopped up the sweat, felt the grit and dirt on her skin. Dear God, she had killed a deer. Or had she? Please don't let it be injured, she thought. Please don't let it be limping through the forest, bleeding from a gut shot.

"Hey!" Jamie shouted. "Get on over here."

She looked up. He was waving at her. Using both hands, she managed to get to her feet. Her legs shook. She walked unsteadily to the creek. Jamie was holding the deer's head by one antler. He looked as proud as punch.

"Tell me, am I a great teacher?" he said. "Or am I a great teacher?"

She smiled. "Maybe it was beginner's luck."

"No such thing."

"I suppose the field dressing comes next," she said.

"That's right." He dropped the deer's lifeless head and took the hunting knife from the scabbard on his belt. "Would you like to do the honours?"

***

They each hauled a skinned and gutted deer back to camp using what Jamie called an "Indian-sled": a travois fashioned from tarp and two poles. He dragged the larger red deer, and Erin the fallow. The trek, less than a kilometre, felt interminable. The animal's corpse steadily became heavier. As time passed, Erin's boots could barely clear the ground. She stumbled more frequently over rocks, exposed tree roots and fallen branches. Her glasses were fogged with sweat. She kept stopping to wipe them. Every now and then, Jamie waited for her to catch up.

"Holy Christ," she said at one point. "Are you sure we're going the right way?"

"Yeah, but these are 'deer miles' now. The distance from camp always seems ten times longer once you're dragging a kill." Cheerfully, Jamie clapped her on the back. "Don't worry, mate, you'll get used to it. Everybody does."

No way, she thought. This is the first and only time I'm ever going hunting.

When the trees thinned at last and the campsite appeared in the centre of the clearing, Erin wanted to collapse. She paused to catch her breath. Jamie ploughed onwards. The decapitated deer head, attached to Jamie's travois by a rope around its antlers, bobbed lifelessly against the tarp, the glossy black eyes filmed with dirt and debris, tongue extruded, its nose clogged with blood clots.

Megan stood up from her seat by the fire. "What took you so long?" she shouted. The suspicious edge to her voice would have been apparent even to a stranger.

Go to hell, Erin wanted to say, but couldn't speak. She trudged on.

"Like I told you on the walkie-talkie," Jamie said, "I taught her to shoot."

"I figured you'd be back an hour ago, at least."

"Yeah, but I had to teach her from scratch," he said. "Can you believe it? She'd never fired a rifle before."

"Yeah, I believe it," Noel said. "So quit the bullying."

"Bullying? Hey, old man, I showed her what to do. See this deer? The brocket? That's her doing. Clean shot: one bullet, one kill. She's a fucken natural."

Megan, fists akimbo, cut her eyes at Erin, who was too exhausted to give a damn. On reaching the campsite, Erin stopped and leaned on her knees. Her usual exercise routine consisted of 30 minutes on the recumbent stationary bike, three times per week, as she watched a cooking show on TV and sipped on mineral water. Her lower back ached so terribly, it felt as if several vertebral discs were preparing to rupture. Suddenly, the load lifted away. She opened her eyes. Noel had released the Velcro straps that connected the travois poles around her hips. She felt light enough to float.

"Poor girl, you look knackered," he said.

"I was, about an hour ago," she said. "Now, I believe I'm actually dying."

Noel said, "Jamie, take this deer off her hands, like a gentleman." Then the old man put an arm around her waist and gripped her free hand, gently, as if she were made of glass. "Come along, Dr. Harris," he said. "Let's get you coffee and something to eat."

Thank God the ground was flat. Her raw blisters stung. Limping, she knew she'd lost face, but didn't care. Noel helped her into a chair. Erin slumped over, dark spots swimming in her vision. She fumbled to unlace her boots.

"Is she for real?" Megan said. "Why's she acting like a princess?"

"You watch your lip, Missy," Noel said. "She's not built for the outdoors. She's built for thinking. Granted, she can't rope a calf, but Dr. Harris is a scientist that knows how the universe works, and that's more than any of us can ever say."

"Now she knows how the universe works," Jamie said, "*and* how to hunt deer."

Erin managed a weak chuckle.

"Sure, whatever," Megan said. "Jamie, go hang up the baits."

Noel put his arm around Erin. She leaned into the old man's shoulder. If she could choose a grandfather, she would choose Noel. He pressed a cup of coffee into her hand. The bitter liquid had neither sugar nor milk and was hot enough to scald her mouth, but it was the best drink she'd ever had, like nectar from the gods.

8

Erin stared at her watch and waited for the second hand to tick over: exactly 9.30 a.m.

She gazed around the clearing.

Dead ahead lay the bare lip of the escarpment. Shockingly red against the blue of the sky hung two deer carcasses, spaced far apart, each dangling from eucalypts by their butcher-hooked ankles like a pair of grisly curtains framing an empty stage. On the other three sides of the camp loomed the forest. Erin twisted around in the chair. Behind the camp, the remaining two carcasses drooped from trees about 25 metres apart. As she'd requested, the baits were set at the four corners of a near-perfect square. Their bolt-hole, if required, would be the interior of the car, where they would shoot through open windows. However, the only movement for the entire morning had come from birds. Species that she couldn't identify darted and flitted through the trees, calling to each other. Such a peaceful atmosphere; it was hard to imagine that anything out of the ordinary might ever happen.

She felt an odd combination of disappointment and relief.

What had Russ Walker-Smith called her expedition? A fool's errand? When she'd walk into the university's staff room on Monday morning, empty-handed, so to speak, how might he greet her? With a mocking laugh? A sneer? No, Russ was never one to gloat. Polite to a fault, he would likely never mention her failed expedition and instead, in an off-hand manner, would ask if she'd enjoyed her long weekend.

Dear old Russ.

Thinking of him brought the lab results to mind. Pathogens typically found in Komodo dragon saliva had riddled the corpse of

Noel's heifer. So this expedition couldn't possibly be a fool's errand. She peered expectantly around the clearing again.

Birds warbled. Insects droned. Nothing extraordinary continued to happen.

Erin took another sip of water. Breakfast had been a cold meal of baked beans and bread. Apparently, you don't light a campfire while hunting since animals, quite rightly, associate smoke with fire and tend to stay away. The Robinsons had built a fire pit for later, and everyone's camp chairs were arranged around it. Nearby were low and wide sheets of brown mesh suspended between poles, reminding her of tennis nets, which were intended to disguise their shapes and help them blend in with their surroundings. Hunting seemed to require an awful lot of equipment. The money must be good, though, or why else would the Robinsons do it?

Erin leaned back and crossed her legs at the ankles. The fold-out chair was surprisingly comfortable. She regarded her bare feet, covered in ointment and sticking plasters. At least her blisters felt better. The summer sun continued to warm the air. She unzipped her jacket.

Across the fire pit, Noel whittled a length of wood with a pen-knife. Next to him, Jamie crushed a beer can, tossed it at a garbage bag, and opened the esky for another drink. He cracked a tinny and sipped. How on earth could he stomach alcohol so early in the day? Nobody had mentioned it, so Erin didn't, either. Meanwhile, under the shade of the rectangular awning that ran from the car's roof-rack to a couple of poles, Megan lounged on an air mattress, reading a paperback.

Erin picked at her cuticles, checked her watch again: 9.34 a.m.

Crap. She wished she'd brought something to read. Flies buzzed. Whenever they hovered at her face, she idly swatted them away. Those that twitched over her stained trouser legs, however, she decided to leave. Deer blood belonged to the bush. I killed a living creature, she thought, for no good reason.

Jesus, she felt tired. Lack of sleep, a lingering hangover, the after-effects of too much adrenaline, that brutal hike through the goddamned forest dragging a deer.... She took off her glasses for a moment and rubbed at her closed eyelids.

"Dr. Harris," Noel said. "You need more sunscreen."

"But I'm covered in dirt."

"Dirt won't stop sunburn. You started out whiter than a sheet and now you're turning red."

Erin picked up the bottle beneath her chair. She squirted the viscous liquid into her palm, and tried to drag it across the filthy skin of her face. Oh God, how she longed for a shower: a hot shower with plenty of soap and shampoo. She scrubbed the sunscreen over her crusty throat and neck.

Noel said, "What about your hat?"

Sighing, she pulled the Legionnaire's cap from her jacket pocket and dutifully put it on. "Where are we exactly?" she said. "In the park, I mean."

Jamie said, "About twenty ks from any tourist walk, a fair way off the nearest fire access road. Nobody comes here but us."

"What about Gregory Lee?" she said.

"The park ranger?" Jamie laughed. "He's too busy chatting up sheilas at the picnic grounds to ever go bush."

"Does he realise that you and Megan hunt in the park?"

Jamie shrugged.

"Rumour has it he enjoys your goat meat," Noel continued. "Is that true?"

Glancing up from her book, Megan said, "Well, his wife happens to be Greek."

"Aw, good one," Jamie said, and sucked on the beer can. "Tell the world."

Megan kept reading and Noel continued whittling. Erin checked her watch, and gazed at the carcasses again.

"Don't worry about the deer," Megan said from behind her paperback. "Anything happens, we'll hear the cowbells."

Attaching cowbells to the baits had been Noel's idea, a simple yet ingenious alarm system. The rifles, which Erin couldn't identify by name, were loaded and leaning against the four-wheel drive. Alongside were three canvas ammunition bags with shoulder-straps. Noel and Jamie each sported a holstered revolver. As Jamie had explained during his shooting lesson, you need a handgun to finish off a wounded deer at close range. If you use a high-powered rifle instead, the bullet might ricochet off the ground, fly back through the animal, and straight into your fucken leg, quote unquote. She'd never met anyone who liked to swear as much as Jamie Robinson.

"Here, Dr. Harris," Noel said, reaching over. "This is for you."

He offered the whittled piece of wood. She took it and discovered, to her surprise and delight, that he had carved a little crocodile, about 10cm long, complete with keeled, bony scutes running dorsally along its back and tail. Such detail.... She grazed her fingertips across tiny teeth and claws.

"Oh, it's perfect," she said. "Can I really keep it?"

"Sure." Noel clamped his lips as if trying not to smile. "I've got plenty at home. An old man's got to have hobbies."

"I'll treasure it. Thanks so much."

"My pleasure," he said, and took another stick from his pocket. He must have been collecting them during the deer hunt that morning. "This one looks like it could be a blue-tongue lizard. How would you like one of those?"

She smiled. "I'd love one."

Running his pen-knife along the stick, shearing away a sliver of bark, he said, "You got any good stories about crocodiles, Dr. Harris?"

"Oh, more than I could count."

"So tell us about your first time," Jamie said, grinning. "Everyone remembers their first time."

Megan exhaled noisily. "Aw, give it a rest, will you?"

Jamie sniggered.

Erin couldn't decide whether he was genuinely flirting or just trying to get a rise from his wife. Probably the latter. She turned the whittled figurine over and over in her hands. The memory came back, awful and in full colour, as always.

"When I was very young, back in primary school," she said, "my father worked at an animal park that featured reptiles. It must have been school holidays on this occasion because I spent a whole week there. Anyway, Dad and his crew were moving a saltwater croc from one pen to another. The saltie was medium-sized, light enough for three men to carry. They had already taped its snout so it couldn't bite anyone, but the man carrying its head didn't know what he was doing. No one bothered to tell him. The experience went badly."

She had their attention. Noel stopped whittling. Jamie stopped drinking. Megan placed the paperback face-down on her chest and looked over.

"When holding a croc by the head," Erin continued, "you have to grab it in a tight headlock, and press it against your body as hard as you can. A croc can swing itself sideways with an unbelievable amount of force. Even as a child, I knew this man didn't have the skill to be holding the animal's head."

She had told Dad. He hadn't listened. In fact, had waved her off, scornful.

Erin studied the whittled figurine. Some memories were best left buried.

"Well?" Megan said. "Don't keep us in suspense. How did he hold the croc?"

"By its snout. The croc swung sideways and bashed straight into his face."

"Shit," Noel said. "Then what happened?"

Erin hesitated. Dad had been fired that same day, and couldn't get another job for a long time. Dad and Mother argued day and night. The bank took the house. Forced to live with relatives, Erin got used to cold hostility, to being ignored, resented. Eventually, Dad and Mother found a place to rent. The carpet smelled like cat urine. Mother constantly sprinkled scented talc and vacuumed with aggression, but to no avail. Like the stink, the arguing had never stopped. The animosity had never stopped. Erin blinked, momentarily bewildered. But wait, Noel's question was about that careless man at the animal park.

"He got knocked off his feet," Erin said. "His face was opened from nostril to chin in one long line, all the way through the meat, as if sliced with a box-cutter." She shook off the memory. "When you tape the snout of a croc," she went on, "its teeth are still exposed. The fourth tooth in the lower jaw is quite a bit larger, and overlaps the upper jaw. That tooth is probably what inflicted the damage."

"How did the bloke end up?" Megan said.

"With a broken nose, fifty stitches and a partial set of dentures."

Jamie whistled and sucked on his beer. "Shit, hey."

"Have you ever been injured by a croc?" Noel said.

Erin tucked the whittled figurine into her shirt pocket and held out her hand. "See those scars on my knuckle? A baby saltie bit me. It seemed so helpless; it was making soft chirruping sounds like a hatched bird. Believe it or not, I tried to pat it. I learned my lesson the hard way."

Jamie nodded his head sagely. "Shit, yeah."

"We don't have crocs here, but we've got plenty of snakes," Megan said.

"Ah, big deal," Noel said. "They skedaddle as soon as they hear you coming. No, the biggest danger is wild dogs. I've seen a pack take down a steer and eat the bloody thing while it was still living. That kind of business plays on your mind."

"Jesus," Erin said. "Are there many wild dogs in this park?"

"The place is teeming with them."

Erin looked about the clearing. She'd had trouble spotting deer through the trees. Anything could be skulking out there in the forest, watching.

Megan closed her paperback, sat up and wagged a finger. "Nah, listen," she said, "the worst of all is the feral pig. Some of those bastards are a hundred and fifty kilos or more. They move flat-out. And their tusks? Foot-long razorblades. They've got a bite strong enough to snap bones. And they're not scared of humans, either. If a pig sees you and feels threatened, they'll charge, no worries."

"Then what do you do?" Erin said.

"Pray you've got a loaded rifle on hand."

"And can shoot straight," Jamie added, giving Erin a sly grin.

"Holy Mary," Noel said, voice hoarse and strangled.

His tanned face had turned grey, his eyes staring, glassy and unseeing. His feet kicked spasmodically at the ground. It was a frightening display.

"Noel, oh my God, what's wrong?" Erin said. "Are you okay?"

He didn't answer. His lips pulled back into a rictus.

Heart attack, it must be.... Alarmed, Erin reached out and grabbed Noel's wrist. Didn't she have a first aid kit in her backpack? But what good would that do? It contained nothing but bandages, slings, iodine. She tried to remember the specifics of CPR. Was it five chest compressions to one breath? Eight chest compressions? Quite possibly, it was more. Twenty? Her mind went blank.

"Fuck," Jamie shouted. "Fuck!"

Then Erin finally heard the cowbell.

The cowbell....

Her lungs squeezed down into a ball. Yet she couldn't tear her eyes away from Noel's blanched face. The bell kept jangling in fits and starts.

"Pray for us sinners," Noel muttered, "now and at the hour of our death."

Erin turned toward the bell.

She froze. They all did. The sight was too terrible, too incredible.

Poking above the edge of the escarpment, framed by the cloudless blue of the sky, was the enormous head of a *Varanus priscus*, a metre wide from one ear hole to the other. Dusky grey scales with patches of osteoderms covered its hide like chain mail. The skin bagged in folds about its neck, which was as thick as a tree trunk. The front feet gripping the cliff-top had talons the size of butcher's knives. The proportions of the animal were beyond comprehension.

Breath fluttered out of Erin's body and didn't return.

The forest was quiet. Birds had stopped singing. Only the cowbell sounded.

The lizard touched its snout against the deer carcass, snuffling, nostrils winking. The forked tongue, long and thick as a whip, extruded and retracted. Delicately, the monster took an exploratory bite at the carcass. The cowbell rang.

"Get the rifles," Megan whispered.

Yet nobody moved. Erin felt pinned to the chair. I should get my camera, she thought. Instead, she pulled in a breath and lost it again.

Those round eyes never blinked. The lizard's face wore the blank expression typical of reptiles. And there's the kicker, Erin thought, rapt, her pulse hammering. Compared to mammals, reptile behaviour seems so alien: no visible emotion, no extraneous movement, that eerie ability to remain as still as a rock, a tree, a corpse. Viewing a reptile is like viewing something dead which can somehow function. That's one of the reasons why reptiles had always fascinated her.

But this...this inconceivable beast...was something else again.

It was beautiful in its own dreadful way, perfect enough to almost stop Erin's heart. The *Varanus priscus* skeleton on the steps of the Melbourne Museum had nothing on the real thing.... That skeleton, assumed to be the reconstruction of an adult, must be that of a juvenile....

Wow, Erin had been right all along.

The modern-day *Varanus priscus* was real.

The lizard made rumbling noises, reminiscent of a truck moving through its lowest gears. The tongue disappeared into a sheath that jutted like a pipe from the sublingual caruncle. Erin gasped. The creature had a hyoid apparatus, the same structure of bone and cartilage found in members of the Varanid family, including the Komodo dragon and the perentie. Scientists who pegged *Varanus priscus* as an ancestor of the perentie might have a case after all. Next, she noticed the parietal "eye" atop its enormous head. The Komodo dragon had a similar-looking organ, believed to help regulate circadian rhythms and body temperature.

But how could such a sizeable lizard scale a cliff?

Only juvenile Komodo dragons could climb vertical surfaces, such as trees. By adulthood, they became too heavy. The *Varanus priscus* should have appeared out of the forest. Instead, the lizard had climbed the cliff, a theoretical impossibility. By the girth of its skull, its body must be close to 10 metres long, meaning it weighed at least two tonne. Much larger than any reptile Erin had ever seen, larger than the biggest saltwater crocodile ever recorded, larger than any comparable beast in modern history....

The lizard opened its mouth, the jaws separating widely. So it had a movable intramandibular hinge, just like the Komodo dragon. Unlike the Komodo, however, no gingival tissue covered the teeth. Each recurved, serrated and pointed tooth lining the cavernous red maw drooled with ropes of saliva. Erin felt her stomach fall away. She knew what was coming, yet couldn't avert her eyes.

Dipping its giant head, the lizard scooped the decapitated carcass neck-first into its jaws. It bit down. A quarter of the carcass disappeared down its gullet. Snap, snap. Its set of backward-facing teeth acted like a ratchet, drawing in the meat. The armoured skin of the throat expanded to accommodate the deer's passage. With two more chomps, the carcass disappeared. Only the slim, dangling back legs remained, which were ripped free from their butcher-hooks and devoured.

Unbelievable...an entire deer consumed in less than seven seconds.

Erin, giddy and sickened, contemplated fainting.

The lizard tilted its jaws and broke the rope that had tied the carcass to the tree. The cowbell fell to the ground. The lizard regarded it for a moment, then lifted its head and swung it from side to side.

Could it see them?

Erin held her breath. No, probably not. While varanids in general have good daylight vision, the vision of the Komodo dragon is designed more to track movement rather than to distinguish stationary objects. And no one had moved a muscle since its spectacular appearance just half a minute ago. The *Varanus priscus* lapped out its extensive tongue, drew it back in.

Oh God.

The lizard was sniffing them.

A chill moved through Erin's body, a slow and shuddering electric shock that loosened her bladder. No one had yet grabbed a firearm. They were defenceless. If the beast crawled up from the escarpment and into the clearing right this very second, they were doomed. At top speed, an adult Komodo dragon can run about 20km per hour over a short distance. How much faster might a *Varanus priscus* travel? Her estimation of a 50 metre "safe zone" between the campsite and each deer-bait now appeared ludicrously inadequate. The lizard would be amongst them in a heartbeat. It would swallow each one of them, alive, faster than it had swallowed the carcass.

Get out of the goddamned chair, she thought.

Yet she couldn't budge. Wet warmth spread across her backside. Jesus, she realised in surprise, I'm literally pissing my pants. She had assumed the term was a figure of speech, not an actual symptom of terror. Well, I stand corrected, she thought, and inexplicably felt like laughing. If they survived this encounter, how on earth would she explain the urine-soaked chair?

The lizard clapped its jaws together, *thock,* a resounding, hollow noise. Then it ducked its head and was gone.

9

The sight of clear blue sky broke the spell.

"Let's go get that motherfucker!" Megan shouted.

She leapt up, snatched an ammunition bag and a light brown, long-barrelled firearm, and began sprinting toward the cliff edge. Jamie threw his beer can to the dirt and followed suit. The couple was either fearless or crazy.

Erin noticed that she still held Noel's wrist. "Are you all right?" she said.

He patted her hand and stood up, grey-faced, looking shaky on his feet. "To be honest, no.... I've just seen Lucifer himself."

"It's not called the Devil dragon for nothing." Tears blurred her sight. "Oh Noel, thank you, this is honest to God the best thing that's ever happened to me."

He offered a quizzical smile, and said, "Each to his own."

Grabbing a rifle, he broke into a trot after the Robinsons. Erin could only marvel. How did they have the guts? What if the lizard was lying in wait? Dry-mouthed, Erin took her camcorder from her backpack and forced herself to hurry across the clearing after the others. Nobody had fired a single shot.

"Is it out of range?" she said as she caught up.

"Nah," Megan said. "The prick's gone."

"Gone?"

"Yeah, somehow it's disappeared."

Noel said, "It must be fifty, maybe sixty metres to the valley. Dr. Harris, how could the monster climb down so fast?"

"I don't know. Maybe there's a cave."

Megan shook her head. "No caves. Solid granite all the way."

"And it'd have to be a big cave to fit a bastard that size," Jamie said.

"It doesn't make sense," Erin said. "Look, I don't have an explanation."

She felt dazed. Had a *Varanus priscus* actually appeared in this very spot only moments ago? It seemed impossible. She reached the lip of the escarpment, stumbling over the rocky ground in her bare feet. Jamie gripped her arm.

"For fuck's sake, watch it," he said.

"I'm okay. I won't fall, promise."

"Better not. It's a long way down."

Cautiously, she approached the edge.

She had expected a sheer drop in a straight line to the ground. The cartoon cliché of a cliff, she realised, chiding herself. Instead, there was a long, gentle gradient comprised of granite boulders. The boulders were colossal, the size of houses, and stacked together higgledy-piggledy as if a careless giant had thrown them by the handful. Jammed into every fissure and crevice along that wide and deep gradient were plants: eucalypts, shrubs, grasses, even lichen wedged within the tiniest of cracks. At the sweeping hem of the escarpment lay a sea of trees. Beyond that, hazy and blue on the horizon, sat a long line of hills that resembled ocean waves caught in freeze-frame. Jesus, this park was enormous.

Jamie slung his firearm, jabbed a thumb at Erin's camera. "And what in the name of fuck is that?" he said.

Surprised, she lifted it to show him. "A digital camcorder with optical zoom."

"No! I mean, where's your Remington?"

She didn't, couldn't answer. Picking up the rifle hadn't occurred to her.

Megan shook her head. "Ugh. Have you wet your pants?"

Erin blushed. "It appears so."

The couple stared at her with the same expression: equal parts annoyance and perplexity. My humiliation is complete, Erin thought. I have failed on all counts. And now, oh goddamn it, she felt tears of shame pricking at her eyes.

"Leave her alone, both of you," Noel said, holding her elbow. "Come along, Dr. Harris. You've got spare clothes? Megan, stop being such a bloody sow for once and help this young lady clean herself up."

***

They were clustered around the campfire, each with a loaded firearm. Erin had been assigned the bolt-action Remington 700, the same rifle she'd used to shoot the deer. It frightened her so much that she couldn't move. The rifle felt like a mercury-switch bomb: ready to go off at any moment. The argument continued without her. All she could do was hope. Her fear was that Noel and the Robinsons would decide to call off the hunt. Please God, she thought, the *Harris's dragon* is all I've ever wanted.

"We need the army," Jamie said, yet again. "We need rocket launchers."

Megan said, "All we need is to hold on to our balls."

"Nah, this is about knowing when we're beat."

"There's only one thing to worry about," Noel said, "and that's whether or not we've got the firepower to kill that bastard."

"Oh, we've got the firepower," Megan said. "Hey, the SKK can drop a full-grown boar in its tracks."

"A pissy little .22 can do that, if you aim it right," Jamie said. "But we're not talking about a boar. We're talking about that dinosaur. Pig slugs are too small. Don't bullshit me."

"We've got more than enough ammo, more than enough firearms." Megan's eyes began to shine. "Come on, babe, this is our chance. Don't you see? We've always wanted to go big-game hunting in Africa, haven't we? And it's a pipe dream."

"Nah, we'll get there some day."

"After winning Tattslotto? We can't even afford the Gold Coast."

He considered for a time. "Yeah, but this isn't antelopes and lions and shit."

"No, it isn't," Megan said. "It's better."

Jamie seemed to think about that, and finally shrugged.

Megan laughed. "Come on, what do you reckon all the big-game hunters around the world are gonna say when we bring home this humongous animal?"

The suggestion made him chuckle.

"There, you see?" she added. "So we don't need the army after all."

He took a long swig of beer. "Yeah, we do."

She slapped the can out of his hand. It landed on the ground and glugged out some froth. Without reacting, Jamie simply picked up the can and wiped off the dirt.

"You gave Noel your word," Megan said. "Are you going back on it?"

"I'll go back on anything if it means I'll live another day."

Megan seemed ready to strike him. Erin looked away. And there, some five metres from camp, was her urine-soaked chair, sluiced with water, left in the sun to dry, draped with her wet camouflage trousers. She was perched on the esky in a pair of shorts, miserable, a child forced to stand in a corner of the classroom. It seemed everyone had forgotten her. The debate raged as if she wasn't there. I want this lizard, she thought. And she would never want for anything else for as long as she lived.

"Yesterday, you sat in Noel's kitchen and took his money," Megan said. "Now you're going to pussy out? No way. The Robinson word is our bond. Or it used to be."

Jamie groaned, dropped his head. "Aw, don't give me that shit again."

"And yep, it's always the same with you."

"Oh, here we go...."

"When you make a promise, Jamie, you keep it. Okay? It's not rocket science. You took his money and swore you'd hunt that Devil dragon for him."

"So we'll give the money back."

"We're not wussing out." She turned to Noel. "What do you want to do?"

The old man looked up from the fire. It seemed he had aged ten years. Nonetheless, he jutted his chin. "Me? I want to kill that prick."

Jamie groaned again. "You're both mad."

"You know what I'm mad about?" Noel said, his voice quavering. "Losing my stock, hand over fist. I can't tell you how many letters I've written to the council and the state government about these feral animals and how much they're costing me. No one gives a stuff. I've sent invoices, showing them exactly what I'm losing every week, so much money I can hardly keep my head above water. They have to let hunters into this fucking park, excuse my French, or else the farming community is done for." He gulped, wiped the back of his hand across his forehead, and said, "Mate, I think I'd fancy a beer."

Erin gingerly gripped the rifle and stood up from the esky. Jamie fished out a can, opened it and gave it to Noel, who drank in quick swallows. Erin sat down again. Gently, she balanced the rifle across her lap.

"Once we bring back this Devil dragon," Noel continued, "I'll dump its bloody mug on the front steps of the council building. Then we'll see if those Greenie do-good cocksuckers can deny the need for hunting. And next I'll dump the lizard's bloody dong on the front steps of the Rodeo Association clubhouse and let them try to tell me I'm a crazy fool who can't officiate on bull riding, by God. Seeing things? Hah. I'll show them. I'll show the whole bloody town. Anyone here wants to leave? Go ahead, but not me. I'm staying put until that prick is stone cold dead."

He fell silent, panting, out of breath.

No one said anything, as if stunned by the vehemence of his outburst. Erin had never heard him speak more than a couple of sentences at once, and by the looks on their faces, neither had the Robinsons.

A pair of squawking crimson rosellas flew out of the forest. Everyone jumped. The birds swooped over the campsite and into the blue sky over the escarpment, chattering and screeching. A rustling noise sounded from behind. As if on cue, Noel, Jamie and Megan all half-stood and gripped their rifles. Erin flinched.

"Relax," Megan said, dropping back into her chair. "It's a wallaby."

Erin turned to look. The creature peeked out from between the bushes and darted back amongst the undergrowth.

"Don't worry about the Devil dragon," Erin said. "It's busy digesting its meal."

Megan said, "Yeah, but there are still dogs, or even worse, pigs. If pigs sniff out the bait, they might come running."

Despite the warmth, Erin hugged herself and shivered. Was there no end to the dangers in this godforsaken place? Why would anyone choose to go camping?

Noel said, "No need for alarm, Dr. Harris. One shot can kill a pig."

"Unless you hit their fighting pad," Jamie said. "Then you're stuffed."

"Yeah, but I'm talking in general. Behind the shoulder is best, obviously."

"Nah, mate. Behind the ear."

"If you've got what? A BB gun?" Noel made a derisive *pfft* sound. "You wouldn't even bother with small calibres. Not when the wretches come in herds of twenty or more."

Erin said, "Wait, herds of twenty?"

"I've seen bigger," Megan said. "Once, I saw a group closer to a hundred."

Erin rubbed at her temples, took off her glasses, rubbed at her eyelids. Russ Walker-Smith had been right. She should never have come here.

Jamie said, "I vote we pack up and get the hell out."

"So far," Megan said, "there are two votes against you."

Noel placed a gentle hand on Erin's shoulder. "Dr. Harris?"

She put her glasses back on, looked around. Their faces were strained, pale beneath their tans. She could only imagine how she herself must look. Perhaps like a terrified child. At last, she said, "We were underprepared, without a doubt."

"Yeah, you see?" Jamie said, and slapped his knee as if in victory.

Megan scowled.

"Go on, Dr. Harris," Noel said.

She took off her hat, scraped back her dirty hair, and pulled the hat down tight about her ears. "I have to show the world that *Varanus priscus* still exists."

Jamie snorted. "Even if it kills you?"

"We'll each of us be in the ground someday," Noel said, "whether we make an historical discovery or not."

"Hey, I couldn't give a flying rat's arse about making discoveries."

Megan clapped a hand on the back of her husband's neck. "We know how to hunt," she said. "We've taken down plenty of big bastards, no sweat. And what was our worst injury? Come on, Jamie, what was it?"

After a time, he mumbled, "A sprained ankle."

"Exactly, a sprained ankle, that one time you stepped in a rabbit hole." She leaned toward him. "Don't you want to make something of our lives? Something that lasts? Maybe forever?"

Erin said, "It's true. We'll be famous."

Jamie shook his head and gave a bitter laugh. "Nobody wants out but me? Get fucked, really?" Sighing, he added, "Well, okay. But if we get turned into dinosaur shit, that's because of youse, all right? I'm the innocent party. Remember that."

***

At the lip of the escarpment, Erin took photographs and measurements. The lizard had left footprints. Most of them were incomplete, scuffed, lost against bare rock. But, dear God, one print from heel to claw spanned the best part of 70 centimetres. Erin included not just a ruler but her own boot-shod foot in each photograph. She wished she'd brought plaster of Paris. Next, she took a few shots of the blood-spattered cowbell. She recalled its hollow sounds, and her flesh crept.

She closed her eyes. The pebbled skin of the beast came to mind, the rounded scales arranged in neat, identical rows. Yes, the skin had been mostly grey, but there were flashes of yellow around the bulbous eyes and along the mouth; a faint and iridescent greenish hue to the underside of its throat. What might the rest of its skin look like? A swell of excitement pressed against Erin's diaphragm, snagging her breath. She was the only scientist who had ever seen the colouration of *Varanus priscus*. Already, she could rewrite a chapter or two in the books on vertebrate palaeontology. Her nerve endings began to tingle. The only scientist to have ever seen it.... And the vocalisation the lizard had made, reminiscent of a truck's engine brake. No other scientist in the world but Erin had ever heard it. No other scientist...no other scientist in the entire *history* of modern science had ever—

"What are you doing?"

Erin jumped. Jamie stood next to her. She hadn't noticed his approach.

Recovering, she lowered the camera, allowing it to hang from its strap about her neck. "I'm documenting the sighting," she said. "This might be our only evidence."

"Yeah? Don't you reckon it'll come back later on?"

"Wild animals are unpredictable."

He gazed over the sea of trees far below. "So it's sleeping down there?"

"Possibly."

"Too bad we didn't have one of those tagging-tracker guns," he said, "like they use on sharks. We could follow the beeps, and kill the dinosaur in its sleep."

He moved closer to the edge.

"Please," she said. "Avoid stepping on the print. It's smudged enough as it is."

He ducked back with a silly grin. Was he drunk? More than likely.

"This is what I don't understand," she continued. "If you and your wife hunt regularly in the park, how come you haven't seen a Devil dragon before?"

"We haven't come out to this spot in yonks. Not since the fires."

Oh, that's right, she thought. The park ranger, Gregory Lee, had mentioned that a bushfire had gutted the southwest of the park last summer, driving the animals—including *Varanus priscus*, one would assume—closer to town.

"And we don't come out here that often, anyway," Jamie continued. "Know how much meat you can get from a single deer? Twenty-four cuts. Even if you wanted to eat venison twice a week, you'd need...." He counted on his fingers. "...about four animals for a whole year. And you saw yourself how quick we shot four of them this morning."

Erin felt shocked, a little confused. "But I thought you had paying customers."

"Yeah, about half a dozen, but they can only fit so much in the freezer. So me and the missus come out here two, maybe three times a year, always in the morning and always in the cooler months, when your dinosaur is probably too busy freezing its nuts off to get out of bed."

Erin felt duped.

Christ almighty, just two or three visits per *year*?

She had assumed the Robinsons to be seasoned hunters. There would be picnickers and hikers with more hands-on experience of the park than these two.

"But don't worry," Jamie said, looking at her sideways with a smile. "We've known for years that some kind of big son-of-a-bitch that didn't belong was living out here. Sometimes we heard strange noises."

"Like what?"

He shrugged. "Far-off growling noises. I figured on a tiger."

"Gregory Lee told me a similar thing."

Jamie sneered. "Gregory Lee would tell a sheila anything she wanted to hear."

"Sorry, am I interrupting?" Megan said.

Erin turned. Megan had approached quietly from the rear, two red patches stamped on her cheeks. Sensing Megan's accusation, Erin blushed.

"I'm photographing the Devil dragon tracks," Erin said. "Where's Noel?"

"He's having a lie-down in the car, the poor bugger." Megan glared at her husband. "Doing some field work, are we?"

"If I'm risking my arse, I'm taking an interest in it."

Whatever the frictions in their marriage, and there seemed to be plenty, Erin didn't want any part of it. She said, "He was telling me about the noises you've heard in the park, like from a big cat."

Megan nodded. "We reckoned it was a lion or tiger escaped from a circus. There are stories about black panthers, too. Shit, anything at all could be roaming around in here. Did you know this national park feeds into the State Forest?"

"What?" Erin said. "No, I didn't."

"The southeast corner has a bridge to another hundred thousand hectares."

Despite herself, Erin's mouth fell open. She gazed across the valley, which lay in a blue haze from one horizon to the other. "Oh, my God," she whispered, "so the Devil dragon can hide in a total of one hundred and thirty thousand hectares?"

Jamie laughed into his fist. "Yeah, shit, hey? It's a big fucken place. Travel a few hours from the coast and the bush goes on forever and a day."

10

Their late lunch had sizzled in frypans over the campfire: sausages, chops and eggs. Erin picked at her meal. Why hadn't the Robinsons brought any fruits or vegetables? At this rate, Erin would be bound up for days, which, come to think of it, was a good thing considering she was in the bush. Urinating was scary enough. Then she remembered wetting her pants. Goddamn it. She sighed, putting down her fork. At least she was wearing trousers again and sitting in her dried-out chair, which didn't smell at all.... She felt her cheeks starting to burn again with humiliation.

"Better eat up," Jamie said to her, sucking at a lamb chop. "You never know, you might need your strength."

Noel said, "There's no way of telling if the Devil dragon will turn up again."

"But it probably will," Erin said. "It knows that carrion is available here."

Megan said, "Yeah, but it's got a big stomping ground, right?"

Erin nodded. If she were a betting woman, however, she'd stake everything she had on the *Varanus priscus* returning. The Remington lay at her feet. Could she remember how to chamber a cartridge? How to aim and shoot? Reload? Yes, she felt confident that she could perform satisfactorily under normal conditions. But if confronted by that apex predator? She had no way of telling.

Nonetheless, she itched to see the lizard again.

Just the thought of it suffused a warm, tingling glow through her body. Oh, the glorious path that lay ahead of her now, the many preparations she would need to make. My whole life will change, she thought, and her heart beat faster. The Big Three biology journals—*Nature, Science,* and *Ecology*—would certainly vie to publish her first report. No matter which one got the scoop, her lizard would be on the cover of every herp journal across the planet, including the most prestigious: *Copeia, Journal of Herpetology,* and *Herpetologica.* And yes, her face would surely make the cover of *National Geographic, Newsweek, Time,* and so many more. Maybe she'd get contact lenses and ditch the spectacles.... Naturally, the Herpetologists League, the Society for the Study of Amphibians and Reptiles, and the Australian Society of Herpetologists would invite her as a key-note speaker. A speech, she'd need to prepare a speech, perhaps hire a professional writer for help. Herps and cryptos and weird science enthusiasts would fly in from all over the world to hear her talk and get her autograph, have their photograph snapped with her. God, the research programs that *Harris's dragon* would create, the grants....

"Noel, snaffle another chop," Megan said. "Plenty here."

"Thanks, I'm fine."

"Suit yourself."

Sighing, Erin put aside her reveries and poked her fork at the food. The rubbery fried egg tasted like wood smoke. Megan, the only one with an appetite, grabbed a second helping of everything. Noel took the knife from his pocket and started whittling again, whistling softly.

Jamie threw his paper plate, chop-bones and all, onto the fire and lit a cigarette. He kept looking up. Erin knew what was bothering him: the sun's slow creep toward the horizon. Already, the stinging heat in the air had softened. Cool breezes fanned across the campsite from the escarpment, rattling through the forest around them. Hundreds of blowflies smothered the remaining deer carcasses. An ordinary Komodo dragon could smell putrefying meat from over 10kms away. No doubt, the stench was rousing the *Varanus priscus* from its nap, calling it back to their campsite. Erin checked her watch: 5.13 p.m. A tremble of anxiety jittered along her spine. Or was it excitement?

Jamie said, "I reckon a couple of beers would do the doctor some good."

"Leave her be," Noel said. "She's not a pisspot like some I won't mention."

"Whatever." Grinning, Jamie drew on his cigarette.

The temperature continued to drop. Megan finished her meal and began to stoke the fire. Erin zipped her jacket.

"Here's another one for your collection, Dr. Harris." Standing up, Noel leant out, holding a wooden figurine. "It was going to be a blue-tongue lizard, but this is better, I think."

"Thank you, Noel. You're very kind."

She took the figurine and caught her breath. About 15cms long, it was undoubtedly *Varanus priscus*. No mistake, the figurine had the boa-like flattened head, sturdy body, stout bowed legs, and thick tail of the lizard. Noel had nicked the figurine all over in uniform rows, probably using the very tip of his pen-knife. So he'd noticed the chain mail pattern too. Nothing got past Noel Baines. She couldn't help but smile. She would cherish this figurine for as long as she lived.

"Do you like it?" he said.

"I love it. My God, it's the perfect memento. Teach me how to whittle."

Jamie laughed. "Aw, you'll be busting brumbies next, just you wait."

"No, I'm serious," Erin said. "I want to know how to do it."

Noel fidgeted in his chair, flushed, clenched his lips to stop himself from beaming. "Well, shit. Have you at least got a pen-knife?"

She patted through her pockets. "I have a Swiss Army knife somewhere."

"Yeah?" Megan arched an eyebrow. "You don't seem the type."

"I bought it while you were gathering my supplies at the disposal store."

Jamie stood up. "Well, I'm off to drain the spuds," he said, and wandered toward the trees.

Extending a hand to Erin, Megan said, "Give us the Swiss Army. Does it come with a toothpick?"

"I don't know," Erin said, giving it over.

"The best ones have a toothpick." Megan inspected the knife, smiled, and drew out a length of wood with a flourish. "You see? Right near the bottle-opener. There's a pair of tweezers too, did you know? You've got to be careful, but. The toothpick and tweezers aren't attached, so they're shit-easy to lose."

"It's simple enough to buy replacements," Noel said. "I can show you a few basic techniques, Dr. Harris, but you can't really whittle with that particular toy. For starters, you need something with a curved handle to help keep your paring motions under control."

Sheathing the toothpick, Megan said, "Did you know you can get a Swiss Army knife that has everything on it but the kitchen sink? I'm talking maybe ninety or something tools on it."

Erin smiled. "Yes, but does it have a toothpick?"

Jamie's voice cried, "Look out!" and then he was running from the bush toward camp, his face white, eyes wide and staring.

Behind him, the noise through the undergrowth thundered like an oncoming locomotive. Branches splintered. Frightened birds screeched and flapped into the sky. Erin dropped the figurine. Noel and Megan jumped to their feet and, as one, lifted their firearms and swung them toward the rear of the campsite. Fumbling, Erin grappled for the Remington. Her fingers seemed frozen into claws. Panting, Jamie grabbed a rifle.

"Aim for the bastard's head and chest," Megan yelled.

Erin had one clear and distinct thought before chaos broke loose across the campsite: how many bullets will it take to stop a charging *Varanus priscus?* She grabbed her rifle and stumbled out of the chair.

At top speed from the bushes charged a group of enormous black pigs.

For a split second, Erin felt relieved. Of course, *Varanus priscus* was an ambush predator; it would never give away its position, especially not in such a clumsy way. Why, its prey would simply bolt. Then she saw that some of the pigs were the size of bears, had dagger-like tusks, and were heading straight at her.

She screamed.

Shooting erupted from every side. A pig's skull aerated into a puff of red mist. Snout-first, the animal's momentum ploughed it along the dirt and into the fire. Another pig went down, then another. More of them ran out from the forest, darting in all directions, squealing and grunting.

We're overwhelmed, Erin thought. The hair on the back of her neck lifted.

A massive boar rushed at her. With a shriek, Erin fired from the hip. The punch of the rifle's stock doubled her over. Had she hit the pig? One swipe of those tusks would split her like a Bowie knife. With sweating hands, she ejected the spent shell and reloaded. The pig closed the distance between them before crashing to its knees with a grunt. Blood spurted from a hole in its brow. Her surprise froze her for a moment.

I got it, she thought. Jesus, *I actually got it*.

Noel's anguished yell spun her around. A boar had him on the run, bucking its head at the old man's legs. Erin lifted the Remington. Time spun out in a long, lazy thread as a fresh surge of adrenaline flooded her system. Everything went into slow motion. She put the stock to the meat of her shoulder. Jamie's lesson at the deer hunt came back to her in vivid technicolour.

Stand like a boxer....

Sight down the scope using the crosshairs....

Aim for the base of the animal's neck....

Gently squeeze the trigger....

Boom.

The recoil of the rifle against her body tightened the loose spool of time, snapping it back to normal speed. Blood vomited from the pig's mouth as it fell. Wow, she marvelled, reloading. Excellent shot. Noel scrambled to his feet. His trousers were ripped. Had he been gored? She couldn't see any blood on him. He picked up his rifle and kept shooting. She caught a glimpse of Jamie and Megan, standing back to back in perfect formation, firing over and over. The concussion of every shot hurt her ears. The campsite still boiled with frantic, angry, screeching pigs.

How many could there be?

She raised the Remington, locked her sights on a small pig. Something crashed into her from behind. Her feet flew out from beneath her as if she had been hit by a car. Airborne, she contemplated the pale sky. Then she landed heavily on her back. Winded, she lifted her head. The pig that had charged her turned for the attack.

She had to shoot now or get mauled.

There was no time for correct procedure. Supine, Erin scrabbled to aim the rifle between her knees. She couldn't brace the stock anywhere on her body. Jamie's words of warning came to her panicked mind: *If you pull the trigger now, the recoil from the scope will punch those fucken spectacles and your eyeball right out the back of your fucken head.* Dear God, she thought, don't let me lose an eye.

The pig opened its jaws, ready to bite. The roof of its mouth was deeply corrugated and red, the four tusks hideously long and yellow.

Squeezing her eyes shut, she pulled the trigger.

The Remington's recoil pad punched into her breast. The pain took her breath. Something heavy trod on her foot. She had missed. Now she would be disembowelled. Frantically, she scrambled back on her elbows. The pig's black, wiry bristles scraped at her bare skin between sock and trouser hem.

One shot left.

As she shifted the bolt, a shadow moved across her.

"They're all dead," Jamie's voice said. "Calm down. Switch on the safety."

Erin struggled into a sitting position.

The shooting had stopped. The campsite and surrounding forest were quiet. At her feet lay the dead pig. Her shot had erupted out the back of its skull.

Jesus.

She looked around.

Slaughtered pigs were everywhere. Literally *everywhere*. Some of the smaller ones, the piglets, had smears of gory paste instead of heads. Bile rose in her throat. With determination, she swallowed it down. No way. She'd already peed herself in front of these people. She'd be damned if she'd vomit, too.

"Did you hear me?" Jamie said. "Flip the safety on. I don't want to get shot in the face."

She complied and pushed the rifle to the ground. Her body ached from bruising and muscle tension. Jamie offered his hand. She took it. As if she weighed nothing at all, he lifted her to her feet. She wobbled. He put a steadying arm about her waist and walked her back to the campfire. All of the chairs had been knocked over. He righted one and set her gently into it. Then he picked up the other chairs.

Standing on the other side of the fire, Megan lowered her rifle. With that erect posture and flinty gaze, she appeared to Erin as a warrior, an Amazon. She couldn't imagine Megan being afraid of any living thing.

Noel slapped his bush hat against his thigh, knocking out clouds of dust. Putting his hat back on, he said, "Are you okay, Dr. Harris?"

"Three," she whispered. "I got three."

Jamie picked up her rifle, checked it, and nodded. "Good job."

"Holy shit," she said, wiping a forearm across her sweating brow. "Noel, did that pig get you? I shot it but I think it got you."

"That's true, it did."

"Let me see," Megan said, slinging her firearm by its strap over one shoulder.

Noel propped his foot on a chair and lifted his ripped trouser leg. A laceration eight centimetres long ran parallel to his shin bone. Blood pumped in lazy rivulets toward his once-white sock.

"Aw, nasty," Jamie said.

"It's my own fault." Noel spat at the dirt. "I tripped, gave the bastard a free go."

Megan headed to the car. "I'll get the first aid kit. Noel, get some ice on it. That'll help stop the pain."

He did as he was told, retrieving a handful of wet ice chips from the esky. Limping back to a chair, he sat down, pulled up the torn trouser leg, and held the ice against the wound. Blood continued to ooze.

A wave of nausea swept over Erin.

Had she ever experienced something this wild, this dangerous? Not a chance. Each one of her field trips had been an exercise in planning and precision. Even that time she and a group of researchers had caught Mulga snakes, the *Pseudechis australis*.

While ostensibly the same species, southern Mulgas are much more docile than those in the north; hence, the field study to discern the reasons behind the difference. Crazy things had happened. The Mulga is a heavy snake with the highest venom output per bite of any snake in Australia for its size. When it strikes, it tends to hang on and chew, injecting massive amounts of venom into its victim. Fun, exhilarating and perilous stuff.... But child's play compared to this experience.

Woozy, Erin slumped back in the chair.

"Dr. Harris," Noel said, alarmed. "You're not fainting?"

"No, I'm fine," she said. "Don't mind me. I'm just having a rest."

Megan knelt in front of Noel with the first aid kit. Noel let go of the ice chips and looked away.

"Don't forget the iodine," Jamie said.

"I know what I'm doing. Shut up and get him a beer."

Jamie opened the esky, paused, and glanced at Erin. "You want a drink?"

"God, yes, please."

He cracked a tin and handed it her. She gulped too quickly. The beer fizzed on the way down, forming a bolus that hurt her oesophagus as sharply as a swallowed razor. Wincing, she tried to burp. Not a chance. As soon as the bolus passed through the sphincter into her stomach, she might be able to manage another sip.

"You right?" Jamie said.

"Yes, for Christ's sake, yes."

Handing a can to Noel, he said, "I guess she's not used to beer."

"Leave her be."

Megan had cleaned the wound. Now, she pulled the edges of it together with butterfly plasters, wadded a length of gauze and pressed it against the wound, and secured the gauze with a bandage. After tying off the bandage, she took out a roll of duct tape. Erin couldn't believe her eyes. Duct tape? Megan began to wind the tape around and around the bandage. Upon reflection, Erin decided that duct tape would make quite a good waterproof dressing.

She looked about the clearing. "What are we going to do with these pigs?"

Jamie shrugged. "Chuck 'em over the cliff for more bait."

"You can't sell any for meat?"

"Are you shitting me?" He wiped the suds from his mouth with the back of his hand. "Well, to be fair, some people eat wild pig, but these fuckers are loaded with worms and flukes. I'd rather eat road kill."

"Never eat omnivores," Megan added. "You're asking for trouble."

Blowflies were already landing on the corpses.

Erin closed her eyes. "I've never seen so many dead things at once."

"Nah. Fair dinkum? But there's only...." Jamie did a head count with his pointer finger. "About sixteen."

"Sixteen? That's all? Are you sure?"

"Positive." He grinned, radiant. "Your first always feels like the biggest."

"Yeah, funny," Megan said as she packed the first aid kit back in the car. "Stop being the joker and tell me where you stashed the antibiotics."

"Uh, in one of the toilet bags, I think."

"How many times do I have to tell you? The antibiotics go in the first aid kit."

Erin said, "You've got a stash of prescription medicines?"

"Bites from a boar can poison your blood," Megan said as she fossicked through various bags. "They carry lots of diseases. When we hunt, we always bring antibiotics."

"How? They're prescription-only."

Megan shrugged. "We get them from Tania O'Farrell."

"The vet? But that's against the law. The town vet gives you antibiotics?"

"Sure," Megan said, flourishing a pill box, "in exchange for free venison."

Erin couldn't believe it. What the actual hell...? She removed her glasses and rubbed at her eyelids. When she looked up, Noel was taking a couple of pills from Megan's open palm. He swallowed them with a swig of beer. Antibiotics were bacterium-specific. Didn't these hunters realise?

Oh, Erin felt tired, so very tired. She put down her beer can. "I think I might rest," she said, and moved toward her tent.

"No worries," Megan said. "Okay, first things first, let's reload."

Erin lay on her air mattress and tried to relax. Her muscles wouldn't stop trembling. She listened to the unfamiliar metallic noises, which must be Noel and the Robinsons reloading their firearms.

After a while, Jamie called out, "Hey, Erin, you wanna come out for this?"

No, she thought, I don't want to come out ever.

Reluctantly, she exited the tent.

Jamie lit a smoke, held it between his lips, and picked up the nearest pig by its back feet. "I'm piffing these fuckers over the cliff. Anybody want to help?"

"Yeah, I will," Noel said.

The old man stood up and stamped his injured leg into the ground a couple of times as if to check its soundness. Then he took hold of a nearby pig's trotters and walked with effort toward the escarpment. The hauled corpse jetted spurts of blood into the dirt. Rafts of disturbed blowflies flitted and buzzed along the wet trail.

"Oh, Christ," Erin murmured, and slumped into her camp chair.

"Drink some water," Megan said. "You'll feel better."

"I don't think I can stand up."

"That's okay. You stay there and get your wind back."

Megan grabbed a pig's hind leg and dragged the corpse behind her. Stunned, Erin watched Noel and the Robinsons turn the clean-up into a race. "Heave ho" was the laughing phrase they shouted. For the larger pigs, the Robinsons hauled on a leg each. The carcasses kept disappearing over the precipice, each one bouncing loudly and wetly against the rocks. Bile rose in Erin's throat. She chased it down with beer.

Goddamn, she thought. God*damn*.

Looking at the ground between her feet, she noticed the Swiss Army knife, and pocketed it. Then she saw the whittled figurine of the *Varanus priscus*. Gasping, she snatched up the figurine and turned it over in her hands, quickly wiping away the dust. It was still in one piece, thankfully.

She contemplated the figurine's wide, flat visage.

Now would be the perfect time for the lizard to strike, she thought. *Everyone's guard is down.* She watched Noel and the Robinsons, each one preoccupied with their pig-slinging competition. Erin pocketed the figurine and went over to retrieve her Remington. She slung it by its strap over one shoulder. From her backpack, she took out two boxes of cartridges and zipped them inside her jacket.

She sat down and studied the surroundings. Shadows lengthened in the forest. Fewer birds called from their hidden places. The sky began to look bleached around its edges. Rather than attacking the camp, perhaps the pigs had been running from something...something larger and more ferocious....

"Keeping an eye on things for us, Dr. Harris? Good girl."

She turned in her chair.

Noel tipped his hat, and grabbed hold of a nearby pig by its leg. "That was fine shooting, by the way," he said. "Much appreciated. You're a natural hunter."

"Thanks," she said, genuinely pleased. "So, who's winning the race?"

"Jamie, but we reckon he's counting each one twice, the blasted so-and-so."

The old man limped toward the escarpment. The pig left long, shallow furrows in the dirt all the way. Noel released the carcass at the lip of the cliff, and rolled it over with his foot.

Erin rubbed at the growing tension in her shoulders.

Sixteen dead pigs strewn down the face of the escarpment would be an irresistible lure to the *Varanus priscus*. *It will come back to our camp*, she thought. *Maybe it was already stirring from its burrow, slipping its forked tongue in and out.*

11

Everyone huddled around the campfire. Inside the pit ringed with stones, Jamie and Megan had built what they called a "pyramid fire": eight layers of wood stacked in a cross-hatching pattern, the heaviest branches on the bottom and the lightest kindling at the top. Megan had lit the kindling so that the pyre would, paradoxically, burn downwards. If well-constructed, a pyramid fire should burn the whole night long without needing attention. The more you know, Erin thought wryly. But then again, everything about this day had been a near-vertical learning curve. Only one day? It felt like she'd been stranded out here for weeks. What would Russ Walker-Smith say? He'd be shocked, no doubt; shocked at her new-found abilities to camp: pissing in the woods, hunting, shooting. To be honest, she was a little shocked herself. To think only yesterday she was wearing Capri pants.

"Why did the pigs attack us?" she said. "I thought pigs only attack when they feel threatened."

Megan shrugged. "Could be Jamie trespassed into their foraging territory when he went to take a piss."

"Yeah, but nah," Jamie said. "You never can tell with ferals, pigs in particular. They're crazy buggers. You think you've got them pegged 'til they do something weird. It's the inbreeding."

Erin checked her watch: 9.37 p.m. and a cold night, too. No chance of the *Varanus priscus* appearing until the morning. She sighed, relaxed, and sipped her coffee. A sheet of a million stars shimmered overhead. She looked up and marvelled.

"The night sky at home is never this dramatic," she said.

"That's on account of the city lights," Noel said, and stood up. The joints of his knees popped and creaked. "I'm off to bed," he added. "Jamie, set an alarm for no later than five-thirty."

"No worries."

"How are you feeling?" Erin said, hoping Noel wasn't developing a fever.

"Right as rain," he said, shuffling away.

When Noel was out of earshot, Megan said, "Don't fret. He's as tough as an old boot, that feller. Back in the day, he used to be a champion bull rider."

"Really?" Erin said. "He never told me."

"Oh, he's got heaps of trophies and medals from rodeos all over Australia. This was before helmets and Kevlar vests and knee-pads and what have you, when cowboys rode in hats, shirts and jeans. Most of them got their heads and ribs kicked in. Noel got a few busted bones over the years, too, but not many. He always kept riding. One season he rode with his free arm in a cast from elbow to wrist."

It was difficult to picture Noel as a young man, let alone one who rode bulls. His depth of resentment toward the local Rodeo Association for passing him over as a judge this year suddenly made a whole lot more sense.

"Did you ever see him compete?" Erin said.

Megan nodded. "When we were kids; lots of times."

"He was awesome," Jamie added. "People reckoned he had some kind of telepathic shit going on with the bulls."

Megan laughed. "No, he just had the knack of holding the flank-strap for eight seconds, that's all. Built that way, I guess. He never let go. If he got thrown, it was because the strap let go of the bull first. Hey, babe, you remember his fancy chaps?"

Jamie nodded, smiled, and took a sip of beer. "Gold and black with a bright green fringe. Who could forget?"

"And he'd get invites to every rodeo in Australia. He pulled the crowds. Fans used to follow him from North Queensland to Victoria, every event, every season."

"Wow, I had no idea," Erin said. "I guess he was a celebrity?"

Jamie said, "A legend."

"And he had his fair share of groupies." Megan shot a cold glance at Jamie. "But he didn't cheat on his wife, rest in peace. Not even once. Can you imagine? Women throwing themselves at him, and he didn't go for it. And I'm talking young and beautiful women, not worn-out, fat, drunken sluts."

Jamie stared into the fire and belched. Megan kept glaring at him.

Erin took this as her cue. "Well, goodnight," she said and stood up.

"Hang on, don't forget your rifle," Megan said. "You never know."

***

The quarter-moon shone through the nylon of Erin's one-man tent. She shivered, but not from the cool night; the hooded sleeping bag fitted snugly. Had she been imagining things? She strained her ears. All she could hear was Noel's vigorous snoring from his tent nearby, the trill of a lone cicada, the occasional breeze clattering at leaves. Yet her heart kept slamming against her ribs.

Oh, there it was again.

The guttural, rasping snarl raised goose bumps across her flesh. It was a *Varanus priscus*, perhaps the same one they had seen. Could any other animal sound so otherworldly, so primeval? Yet the Komodo didn't make loud vocalisations.... The snarl seemed to come from far away. But how could she know for sure that it was far away? In the city, noise was measured on a different scale—music playing next door, a car horn honking in a parallel street, a dog barking in a yard across the highway—but out here? She knew that sound travelled a long, long way through water. Perhaps it was the same in a forest. Perhaps the *Varanus priscus* was 10 or 20 kilometres away, maybe even 30 kilometres or more....

Oh God, there it was again.

Did it sound closer? Farther? She couldn't tell. The nylon of the tent looked flimsier than tissue paper. Her scalp began to prickle and crawl, as if anticipating the crunch of teeth. Why the hell had she decided to camp in this godforsaken park? Reaching an arm out of the sleeping bag, she groped around the tent's groundsheet until her fingers touched the Remington. It was loaded and ready to go. Two full magazines lay alongside. She had never before understood the attraction of guns. Now she did. If she weren't so afraid of accidentally blowing off her own head, she would sleep with the Remington cradled in her arms like a teddy bear.

Then she smelled smoke.

Not from the campfire, still burning lazily, but from a cigarette.

Thrashing her upper body out of the sleeping bag, she unzipped her tent and stuck out her head. Jamie sat in one of the camp chairs. He had two of the light-brown rifles leaning against either side of his chair. Fully dressed including coat, beanie and boots, Jamie glanced at her while sucking on his cigarette.

"So it woke you up too," he whispered.

She nodded.

"That's the Devil dragon, right?" he added.

"I don't know. I've never heard these kinds of vocalisations. But if it's not the Devil dragon, what else could it be?"

Jamie exhaled a long stream of smoke. "No fucken idea."

The roar sounded once more. This time, however, Erin didn't feel quite as frightened because Jamie was with her. Things are always more frightening, she thought, when you have to face them alone.

"How close is it?" she said.

"Dunno."

"That's not very reassuring."

"It wasn't meant to be." He regarded her for a time. "I thought your Devil dragon slept at night."

"Well, that's the habit of the Komodo. My supposition was that the Komodo dragon and Devil dragon shared an ancestor. I assumed their habits would be similar."

He rolled his eyes and dragged on the cigarette.

"Is that why you're out here?" she said. "To stand guard?"

"If it's awake, it might come back."

Erin shivered. Yes, it might. Her assumptions on peak activity times must be wrong. Clearly, *Varanus priscus* was poikilothermic. Having the ability to tolerate wide extremes of environmental temperatures would allow it to be active in colder weather. Alternatively, the lizard might be exhibiting gigantothermy, its sheer size slowing the loss and gain of heat to the surroundings. Why hadn't she figured on these possibilities before? Yet it didn't seem feasible that the *Varanus priscus* could be roaming around in this kind of weather. How cold was it right now? Seven or eight degrees? At any rate, unseasonably chilly for the first week of summer.

"Is the overnight temperature always so low in the park?" she said.

"Dunno."

"Huh? What do you mean?"

Jamie flipped the cigarette butt onto the campfire. "I mean, we've never camped overnight here."

Shocked, Erin said, "You're kidding."

"Nope."

"This is the first time ever?"

"That's what I just told you."

She felt a surge of irritation. Some guides the Robinsons had turned out to be. Only three or four visits to the park every year and zero night-time experience.

"Hey, don't give me that snitchy face," he said. "We didn't tell you otherwise."

"I had the impression that you were well-versed on this park."

Jamie gave a derisive snort. "And we had the impression that you knew what the fuck you were talking about."

"The Devil dragon took the deer bait, didn't it?"

"Yeah, but what's the bastard doing awake?" He pushed up the sleeve of his jacket and glanced at his watch. "It's half-three in the morning."

Good point. Finally, she said, "Look, I'm sorry. I don't know."

He sighed, shook his head, and stared into the fire.

A blood-chilling shriek echoed out of the distance. Erin flinched. Oh God, a woman screaming for her life; perhaps a camper, a lost hiker—

"Hey," Jamie said through his teeth, "it's a pig."

The shriek came again. Now Erin could recognise the high-pitched, porcine squeal. But there was no mistaking the animal's terror. Abruptly, the squeal cut off.

That seemed even worse.

The brief, grating hiss of the *Varanus priscus* shot a panicked flood of adrenaline into Erin's limbs. Even by the dim firelight, she saw Jamie tense. They locked frightened eyes for a moment.

At last, he said, "It's eating that pig, isn't it?"

"Yes, I think so."

"Headfirst."

"Yes, in the manner of a snake."

Jamie grimaced, wrinkling his nose.

"Try to think about something else," she said.

He reached for his cigarette pack. "Dunno how the others can keep sleeping."

Erin propped her chin in her hands and stared at the fire. Jamie lit his smoke and worked on it in silence. The forest remained quiet. Despite herself, Erin couldn't help but picture those toothy jaws working steadily, inexorably, like a ratchet. By the time Jamie tossed the butt onto the pyre, she had her mind made up.

"What kind of weapon is that?" she said, pointing at one of the rifles propped against his chair.

"It's a firearm, not a weapon."

She shrugged. "Firearm, weapon; what's the difference?"

He seemed to take offence. "A lot. A weapon can be anything. Not just a gun or rifle, but a fist, knife, can of mace, length of pipe, nunchakus, bomb, chainsaw, even a paperclip if you use it to hurt somebody. A firearm shoots a cartridge using gunpowder, okay?"

But a firearm still qualifies as a weapon. How ridiculous to nit-pick. Erin contemplated retreating and zipping her tent closed. Instead, she swallowed her annoyance and said, "My apologies. It's a firearm. Can you teach me how to use it?"

Incredulous, he picked up the rifle. "This?"

"Why not? I did okay with the Remington, didn't I?"

After a moment, he said, "Sure, okay. This is an SKK semi-automatic. It shoots a 7.62 by 39 cartridge, but I don't expect you'd know what that means." He turned the firearm in his hands so that the barrel pointed at the sky. Indicating various parts, he continued. "There's the bolt. This here's the thirty-round detachable magazine; easy to swap in and out. And this, I fitted myself: an optic red-dot sight. You know what that means?"

"I imagine it means you aim the red dot where you want to shoot."

He smiled. "Yep, that's right. But it's not a laser sight. Whatever you're aiming at doesn't get lit up with a red dot. It's like crosshairs on a regular scope. You only see a red dot when you're looking through the eye piece."

"The reticule?"

"Yeah, the sighting scope, mounted right on top here, see? Come on out. I'll show you the rest."

"Give me a second."

She ducked back into the tent, zipped it closed and climbed fully out of the sleeping bag. The Remington seemed like a pea-shooter in comparison to the SKK. The close confines of the tent made dressing a struggle, but she was nonetheless out by the campfire in under a minute. She dragged over a chair and sat opposite him.

"Here's the safety," Jamie said, pointing. "Whatever you do, don't touch it."

"I promise."

Then he presented the firearm in both upturned hands, gently, in a manner that suggested a father offering his baby for a cuddle. Erin almost smiled. As she reached out, he suddenly pulled the rifle away with a stern frown. Had he changed his mind?

"Listen," he said. "Don't touch anything yet. No shitting around. Just hold it and get a feel for it while I tell you how things work. Okay?"

"Okay."

Satisfied, he presented the rifle again. She took it. The dead weight of it dropped her hands to her knees. "God, it's heavy."

"Heavy? Not even four kilos." He grinned. "But you're built on the small side, aren't you? Shit, I could carry you around in one arm."

Was he flirting? She couldn't tell. No, probably not. She looked down at the rifle. It was just shy of a metre long, and with what looked like ventilation holes on both sides of the barrel. Perhaps that was to prevent the rifle from overheating. The trigger lay directly in front of the stock. The sighting scope was bulky and short.

"What do you reckon?" Jamie said.

"That it could cut down a tree."

He sniggered. "No firearm can cut down a tree."

God almighty, she thought, do I really want to shoot this evil device? Then she remembered the squeals of the doomed pig, the snarl of the *Varanus priscus*. "What do I have to do?" she said.

"Explain to me this cosy little twosome," Megan said, walking out of the shadows into the light thrown by the fire. Her eyes were stony. "You thought I wouldn't hear you whispering? You're pathetic."

"Babe," Jamie said, "she asked me how to use the SKK and I'm showing her."

Impatiently, Erin snapped, "Oh, please, let me make three things absolutely crystal-clear. Number one, I'm not interested in your husband. Number two, he's not interested in me. Number three, the *Varanus priscus* is exhibiting poikilothermy, gigantothermy, or possibly even both—"

"Hang on, what? And say it in English."

"The Devil dragon is exhibiting the ability to function over a wide environmental temperature range, which means that it's active at night. Didn't you hear it roar?"

Bracing, Megan glanced about the campsite.

"Aw, relax. It's out Woop Woop somewhere," Jamie said.

"But awake?" She stared at Erin. "Isn't it meant to be asleep?"

Erin gave an apologetic shrug. "The Devil dragon seems to differ from the Komodo dragon in ways that I didn't expect."

"Terrific." Megan exhaled and sat in a nearby chair. She didn't look suspicious any more, just annoyed. Pointing at the rifle, she said, "How are you going to teach her without scaring Noel? He's a sick old man. He needs his sleep."

"Sick?" Erin said. "From his gored leg? He's developed a temperature?"

"No, I mean sick in a big way. Never you mind."

"Cancer?" Erin ventured. She felt her heart sink.

"The point is," Megan continued, "you can't shoot without waking him up."

Jamie said, "I wasn't planning on her doing any shooting until daybreak."

"This is a theory lesson," Erin said.

"Well, let's get started." Megan checked her watch. "There's a heap to get through, and the alarm is going off in about ninety minutes."

***

After about a quarter hour of tuition, Erin begged off. Tiredness had finally overwhelmed her. Crawling back into her tent, she stretched out on the air mattress—fully dressed, boots and all—and fell into a deep and dreamless sleep.

A gunshot jerked her awake.

She grabbed the Remington, put on her glasses, thrashed to turn around within the confines of her tent, and pulled open the zipper.

Across from each other at the campfire, both holding fry pans, sat Jamie and Megan, cooking bacon and eggs. They turned to her and smiled.

"What's up, Dopey?" Jamie said. "You look like you've just shit yourself."

"The shooting—"

"Oh, that's Noel." Megan waved a pair of barbecue tongs at the escarpment. "He reckons he saw a feral dog. The old bastard's got it in his head to kill the damn thing. There's only about a million others out there but you can't tell him squat."

Erin squinted into the weak, dawning light. Sure enough, there was Noel, close to the cliff edge, sighting along a rifle and aiming into the forest. Another shot rang out. Erin exhaled a long breath. A feral dog? Putting down the Remington, she flopped onto the air mattress, exhausted. Her heart still hammered.

"What time is it?" she mumbled.

Megan checked her watch. "Five forty-eight."

The others had been up and about for some 18 minutes. And Erin hadn't heard a thing. The *Varanus priscus* could have clawed through her tent at leisure and eaten her while she'd slept. Christ almighty. Erin reached under her glasses and rubbed at her gritty eyes.

"I thought we weren't supposed to light fires in the morning," Erin said. "In case it scares the Devil dragon away."

"Nothing would scare that bastard away," Jamie said.

12

The Robinsons attended happily to their respective fry pans. They must have somehow smoothed over their recent hostility. Weird, but who could understand the complicated dynamics of a marriage? Certainly not Erin; her longest romantic relationship had lasted all of five months. Despite their earnest and resolute efforts, she and Russ Walker-Smith had made terrible lovers. They had decided, mutually and with great relief, that they were much better suited as friends and colleagues.

Erin looked about. The lightening sky was the colour of a mauve bruise. Scudding clouds skipped high overhead on unfelt breezes. Galahs chittered somewhere in the forest. Erin crawled out of the tent. Oh, she felt like death warmed up. She struggled to stand. Her body ached. And her feet? The blisters hurt even more than yesterday. Sweat and grime crusted her skin.

"You okay?" Megan said to her.

"Because you don't look it," Jamie added.

Erin couldn't conjure a pithy reply. She lowered herself gingerly into a chair and watched Noel over by the escarpment. He shouldn't be over there. It wasn't safe.

Jamie squinted up at the last stars glimmering faintly. "Yep, today's a good day for hunting. I can feel it. We'll get the fucker this morning, just you wait."

Megan laughed softly and nodded. "Too right, babe."

Erin kept her gaze on Noel. If the *Varanus priscus* appeared now over the lip of the escarpment, it would catch him with no difficulty. Noel, she silently begged, come back to safety. And, as if hearing her plea, Noel turned, rifle by his side, and began to limp toward the campsite.

Erin watched his progress. Yes, he was tough, but apparently ill with something serious. And for a man in his seventies, that probably meant prostate cancer. She felt a tightening in her throat. Once this expedition was over, she'd earlier resolved to stay in touch with him. Now, she was determined to do so. She patted at the twin whittled figurines buttoned inside her shirt pocket: the crocodile and the *Varanus priscus*. Right at this moment, Noel felt close, as close as family. Then again, she reminded herself, ordeals tend to mess with one's emotions. People who undergo frightening experiences together always feel a temporary bond, regardless of whether their personalities are complementary. But she shouldn't get ahead of herself....

"The bloody mongrel nipped away," Noel said. He propped his rifle against a chair and sat down. "We should come out here one weekend and bait the whole bloody place."

"What about the natural wildlife?" Megan said. "You want to be the one who kills off the last ever spotted-tail quoll?"

Noel grumbled, adjusted his hat, and stared morosely into the fire.

"We should keep away from the cliff," Erin said.

"Oh, we told him that already," Megan said. "He doesn't care."

Noel spat at the dirt. "Hell's bells, I've got my rifle and sidearm."

"But the Devil dragon is more active than we thought," Erin continued. "And those pig carcasses are extra incentive for the lizard to come back. We need to stay well away, close to the campsite, to give us time to shoot before it reaches us."

Noel crossed his arms. "I've hunted an animal or two, thanks very much."

"Wait," Erin said. "I don't doubt your shooting prowess."

"Next, you'll be telling me how to tie my shoes." He looked away, his jaw set.

The Robinsons exchanged amused glances. Erin didn't understand why. Maybe Noel got into moods from time to time, and they found his sullenness comical. Or maybe they were laughing at the way she'd accidentally insulted him. She couldn't read the signs. Despair settled around her.

"Okay, let's eat," Megan said at last. "Sausages, bacon, eggs, baked beans."

"Is there anything else?" Erin said.

Agitated, Noel adjusted his hat. "You're welcome to cook us a gourmet meal."

Wounded, Erin said, "I just meant cereal or fruit."

"Aw, don't mind him." Megan passed around the paper plates. "He's shat off that he didn't kill the dog. Isn't that right, you cranky old fart?"

Noel grunted and started to eat.

A sting of tears warmed Erin's eyes. I want to go home, she thought, as she gazed down at her breakfast; I want to be back at the university.

"Tuck into your brekkie," Megan said. "You've got your shooting lesson next." To Noel, she added, "We're going to teach her how to use the SKK."

He gave a disgusted tut. "Waste of time. It'll knock her down flat."

"We'll see," Erin said.

Jamie laughed. "Shit, hey. Now that's the spirit."

***

Since they all wore ear protection, each one of them was shouting.

"Stand like a boxer," Jamie said. "Bend your knees. Put your weight on the front foot, like you did with the Remington. Now place the stock into your shoulder. Good. Hold the barrel with your left hand. A little farther along. Yeah, that's it. Lean forward from the waist. Clench up, like you're getting ready for a punch to the guts."

"She's going to hurt herself," Noel said. "I don't like this one bit."

"Shut up, old man," Megan said. "She's doing fine."

"Just wait 'til she fires."

"Ignore him, girl," Megan called out. "You're showing great form."

Jamie turned to Noel and Megan with his hands on his hips. "How about the jokers in the peanut gallery shut the fuck up?"

Rigid, muscles trembling from the weight of the SKK, Erin tried to ignore the runnels of sweat trickling along her scalp. Noel and the Robinsons had moved the bare minimum of equipment—chairs, rifles, ammunition bags, esky—nearer to one side of the forest. About 20 metres in front of her, Jamie had lined up six empty beer cans along a low-lying tree branch, like ducks in a shooting gallery. The cans looked very far away. Erin had asked to get a little closer, but the Robinsons had only laughed, good-naturedly, as if she'd been joking. The escarpment lay to her left. She kept it in her peripheral vision. The *Varanus priscus* could appear at any second.

Now, her shoulder muscles burned and shook. This stance would soon become untenable. "Now what?" she said.

"Pull back the rod like I showed you," Jamie said.

She did. She heard and felt a cartridge feed up from the magazine.

"Let go of the rod and let it slide home," he continued. "Now you're ready to fire. Where's your pointer finger?"

"On the trigger guard."

"Good stuff. Put your cheek on the stock. Lightly, hey, don't rest the whole weight of your bloody head on it, all right? Now look through the eye piece. Centre the red dot on the first beer can, the one on the far left. Got it?"

Erin's arms trembled. "I think so."

"Well, you either have it in your sights or you don't," Noel said.

"Oi, shut it," Jamie responded, "who's rooting this cat?" To Erin, he continued, "Okay, the safety is off, right?"

"Right," she said. Her heart started to boom like a kettle drum.

"You got that red dot on the beer can?"

To be honest, the dot was wavering. Instead, she said, "Yes, I've got it."

"Make sure you're clenched in the guts, with all your weight on your front foot. Brace for the recoil. Put your finger on the trigger. Ready?"

No, but she gave a tight nod anyway.

"Shoot."

Erin pulled the trigger. A loud crack rang out. The rifle shoved into her shoulder, but she didn't overbalance. Panting, she lowered the firearm. There were still six beer cans on the branch. Goddamn it.

"Take your finger off the trigger, remember?" Jamie said. "Put it back on the trigger guard. Good, that's the way."

"She missed," Noel said.

"Yeah, but you reckoned she'd fall over." Megan held out an upturned palm. "That's fifty bucks, mate."

Noel chuckled, his bad mood gone. "Put it on my tab."

Jamie approached Erin and patted her on the back. "Great job. Have another go. You don't have to cock it again. This is a semi-automatic, so it's still loaded. There are still twenty-nine more bullets. This time, lift, aim and shoot, as quickly as you can, so you're not straining to hold it up. Okay? Let her rip."

He stepped back.

Catching her breath, Erin prepared herself. Then she hoisted the rifle, sighted the beer can and squeezed the trigger.

Bang...tink...and the can flipped into the bush.

For a moment, Erin froze in surprise.

"I hit it!" she yelled, and spun toward Jamie.

"Finger off the trigger," he barked. "Lift the rifle. Put the safety back on. Shit, woman, you want to kill us all?"

Chastened, she did as she was told. Jamie took the rifle from her and turned to the others, his blue eyes shining.

"Eat shit, you old bastard," he said and laughed. "What did I tell you?"

Everyone removed their earplugs. Erin took off her earmuffs.

"That's another fifty you owe," Megan said, shoving at Noel with her elbow.

"And I'm damned happy to pay it." Noel got up, limped over and held out his hand. "Dr. Harris, for a city woman, it looks like you've got a big country streak."

They shook hands.

Megan came over and shook with her too. Erin felt delighted. Who would have thought that she could ever feel this happy about shooting a weapon? No, a firearm, she corrected herself;

specifically, a semi-automatic rifle. God almighty, what would Russ Walker-Smith think of her now?

With a sly parting grin, Noel began to shuffle toward the campsite proper.

"Where are you going?" Megan said.

Without looking back, he raised an arm with a waggling finger, in a *just you wait and see* gesture.

Megan added, "What's the old bugger up to?"

"Fucked if I know," Jamie said.

By the car and under the shade of the awning, Noel bent over and fossicked through the food bin. Then he hurried back, smiling.

"What's he got?" Megan said. "I can't see."

Jamie shrugged. "Dunno. Some kind of prize? A chocolate bar?"

But Erin didn't care what he carried; she was too busy assessing his limp. It seemed worse. Perhaps that explained his short fuse: a soaring temperature from an infection. She needed to remove the dressings and inspect the cut on his leg, and soon.

Puffing, Noel approached, one arm behind his back and eyes twinkling.

"Here's a challenge for you," he said to Erin.

He lifted his hand and, with a flourish, revealed a chicken egg. The Robinsons burst into guffaws. Erin, out of her depth, wasn't sure how to react.

"You want her to shoot that itty bitty thing?" Jamie said. "Get stuffed. Shoot it from where? Off the top of your head?"

"Hah, good one," Megan said. "Like William Tell."

Jamie frowned. "Like William who?"

Noel said, "Dr. Harris, if you shoot this egg off that tree branch, I'll give each one of you a hundred bucks."

Erin felt her spirits drop. She couldn't succeed. Were they laughing at her again? She said, "You can't possibly expect me to hit something so tiny."

"Give it a try, anyway," Jamie said.

"Yeah, come on, for shits and giggles," Megan added. "Lighten up. There's money in it and nothing to lose. Hey, Noel, this isn't a bet, is it? If she misses, do you expect a pay out?"

"Nope," he said, trotting away toward the forest.

"Even better." Megan slapped Erin on the backside. "See? It's not a bet. Shoot or miss, it doesn't matter. You go, girl."

Disheartened, Erin faced the line of beer cans. Noel, limping heavily, reached the branch and waved at them. The Robinsons waved back. Erin's arms hung limply. If this was a joke, she didn't want to participate. She felt too sore, tired, humiliated.

Jamie, offering her the SKK with the barrel aimed at the sky, said, "Don't lower the firearm until he's clear. Got it? And flip off the safety before you shoot."

"Hold your core tight," Megan added. "Don't hurt your back."

Reluctantly, Erin took the rifle. "I can't hit a goddamned egg."

"Oh, what's the harm?" Megan said. "Jeez, when are you planning to yank that stick out of your arse and enjoy life for a change?"

By shooting an egg? Oh, give me a break, Erin thought.

Noel was still trying to balance the egg next to the line of beer cans.

"Shit, what's taking him so long?" Jamie said.

"It must be rolling about," Megan said. "He can't find a dip in the branch."

Erin sighed. "I can't hit a target that small."

"Aw, come on, Erin, what's with the negativity?" Jamie said.

"Yeah, show a little faith," Megan said.

Finally, Noel found a resting place for the egg. Slowly, he let it go. When the egg didn't fall, he faced them all and gave two thumbs up. A shadow fell across him. Momentarily, Erin thought that a cloud must have covered the sun. But no. From between the trees, noiselessly, smoothly, jaws agape, the giant head of a *Varanus priscus* appeared directly over Noel.

Erin screamed.

Noel looked up. Flinching, ducking into a crouch, he flung both arms over his head in a protective stance. No, Erin thought, draw your handgun; fire directly into its mouth. Each bullet would penetrate the monster's palate, smash through the parietal bones, enter the braincase, and tear the brain tissue....

Shoot, she tried to yell. Her throat was locked.

Everything happened so fast.

The vast jaws with their dagger-like teeth descended, enclosing Noel to the hips. The monster lifted its head. Noel kicked as he left the ground. Beyond dread, Erin couldn't look away. Noel must be aware and conscious inside that terrible mouth. The monster took its first, delicate bite.

Oh, God.

The bite of the Komodo dragon is weaker than that of an average housecat...she had read that somewhere. It doesn't crush its prey like a crocodile. If it tried, it would break its own skull. No, the Komodo dragon relies on the bridge-like design of its jaws to distribute bite pressure, its serrated and recurved teeth to draw in prey, its powerful throat muscles to force the prey along its gullet. The Komodo is an inertia killer...Erin had read that somewhere. She had read it...*weaker than a housecat....*

But this wasn't a Komodo. This was something else, a beast from hell.

Dark red blood spurted. Noel's legs thrashed. One shoe flew off into the bush.

The *Varanus priscus* tipped its snout at the sky. Noel's legs dangled. As a dog eats a steak, the lizard opened its mouth and tossed its enormous head, over and over. Gravity kept dropping Noel's body deeper and deeper into the maw.

Erin's heart skittered wildly.

Jesus, please let him be dead. An image of Noel's face suffocating against the constricting tissue of the monster's gullet ripped a strangled, muffled scream from her. Oh, let him be dead. Let him be dead already.

A rush of disturbed air fanned past her. It was Megan, sprinting toward the monster with an SKK held up to her face. And that cacophony of explosions...that must be Megan firing bullets. For a long, dazed moment, Erin was seated in the front row of a darkened movie theatre, watching this unfathomable horror play out on the screen. She half-expected to hear the thrilled shrieks and murmurs of the audience.

Jamie suddenly appeared in her visual field.

"Come on!" he yelled, wrenching the SKK from her leaden grasp.

And then he was running, too, shooting.

The blank shock fell away. Galvanised, Erin snatched up the Remington that was propped against her chair, and charged at full-speed after him. The Robinsons were almost upon the monster. Where did these people get their courage?

The huge, pebbled head with its bloodied snout turned to face them.

Noel's feet were gone. Where were his feet? Had the lizard totally devoured him? Erin felt a swing of vertigo. Christ almighty, the monster had eaten him alive.

The Robinsons were still firing. Megan paused, discarded the magazine, replaced it with another, and was shooting again. Next, Jamie did the same. Both of them had ammunition bags slung over a shoulder. Erin hadn't thought to pick one up. Were their bullets striking the lizard or not? Yes. The *Varanus priscus* snapped repeatedly at the air, as if swarmed by wasps.

Erin cocked her rifle.

Sighting through the scope, the lizard's eye looked close enough to touch. The eye was eerily human in appearance: a round, black pupil with a scalloped pupillary ruff, a hazel iris with radiating structural folds. Eyes the same colour as mine, Erin thought in detached wonder. The only alien feature was the collarette immediately surrounding the pupil, which was a bright, almost lime green.

She pulled the trigger.

The bullet hit at or around the orbit bones. For a millisecond, she actually saw the hole erupt. Then the colossal head swung away and out of her scope. She lowered the rifle with deadened arms.

Got you, she thought, stupefied.

Motherfucker, *I got you*.

A kind of crazed elation sang through her veins. She ejected the spent cartridge, went to reload. Nothing. She tried again, perplexed. She studied the rifle's bolt. Had it jammed? And in a sickening rush, she recalled that the rifle had had only one bullet left. Yesterday, using a four-bullet magazine, she had killed three pigs with three shots. She patted frantically at her jacket, searching for the magazines stashed in her pockets. Oh shit. Both magazines were lying on the groundsheet in her tent.

She held an empty rifle.

13

The deafening noise of gunfire came back to Erin's awareness. She looked up from her rifle. Where was the lizard? Gone: now there were only eucalyptus trees. The five beer cans were still lined up along the low-lying branch, and beside them sat Noel's egg, upright and perfectly balanced, as if nothing out of the ordinary had ever happened.

The Robinsons stopped shooting.

"After it!" Megan yelled, and ran into the forest.

So the lizard had retreated.

Jamie paused to load a magazine. "You coming?" he yelled to Erin.

If she wasn't scared enough already, the look of him almost stopped her heart. His face was grey, his lips pulled back into a trembling grimace, his eyes bulging so wide that the whites of the sclera showed all the way around. He's terrified, Erin realised. He's terrified out of his mind, but he's going after that monster.

"Yes," she said, "I just need more bullets."

"Hurry up."

He sprinted into the forest after his wife.

Erin turned and raced back to the makeshift camp. Sporadic gunfire sounded. The Robinsons must have the *Varanus priscus* in sight. Gasping, almost retching, Erin fell to her knees and tore open the two remaining ammunition bags. She hunted through them and found six loaded magazines for the Remington. With shaking fingers, she swapped the spent magazine for a fresh one, and pocketed the rest.

She fought to stand up. Her legs felt boneless.

When she looked toward the forest, it seemed to stare back, daring her to enter.

*Hic sunt dracones...here be dragons...*the Hunt-Lenox map of the world came to mind, its ominous warning stamped in Latin across the Indonesian islands occupied by the Komodo. *Hic sunt dracones....*

Apart from the occasional gunshot, there were no sounds. Not one bird call, not a single drone from an insect. The pulse thudded in Erin's ears. Her feet wouldn't move. I can't do it, she thought. I can't go in there. Hot tears rose. Steeling herself, she pressed a hand against her shirt to feel the twin wooden figurines. She took a number of deep, ragged breaths. Then she cocked the Remington and sprinted across the clearing.

The bush enclosed her like deep water.

Erin stopped dead. Goddamn it, her compass was in her tent. If she returned to the campsite proper to retrieve her compass, the Robinsons would have an even longer head start. But if she went into the forest without a compass, she might get lost.

Now what? Shit. Couldn't she do anything right?

She put a hand to her forehead and squeezed at her temples, trying to compose herself. I will do better next time, she promised. If I get another chance, I will make sure that I always have my equipment on my person at all times....

...If there was a next time, if she got another chance....

She wanted desperately to go back for the compass. Jesus, her poor sense of direction meant that she regularly got lost while driving in the city, even around the streets of her own neighbourhood. Urban areas, however, feature recognisable landmarks. If necessary, you can drive around until you stumble upon a familiar building, a known intersection....

She had to decide. Go forward with a chance of catching the Robinsons, or retreat for the compass? Precious seconds were ticking by.

Out of nowhere, she thought of Dad, how he used to savour her every defeat, no matter how small. It gave her strength. Or was it foolhardiness? With the Remington hanging from her shoulder by its strap, she held it across her chest, barrel upward, as Jamie had instructed.

"Megan?" she called, and waited. No response. "Jamie?"

Distant gunshots sounded. Clenching her teeth, Erin walked forward. By keeping on a dead straight path, she could theoretically turn 180 degrees at any time and make a beeline to the campsite. As long as she didn't meander, she wouldn't get lost. Sweat dripped into her eyes. Quickly, she swiped it away, gripped the Remington again. She couldn't allow herself to get lost. This park was 30,000 hectares, feeding into another 100,000 hectares of state forest. No, by Christ, she would not get lost.

I won't get lost.

Gunfire sounded, a quick flurry, echoing as if coming from very far away. Erin stopped to listen. Which direction? She couldn't tell. All around her, as far as she could see, was the same iteration of trees, shrubs, rocks, dirt, as if she stood within a carnival of mirrors. She looked behind her. Already, the campsite had disappeared. Fear stirred inside her belly. When she and Noel had found the lizard's gastric pellet in the scrub at the rear of his property, Noel had said: *We can't go far into the bush without a compass. Spin around twice and you're lost.*

She faced front. One at a time, she wiped her sweating palms against her camouflage trousers.

"Megan?" she called, louder this time. "Jamie?"

No reply. She continued on, resolutely putting one foot in front of the other.

Perhaps she could leave a trail for herself.

Slinging her rifle, she took out her Swiss Army knife and opened the largest blade. Vigorously, she attempted to carve a large "X" into the nearest tree. It was hard going. After a couple of minutes, she stepped back to take a critical look at her handiwork. The dark fissures and furrows of the bark perfectly camouflaged her measly "X". Forget it; marking a trail like this would be a waste of time.

And now Megan and Jamie were even farther ahead.

She pocketed the knife and broke into a shuffling trot. The uneven ground, with its random scattering of rocks, tree roots, dips and hillocks nearly turned her ankles a few times. Besides that, her blisters were stinging. Why hadn't she thought to replace her dressings this morning? No doubt, her socks were spotted with blood....

"Stop it," she said through her teeth. "Stop whining."

Because she was alive and Noel was dead.

The awful memory rolled over her in a wave.

Oh God, Noel was *dead*.

She saw again his pitiful attempt to save himself, his arms flung overhead. And those terrible open jaws.... No, she had to cut off the memory right there. It was too horrible to contemplate.

Grimly, Erin kept pushing herself forward.

He must have suffocated....

Don't think about it.

Yet suffocation takes minutes. The *Varanus priscus* had swallowed him in mere seconds. Did Noel scream? Was he screaming as the monster's throat muscles worked his body down its gullet?

Erin shuddered. Think about something else.

By now, the powerful digestive acids would have eaten through his soft tissue; were dissolving his bones into soup.

Jesus, no, she had to block these images from her mind.

Within moments of being swallowed, Noel's head would have passed through the oesophageal sphincter and into the stomach. Had he been alive at that point? Considering the brief time frame, yes, more than likely. He must have felt the acid boiling and burning through his scalp, into his skull, searing his cerebral cortex until the blessed unconsciousness of brain damage, the relief of death....

Erin's eyes fluttered shut. Without warning, she buckled over and heaved her breakfast into the dirt. When she finished at last, she leaned against a tree, gasping and spitting.

Noel is dead, she thought, and it's my fault.

She had sold him on this crazy hunt. If she hadn't contacted him about the *Varanus priscus* attacking his heifer, he would be safe on his farm right now, tending to his cattle, making breakfast for his daughter—

Oh God, his daughter.

A flash of agonising shame and grief took the strength from Erin's limbs. His pregnant daughter, Kylie.... Noel would never meet his grandchild. How would Erin explain his ghastly death to his family? What on earth would she say to Kylie?

The sharp rapport of a single gunshot echoed in the distance. It acted like a slap to the face. Erin had to quit the hysterics and catch up to the Robinsons. They had known Noel for years, but weren't struck helpless by self-recriminations and torment. No, they were in pursuit of the monster that had killed him. Erin ought to show the same fortitude. She wiped her mouth with the back of her hand. A quick check of the rifle—the safety off, a cartridge in the chamber—and she broke into a trot.

"Megan?" she called. "Jamie? Where are you?"

No answer.

Occasionally, Erin had to deviate around a tree or rock. As soon as possible, she would correct her course. Please God, let me be running in a straight line, she thought. Just don't let me get lost. Her mouth felt sticky and dry from vomiting, and she didn't have a water bottle, either. Holy shit, she thought, I'm an idiot. An idiot who deserves to die of exposure.

"Megan?" she shouted again. "Jamie?"

No response.

Noel had balanced the egg and turned to them, smiling, with two thumbs up.

Don't think about it.

"Megan? Jamie?"

Erin was gasping now. Slow down, she thought. Her legs were trembling. She leaned against a tree to catch her breath. And that's when she heard it.

Slow, purposeful steps through nearby leaf litter.

Her heart jumped into her mouth. Lifting the rifle, she stared about in all directions at trees, shrubs, rocks, dirt—everything the goddamned same.

The rustling sounded closer.

From somewhere behind her.

The steps were too fast and too noisy for the *Varanus priscus*. Could it be a feral pig? Or worse, a dog? Noel's words came back to her: *The biggest danger around here is wild dogs. I've seen a pack take down a steer and eat the bloody thing while it was still living.* Erin swallowed hard, turned slowly—don't lose track of which way you're facing, for Christ's sake—and sighted along the rifle, placing the stock against her shoulder. Her finger stuttered against the trigger guard.

"Come on," she whispered. "Come on out, so I can shoot you in the face."

The rustling stopped momentarily, and then started up.

A flash of movement through the branches...and there it was again.

She placed her finger on the trigger.

The creature advanced. She could see fur. Short, coarse and reddish-tan in colour, like the brindled coat of a Staffordshire bull terrier. Erin curled her finger around the trigger. I've shot pigs and a *Varanus priscus*, she thought, so I can shoot you, dog. The creature emerged from the bush and startled. For a moment, they stared at each other, equally bewildered and alarmed.

Erin lowered the rifle. It was a goat.

Nothing but a goddamned goat.

"Get out of here," she said, waving an arm. "Go on, get."

The goat reared its horned head, turned tail and scampered back into the bush. Erin wiped the sweat from her brow.

Holy shit.

Now....

Where was she, exactly?

A soft exhalation escaped her, almost like a moan. She had turned 180 degrees to confront the goat, hadn't she? Which meant that she was aimed at the campsite, right? But she couldn't be sure that her turn had been exactly 180 degrees. Perhaps it had been 170 or even 160. Enough to throw her off course; enough that she would bypass the campsite entirely, and walk on and on through the bush until she dropped dead from exposure, dehydration or heat exposure, assuming that a pack of wild animals—or a *Varanus priscus*—didn't get to her first.

"Megan!" she screamed at the top of her lungs. "Jamie!"

Why wouldn't they answer? Surely, they couldn't be out of earshot.

She closed her eyes, tried to still her racing mind. *Be rational.* What would be the smartest action to take? There was only one answer: return to the campsite. She couldn't catch up to the

Robinsons at this rate. And the longer she rambled through the forest, the greater the chance of getting lost.

Fine, she thought, I'm facing the way I came in. Start walking.

Yet, she hesitated.

Should she correct her position? Assume that her present angle was wrong? She tried to recall the precise moment when she had spun around. No use; whether she had turned 180 degrees or not, she couldn't remember. I will do better next time, she thought, if I get a next time. She stared down at her boots. They were both spattered with her vomit. Not the most reassuring sight.

Well, she couldn't stand here for the rest of her life.

She began to trot back to where she thought she had come.

After a while, she gave up trying to recognise the scenery. Why hadn't she checked her watch upon entering the forest? That could have given her a rough estimate of how long it might take to get back to the campsite. Oh, she wasn't cut out for this, for any of it. She was designed for lecture halls, paved roads, GPS, air-conditioning, potable water straight from the tap. This is hell, she thought, trying to hold back tears of panic. Hell on earth, and I don't know what I'm doing.

Faster, she had to run faster. Twigs and low-lying branches whipped at her.

She stumbled over a rotten log, fell, and landed face-first against the stock of the Remington, splitting her chin. Her tongue automatically ran over her teeth: all there, none loose. Scrambling to sit up, she pressed at her chin momentarily with both sets of fingers and stared in amazement at the blood covering them. She must need stitches. But it could have been worse, much worse. She could have shot herself. The Remington's safety was off.

Sobered, she got to her feet.

No more running. No more freaking out.

She would walk from now on. If it became clear that she was lost, all she had to do was treat the rifle like a flare gun and shoot it every now and then. Megan and Jamie would eventually find her. Don't worry, she thought, there is plenty of ammunition. She would be okay. Assuming the Robinsons weren't lost, too.

Or being digested within the belly of the beast.

"Megan?" she yelled. "Jamie?"

No answer, no gunshots, nothing.

She hurried on. More trees, more shrubs, more rocks, more dirt....

Her will and testament came to mind. The decision to draw it up had been spurred by her father's suicide a few years ago. A lawyer in the local shopping mall had helped her to draft the simple document: everything to the university. If she were to die this weekend, she hoped that Russ Walker-Smith would remember to pick up his birthday gifts from her apartment: the keychain with a biohazard emblem, the reprint of Ernst Haeckel's engravings of diatom formations. What meagre bequests. I wish I had a family, she thought. Who would come to her funeral besides Russ? The university Dean, a few of her students, perhaps. Oh, don't be ridiculous, she chided herself. If she died out here, no one would find her body, making a funeral a moot point. Unexpectedly, she laughed, a little wildly.

On and on, her tired feet shambled through the leaf litter. She was causing too much noise. Predators would hear her for miles around.

She kept walking, walking, walking....

Her heart gave a spasm. The bush had thinned out.

She broke into a sprint and stopped when she entered the clearing. It happened suddenly, like a popped balloon, the shock of it giving her no time to mentally adjust. I'm hallucinating, she thought. But no, some 20 metres away stood their chairs, ammunition bags, esky, and beyond that, the car with its awning and the fire pit.

Erin dropped the rifle, collapsed to her knees and clenched at the dirt with both fists. Dirt had never felt so precious. Regaining control of her senses, she grabbed the rifle, stood up again, and shuffled into the clearing.

In three trips, she returned everything to the campsite proper. Then she slumped into a chair and contemplated the cold ashes of the fire. Nearby, the frying pans reminded her of their meal; the Robinsons cheerfully looking forward to the hunt, Noel trying to shoot a wild dog. Erin poked at the coffee mugs with her boot. It all looked so normal. The beer cans and the egg continued to sit undisturbed on the tree branch.

How could Noel be dead?

Stop thinking about it.

A sudden realisation froze her breath. What if Noel had been alive when they had shot at the *Varanus priscus*? What if their bullets had penetrated the armoured hide and killed him? Erin put her face in her hands. We could be murderers.... But wait, getting shot to death would be quick and painless, infinitely better than suffocating or being digested alive. A queasy churn rolled through her. She grabbed a water bottle from the esky and took a long drink.

Christ, just stop thinking about it.

She stared into the fire pit. Minutes continued to pass. There hadn't been any gunshots for a long, long time. Where were the Robinsons? They couldn't be lost. The couple was far too capable for such a rookie error.

Then what? Had the *Varanus priscus* turned around, charged, attacked?

What if the couple didn't return?

Squawking and screeching, a flock of budgerigars zipped overhead from one side of the forest and disappeared into the other. Their bright green colours brought the eye of the *Varanus priscus* to mind.

At least Erin had shot the lizard. But that was a small comfort. God alone knew how many bullets the Robinsons had sunk into its skull and throat, into its retreating form as it had lumbered away into the bush. Could the *Varanus priscus* be mortally wounded? Or were the bullets as trifling as flea bites? Erin didn't know. And she called herself a scientist. With no idea of what she was doing, she had plunged into this hunt, and led a sick old man to his horrible death.

Oh Russ, she thought, you were right. Why didn't I return to the university and apply for funding? This should have been a proper scientific expedition instead of an ad hoc hunt. She stared at her hands. They had blood on them.

14

The sun hung hot and bright. Erin had shucked her jacket about an hour ago and was sitting in a camp chair, the t-shirt sticking to her back.

It occurred to her, gradually, and in a creeping manner that caused the hairs on her arms to rise, that she didn't know the location of the campsite in relation to the rest of the park, or even in relation to the town. If she were alone, how could she find her way back to civilisation? In which direction should she drive the car? There weren't any visible gravel or dirt roads leading out of this clearing. Erin had slept during the drive into the park; for all she knew, Megan had bush-bashed the whole way here.

Don't get ahead of yourself, Erin thought.

She would wait. If the Robinsons hadn't returned by morning, she would drive—lost and hopeless—through the forest, hoping to blunder across a road. Perhaps she would find an area that had mobile phone coverage.

Hungry, she searched the boxes in the rear of the four-wheel drive. She found a packet of salted potato chips. Processed food tasted like crap, but at this point, she just wanted to fill her stomach. The Komodo dragon has an expandable stomach, which allows it to consume up to 80 percent of its body weight in one sitting....

Don't think about it.

Erin ate the chips one at a time. Every now and then, she glanced up at the sun. It passed its midway point. She finished the potato chips and put the empty bag into the fire pit. The shadows around her began to lengthen as the afternoon wore on. The loaded Remington sat across her lap. She hummed tunelessly to herself and kept her gaze on the forest. The five beer cans, the carefully balanced egg...the Robinsons would appear where they had disappeared, or they wouldn't appear at all.

Movement through the trees....

What this time? Boar? Dog? Another goddamned goat?

If it was a *Varanus priscus*, she would get in the car and shoot through a few inches of open window until she ran out of bullets, the lizard gave up, or it broke in and ate her, whichever came first. With effort, she stood up, readied her rifle.

Looking round-shouldered and exhausted, their heads hanging, Megan and Jamie shambled into the clearing.

For a second, Erin couldn't believe her eyes.

With a jolt of energy, she dropped the rifle and ran across to them. Jamie grabbed her first, wrapping an arm about her neck and planting a loud, smacking kiss on top of her head. Then Megan pulled Erin into her arms and hugged her. Gasping, the trio stepped back and stared at each other in amazement, as if at ghosts.

"Oh, Jesus," Erin said at last. "I thought you weren't coming back."

"Don't cry, you dope," Jamie said.

Was she crying? Erin touched her cheeks, found them wet with tears.

"What happened to your chin?" Megan said.

"Nothing, I just fell over."

"Come on," Megan said. "Let me fix it for you."

They trudged across the clearing towards the campsite. The defeated postures of the Robinsons spoke volumes, but Erin felt compelled to ask, anyway.

"Did you kill it?"

"Nah," Jamie said. "The prick ran flat to the boards. We couldn't stay on the trail. Fuck only knows how many times we shot him. It didn't bother him much."

Now, that was sobering news.

"So you see?" Jamie continued, addressing his wife. "I told you we needed a bigger calibre, didn't I? Some more mushroom slugs would have come in handy, too. I knew we didn't make enough of them. Not nearly enough."

Perhaps the osteoderms that overlapped the hide were dense to the point of being impenetrable? But no; Erin had seen her single bullet enter the lizard's orbital socket and leave a hole. The *Varanus priscus* is wounded, she thought, but how badly was anyone's guess.

"Maybe we were too close to it," Megan said.

Confused, Erin said, "What do you mean?"

"Hollow-point cartridges can bounce off or not blossom if you're too close."

"Nah, we weren't too close," Jamie said through his teeth. "We shot him and he just didn't give a shit."

"Maybe he's running on adrenaline."

Erin said, "For God's sake, how come you didn't get lost out there?"

From behind her shirt, Megan pulled out a necklace which had a little compass hanging on it like a pendant. "Where's yours?" she said. "In your backpack?"

Erin didn't reply. What for? She was useless and everyone knew it.

They reached the campsite. Jamie sat down, opened the ammunition bags, and took out a number of flat, curved magazines that Erin recognised as belonging to the SKK. Then he took out a couple of yellow boxes.

"What are you doing?" Erin said.

"Reloading the mags. We dropped them on the chase, and picked 'em up on the way back."

He grabbed a magazine. One at a time from a yellow box, he took cartridges and pressed them into the magazine against what sounded like a spring-loaded plate. Until now, Erin had assumed that magazines were single-use items; that they came loaded and had to be thrown away once empty, like disposable cigarette lighters. Wow, her ignorance was astonishing.

"Take a load off," Megan said to her, and headed to the car.

Erin obeyed and sat near Jamie.

"Can I help?" she asked.

He smiled. "Nah, it's okay. I want it done fast."

Megan retrieved the first aid kit. Erin was reminded of childhood, of a schoolteacher attending to a scraped knee and attempting to bribe away tears with a biscuit. Megan unzipped the kit, fussed quickly and expertly with the contents. The iodine on cotton wool stung Erin's chin. Shit.

"Sorry, I know it hurts," Megan said. "But I've got to get the dirt out."

"That's okay."

Would Megan use gauze and cover it with a strip of duct tape? Erin's heart cramped into a tight wad as she recalled Megan tending to Noel's gored leg.

Jamie must have been thinking along similar lines. "Well, fuck," he said, "Noel Baines was a top bloke."

"One of the best," Megan said. She smoothed a plaster over Erin's chin and kept busy for a while putting away the first aid kit, her shoulders hunched. Perhaps she was steeling herself, trying not to cry. Finally she said, "I hope he didn't suffer." Turning to Erin, leaning on the tailgate, she added, "In your opinion, as a scientist, do you think he suffered?"

Yes, Erin thought. He would have suffered a great deal. His death was painful, brutal, slow and terrifying. Instead, she said, "I'm sure he died almost instantly."

Megan sighed. "I should have fired sooner."

Erin should have, too. She felt a wave of shame. When the *Varanus priscus* had appeared over Noel's head, she'd been holding a loaded SKK. Instead of shooting, trying her damndest to save Noel, her arms had turned to water. The twin figurines felt heavy in her pocket.

"Let's pack up, return to town," she said. "The authorities have to be notified."

"Pack up?" Jamie said. "To hell with that. I say we leave everything behind and get out of here now. What if the Devil dragon wants another go?"

Erin said, "It must be thirty-five degrees. It'll seek shade until late afternoon."

Jamie raised a sceptical eyebrow.

Megan punched his arm and said, "I'm not abandoning our equipment. We can't afford it. So shake a leg. We can be out of here in twenty minutes."

The Robinsons seemed to have a set routine on loading the car, so Erin concentrated on packing her own belongings. She put the bags into the back seat of the car, along with the Remington. Then she tried to dismantle her tent. Was there a trick? Why wouldn't it collapse?

Jamie, on the car's roof as his wife handed items to him, suddenly announced, "People are gonna think we killed Noel."

Erin turned to him in surprise. "Why on earth would they think that?"

"Hey, what's a copper more likely to believe? Murder? Or death by dinosaur?"

"Good point," Megan said. "We don't have any evidence."

"What? No, of course we do. I've got photographs of its footprint."

Jamie shrugged. "Who's to say I didn't scratch that into the dirt myself?"

"No, we have three eyewitness accounts...."

"Yeah," Megan said, "like that family driving through the outback that got spooked by a UFO. Remember? I was a kid at the time. Their story was over all the papers, on every news and current affairs show. They were a laughing stock."

"But we're credible witnesses. I'm a scientist...."

"And from now on," Megan said, "you'll be known as the Crazy Scientist."

"Or the Nutty Professor," Jamie agreed.

Despite the tension etched in their faces, the couple managed a shared laugh.

They're right, Erin thought. Physical evidence is what matters. Unsubstantiated accounts, photographs, footprints: all of that means nothing.

"Wait a second," she said. "What about Noel's shoe? I saw it fly off his foot. Maybe it's got traces of Devil dragon saliva."

She hobbled across the clearing towards the set-up of beer cans and single egg, her blisters hurting more than ever.

"You sure he lost a shoe?" Jamie called.

"I didn't see it come off, either," she heard Megan say.

Nonetheless, Erin hurried on. She had to find the shoe. Russ could analyse the fabric. Surely, if the tests came back positive for bacteria or venom similar to the Komodo dragon, that would be evidence enough to bolster their testimonies.

Slowing down, cautious now, she approached the low-lying branch with the beer cans and egg. So many shrubs, so much leaf litter....

In which direction had the shoe flown?

Briefly, she closed her eyes. Once again, she saw Noel's flailing legs. The bile rose in her throat. Concentrate, she thought. Concentrate and remember. It was his right shoe.

Wasn't it?

Yes, she was certain. His kicking right leg had flipped the shoe in a high arc. The shoe had landed perhaps a metre away. If she scrabbled through the undergrowth, she would find it. Falling to her knees, she ran her hands through dead leaves.

Nothing.

Oh Jesus, come *on*....

A creeping sensation prickled at her scalp. She sat up, looked about. Had she heard something? A stealthy footfall? And here she was, defenceless as usual, her rifle at the campsite. Idiot. She stared into the forest. Trees, trees and more trees....

Was there movement?

No, she decided at last. Raw nerves had tricked her.

She went back to searching the undergrowth, frantically now. Her fingers scraped against rocks, snagged on twigs. Death by a thousand cuts, she thought. Her thumb brushed against a different texture, something that felt soft and worn. And yes, here it was...Noel's lace-up, high-top boot. She went to grab it, forced herself to stop. No, she had to pick it up by the rippled sole. The saliva—if present—would probably be on the leather upper.

She stood, turned to the camp and yelled, "I found his shoe."

"What are you waiting for?" Megan yelled back. "Get your arse over here."

Erin hurried away from the forest edge. Again, the hair on the back of her neck rose up. Nerves, she maintained. Stop jumping at your own shadow.

At the campsite, she said, "I need a plastic bag."

Megan found one, handed it over.

Erin placed the shoe inside and sealed the bag. "Maybe there's no saliva at all, but it's worth a try." She tucked the shoe into her backpack. "Where's Jamie?"

"Getting rid of the deer carcasses."

"Huh? What for?"

"Because we're not licensed to hunt here. You think we're going to leave our baits for investigators to find? Jamie's chucking them."

And yes, there he was at the cliff edge, dragging a deer carcass by its butcher's hook: unbelievable. "After everything that's happened," Erin said, "you still care about getting caught for poaching?"

"Shit, yeah. We could lose our licences."

"Lose what?"

Megan popped her bottom lip and huffed out an impatient breath, riffling her fringe. "Okay, look, for three months every year, our kids run the stud while we head up north to pig-shoot. It's good money. It's what saves us from going under." She hefted a couple of folded chairs and swung them into the back of the car. "So, yeah, after everything that's happened, even after Noel getting killed, we still need money to pay our mortgage, keep the stud, and put food on the table."

Erin sighed. "I should never have involved you in this."

"Nobody put a gun to our heads."

"Don't worry. I'll take full responsibility for Noel's death."

"Are you joking?" Megan put her hands on her hips. "Wild horses couldn't have dragged that old bastard away. You tried to stop him, remember? And right there in his kitchen, he told you it was a joint expedition, you and him, no argument. I'm telling you, once he made up his mind, not even the Lord Himself could change it."

Erin nodded, feeling miserable.

"Now listen carefully," Megan continued. "Me and Jamie have the story worked out, and it's easy to remember: we came into the park without any firearms. All right? Our plan was to find the Devil dragon during the hottest part of the day and get footage while it slept. That means we didn't hang deer bait. We didn't teach you to shoot. Noel went for a piss and got killed by the dinosaur."

"Wow." Erin managed a half-hearted laugh. "That's preposterous. Chasing a dangerous reptile with nothing but a camera? Who would believe it?"

"If the three of us stick to the story, then everybody will have to believe it, whether they want to or not. Agreed?"

Erin exhaled a long, tired breath. "Agreed."

"No firearms?"

"Okay, no firearms."

"So that means we've got to pick up the spent casings before we leave."

Erin hesitated. "And spent casings are...?"

"The empty shell casings from all the bullets we fired. It's no use telling people we didn't have firearms if we leave casings all over our campsite, yeah?"

"Yes, of course."

Satisfied, Megan resumed packing the car. Erin struggled on with her tent. Unfortunately, one of the Robinsons would have to help her. Shit. At least she'd be back in the city within a few hours. Her spirits lifted a little. And tomorrow, Monday morning, she would stand behind the familiar lectern in LT5 as usual....

A cold trickle of anxiety rippled through her.

Oh no, she wouldn't be at work.

She'd be with police, SES workers, lawyers, trying to tell the roundabout truth of what had happened, trying to explain the unimaginable circumstances of Noel's death. It would be a scandal. A man killed by an extinct Pleistocene apex predator? Jesus, the media circus would be national, probably global. Oh God, the hashtag frenzy in the Twittersphere, the avalanche of Devil dragon memes, the jokes at her expense made by hosts of late-night talk-shows.... And Jamie may be right; there could even be a murder investigation.

Then another terrible thought struck her.

She could kiss her job goodbye.

The university faculty—and especially the ultra-conservative Dean—would fire her on the spot. The realisation took the strength from her legs. She knelt in the dirt. Her career was over.

Forever the Nutty Professor, she'd be reduced to the entertainment at children's parties, getting booked to show tortoises and frogs to pre-schoolers for the rest of her life—if she was lucky. Notoriety might force her into seclusion, onto welfare.... Unless, of course, the police decided to charge her with murder and the jury convicted her on circumstantial evidence.

She hung her head.

Every which way: doom.

Oh, how Dad would have enjoyed witnessing this defeat. If there was such a thing as an afterlife, no doubt he'd be looking down on her right now and laughing his head off. Tears pricked at her eyes.

She angrily swiped them away.

Self-pity? Ugh, how disgusting, how narcissistic. How dare she cry for herself? Noel was *dead* because of her. She deserved punishment. A ruined career wasn't enough. She ought to be imprisoned. And humiliated for life, too.

Erin jumped to her feet and wrenched at the tent, which stubbornly refused to fold up. "Oh, damn this goddamned thing," she said, her voice cracking.

"What's the matter now?" Megan said. "Have you hurt yourself again?"

Jamie screamed. They spun around. He was sprinting toward camp. Behind him, rising up from the escarpment, reared the huge, flattened head of the *Varanus priscus*. Mesmerised, Erin forgot about the tent. She forgot about everything. All of her petty concerns about work, life and death were meaningless compared to the privilege of seeing this fearsome, wondrous, astonishing creature one more time. It was the same lizard as before—it not only had bullet wounds, but the familiar colourations. In fact, Erin would never in her life forget these colourations.

The *Varanus priscus* hesitated, looked about.

And what do you know, that forked tongue was flicking, whip-like, in and out through a large and perfectly aligned gap in both the top and bottom central teeth. She hadn't noticed this feature before. So this was how the *Varanus priscus* adapted to its dagger-like teeth—by creating a space exclusively for the passage of its tongue. How beautiful and economical.... In contrast, the

Komodo dragon keeps its teeth recessed within gingival tissue to prevent injuring the tongue. That's why the saliva of the Komodo is frequently blood-tinged—from cutting its own gums—while the saliva of *Varanus priscus* is not. Erin would reference this differentiation in one of her many treatises. She had the title for this one already, composed in a flash: *Comparative morphology of the oral cavity of the Komodo dragon* Varanus komodoensis *and* V. priscus*: in particular, the squamate tongue of the* V. priscus *and its movement through upper and lower dental diastema.* No doubt, the Journal of Herpetology would publish that one in record time, probably within two months, so fast that her head would spin. The treatise would make the front cover. She could picture her by-line in bold caps.

"Get in the car!" Jamie yelled, running past her.

The lizard padded one hulking front leg onto the cliff top, and then the other. Had the earth trembled at each footfall? Or had Erin imagined it? The claws were varying shades of black, like banded onyx, and curved like scimitars. The mouth opened a few inches. Drool hung in ropes from the enamel on each tooth. The sibilant growl rumbling from that massive throat was so deep that Erin felt it rather than heard it; a slow, penetrating vibration that shivered through her ribcage, heart and lungs, as if she were standing before giant speakers. Her eyes closed for a moment.

Now, the lizard would climb.

Finally, she would see its whole body for the first time.

15

Instead of climbing any further, the *Varanus priscus* dropped its head, as if resting. The posture brought to mind a tired swimmer holding onto the side of a pool. Perhaps it had eaten a few dead pigs on its ascent, its heavy belly scraping the rocks, its energy diverted away from locomotion and toward digestion.

With effort, the animal lunged forward.

Erin felt an indescribable thrill.

It got one of its back feet onto the cliff top. Oh, the size of the lizard was beyond belief, its body the width of a sedan. And the faint, iridescent green colouration that she'd seen on its throat fanned in a stripe along the body's lateral plane. Most likely, the colouration extended to the tail tip. And was that a yellowish tinge to the scales on the chest? Her fingers tingled. What might it feel like to touch such an incredible animal? On the dorsal side, every bit as hard and bony as it looked, the hide like that of a crocodile. But the ventral side, with that sweep of luminous golden scales like thousands of tiny glistening gemstones, would be surprisingly soft and warm. Somehow, she knew this to be true. And if she slid her palms between the forelegs, she would feel the solid beats of the animal's heart.

The *Varanus priscus* lifted its head. Erin broke from her reverie.

Its elongated tongue lapped out and took a sample of air, tasting everything around it: tasting her. She inhaled sharply. What might she taste like to such a beast? The two tips of the forked tongue retracted into its mouth. Her scent molecules were now contacting the Jacobson's organs within the skull case, being analysed. In a Komodo dragon, the greater saturation of scent molecules on one fork-tip over the other helps to pinpoint the location of prey. Would it work the same way for this beast? The *Varanus priscus* turned its boa-like head.

Oh God, it was looking straight at her.

They locked eyes. A shudder moved through her. She was staring into Death itself, into the eternal abyss. The beast froze, statue-like, and in doing so, turned Erin to stone. She understood that the sole purpose of her life had been to bring her to this very moment. The world fell away.

I see you and you see me....

"What the fuck is wrong with you?"

Startled, Erin recoiled in fright as Jamie pounced. He gripped her about the waist, put his other arm behind her knees and whisked her off her feet. She jolted in his grasp as he ran to the car. The back door was open, Megan behind the wheel, engine running. Erin strained to see the lizard, but Jamie's shoulder was too wide. Hefting her like a sack of flour, he threw her into the back seat. She landed awkwardly on top of her belongings. He slammed the door. When he jumped into the front passenger seat, the engine roared; Megan must have put her foot to the boards. The tyres plumed a cloud of red dust, yet the car bogged, digging into dirt, travelling nowhere.

"Ease up!" Jamie shouted. "Brake, turn the wheel hard."

"Don't tell me how to drive!"

"Turn the fucken wheel and go easy on the juice."

Erin scrambled to look out the window. Oh, God yes, the lizard had crested the cliff top. And its tail, how glorious: some five metres long, or about the average length of a full-grown Australian saltwater crocodile. Extraordinary.

"Wait," she yelled, grabbing her camcorder. "I need footage."

Jamie shouted, "Easy does it. Easy now...."

The car jerked out of its ruts. For a moment, Erin lost her balance. Megan turned and drove toward the escarpment, skimming the tree line. Perfect. Erin slung the camcorder's strap over her head, and tried her best to keep the *Varanus priscus* in frame and in focus. Such a beautiful animal.... As she'd hypothesised, the green scale colouration indeed extended all the way to the tail tip. Exquisite. The colouration must help the beast to blend with its surroundings. Another treatise, perhaps for Copeia: *Significance of ventrolateral colouration in* V. priscus *in regards to camouflage in wet and dry eucalypt habitats....*

For a reason that Erin couldn't fathom, Megan was still driving toward the cliff and, therefore, closer toward the *Varanus priscus*, which was situated on the opposite side. Would the lizard charge? Yes.

Yes, it would.

In fact, it seemed to be preparing to do just that. The *Varanus priscus* lifted itself high on all four splayed legs, extended its neck and lashed its tail; a classic threat display typical of the Komodo dragon. Even the gular inflation....

"Hang on tight," Megan said. "We're almost at the track."

"For fuck's sake, hurry up," Jamie said.

But no, this wasn't the gular inflation of a threat display. Instead of blown tight like a balloon, the throat fluttered in and out as if the animal were breathless. This was hyoid panting, a sign of extreme overheating. The *Varanus priscus* couldn't possibly charge. It would have to find immediate shade or risk expiring from hyperthermia.

"It's okay," Erin said. "Slow down. We're not in any danger."

Megan didn't hear or chose to ignore the advice. The four-wheel drive hammered ever closer to the cliff. Erin kept filming. The *Varanus priscus* swung its head to watch the car's progress. If only there was an everyday object nearby to offer a scale comparison. No matter, video analysis would show the size of the lizard.

The car had still not deviated. Erin glanced out the front window.

Blue sky.

Jesus Christ, were they going to plunge over the edge?

A violent left-hand turn flung Erin across the back seat. She hit her head against the window pillar. Momentarily, she saw stars. Dazed, she sat up and put a hand to her scalp. Her palm came away spotted in blood. She looked up. The car was trundling into the bush, dodging around the meagre scattering of trees that grew alongside the edge of the escarpment.

"You all right back there?" Megan said.

Erin twisted in her seat to look through the back window. Equipment blocked most of the view. Already, the clearing was becoming obscured by eucalypts and scrub. Erin lifted the camera, zoomed, and took her last precious seconds of footage: the *Varanus priscus* tail. Were those alternating bands of yellow and green scales? Amazing. She would have to double-check the footage. Too bad it would be shaky from the car bouncing across uneven ground. If only she could see the tail once more. *A discussion of tail-tip ornamental patterning in* V. priscus...

"Hey," Megan said, louder this time. "Are you okay back there, or what?"

"Slow down," Erin said. "It's not following us."

Jamie clamped his hand on his wife's knee. "Keep it going, babe. If we can fit through these trees, so can the dinosaur."

Goddamn, why couldn't they remember that the *Varanus priscus* wasn't a dinosaur? How many times had Erin told them already?

"No, we're safe now. It's suffering from heat exhaustion. Look out!"

A kangaroo leapt wildly out of their path. Over-correcting, Megan sideswiped a tree, ripping off a mirror.

Jamie said, "Forget it. Keep going, pedal to the metal."

Megan drove, helter-skelter, parallel to the escarpment. The vehicle caromed over a rocky patch. Momentarily airborne, Erin clutched at the armrest. Her rucksack, backpack and—oh shit, the Remington, was the safety on?—jolted around on the back seat. The rifle clattered into the foot well. Fumbling, Erin tried to find the seatbelt clasp. Something thumped against her neck: one of the camping chairs. She shoved at it, hard, sending it backward into the pile of shifting, unsecured equipment.

"Slow down," she yelled. "The Devil dragon is hyperthermic."

The car dodged and wove around trees, fallen logs, boulders. Erin glanced out the side window. The lip of the escarpment was so close that she had to press her nose against the glass to see it. Her stomach dropped.

"You'll go over the side," she yelled. "For God's sake, slow down."

The trees closed in suddenly, a pinch-point. Erin gasped. They would crash. But no, Megan somehow managed to steer a clear path. The remaining side mirror snapped off. The car jounced and kicked.

In the split-second before impact, the flash of reddish-brown through the trees appeared to be a rock. It turned out to be a deer—a big one. In fact, the biggest that Erin had seen. The chugging roar of the diesel engine must have startled it. A *Cervus elaphus*, a mature stag. Erin recognised it as such while it leapt directly into their path. The broad, spiky tines of its brown antlers resembled the naked branches of an oak in winter.

Time stopped.

In her mind's eye, Erin looked again through crosshairs at the juvenile red deer—the brocket—as it placed its spindly legs into the creek. She had fastened the crosshairs of the Remington at the base of its throat and pulled the trigger. She had killed that deer. Jamie had then pressed the knife into her hand and shown her how to dress it. The soft, moist ripping sound of the skin coming away from the flesh returned, producing goose bumps.

And now, in turn, this stag would kill her.

It would kill them all.

The stag loomed large, gaping at them…wet eyes and mouth open wide in terror. Megan seemed to stand up in her seat as she jammed on the brake.

…Too late….

The bull bar hit the deer's flank.

It was as if they had hit a concrete barrier. With a stupendous bang, the cabin filled with white dust as the airbags deployed. Erin slammed into the front seat. Pain flared as blood spurted from her nose. Camping chairs rained down around her. In the next moment, the deer rolled over the bonnet toward the windscreen.

It would smash into the cabin and crush the Robinsons to death.

The deer hit the windscreen. A loud crack sounded. The window transformed into a sheet of a million white stars that bowed into the cabin but did not break. Erin became aware of a swishing noise. The tyres had locked, must be skidding over leaf litter. As the car slid, Erin found that she had her cheek mashed against the side window. She blinked hard. The pain in her nose had made her eyes water. Shit, were they anywhere near the cliff edge?

Yes.

The car was slewing sideways right at it.

A slab of granite the size of a coffee table loomed, but she didn't have time to shout a warning. Not that a warning would make a difference. Megan was pumping the brakes and wrestling the steering wheel to no avail. They were all now passengers in this runaway vehicle.

The car hit the rock, tipped forward and lost the back end.

Erin became weightless. The deer flipped away from the bonnet. Erin crashed into the car's ceiling, along with her rucksack, backpack and Remington. None of this made sense until she realised that the car was rolling. Tumbling loose inside the cabin, smacking her head, arms and legs, she caught a last glimpse out of a window. The blue sky was gone. Now, in a crazy flash, lay the distant hills, the sea of trees, and, oh God, the stony face of the escarpment.

They had plunged over the cliff.

Erin squeezed shut her eyes.

Each impact as the car hit granite felt bone-shattering. Over and over, Erin flailed, thumping her body, limbs, and head. Loose items smacked against her. I'm going to die, she thought in surprise, in wonder. Death had always seemed a faraway problem, something tucked away for old age, and yet, here it was, clutching at her throat and shaking her brains loose. Out of nowhere, Russ Walker-Smith came to mind. For her last birthday, he had given her a fossilised Eocene crocodile egg. She had been overwhelmed, overjoyed. He had blushed at her obvious pleasure. A moment had passed between them, but she had turned away, ostensibly to take a closer look at the fossil. Why had she avoided the kiss? Dear old Russ. So she loved him after all. She locked on the little dimple in his chin, and surrendered to her fate.

The car stopped suddenly.

The deceleration almost snapped her neck.

A creaking noise made her open her eyes. The car had landed upright. She was lying in the back seat, buried under an avalanche of items including freezer blocks, melted ice chips and beer stubbies. The lid must have come off the esky. Well, at least her spectacles weren't damaged. With effort, she looked up at the window. The creaking noise was the car rubbing against a stand of young eucalypt trees. As the car finally settled, the creaking stopped. Erin dropped her head to the seat. She heard the Robinsons unclip their seatbelts. Swallowing, she tasted blood.

"We're on a wide ledge," Megan said. "No chance of falling any farther. Get the rifles. The bastard must be right on top of us."

With all her strength, Erin shouted, "Will you shut up and listen to me?"

The Robinsons flinched.

"The Devil dragon is incapacitated," she continued. "It showed all the classic reptilian signs of overheating. In that state, it has as much chance of running after us as flying to the moon."

The Robinsons fell silent.

"Well, fuck," Jamie said at last. "That information would have come in handy."

"I told you over and over that it was hyperthermic and couldn't follow us."

"You did?" Megan said. "Shit, I didn't hear."

"Look, to be fair," Jamie added, "you've told us a lot of things about this dinosaur that didn't turn out to be true."

"Oh, for the last time, it's a goddamned reptile."

Erin tried to remember the magical feeling that the *Varanus priscus* had aroused, but it had faded like a dream upon waking. As a scientist, she had always doubted the idea of "fascination", the ability of snakes to hypnotise their mammalian prey, but how else could she explain her behaviour? She had stood before the beast like a willing sacrifice. Christ almighty, she had even fantasised about touching it.

Jamie poked his head through the broken front-passenger window and gazed in all directions at the cliff face. "I think she's right. There's no sign of him."

"The car's still running," Megan said. "If we can winch it out of here, we can probably keep driving."

Jamie said, "Or we might be leaking diesel. Until we check that everything's hunky-dory, let's stay on the safe side."

"Agreed." She switched off the ignition. "That also means no smoking while we're down here. Okay. Now let's all of us calm down and take stock. First things first: is anybody hurt? Jamie?"

"Nah, I'm good. You?"

"No worries. What about you, Erin?"

"I don't know," Erin said. "My nose is bleeding."

"That's what happens when you don't wear a seatbelt."

"I was too busy filming." The camcorder was still around her neck. She lifted it and took a few seconds of test footage. It still worked. Thank God for small mercies. She said, "Why didn't you grab your guns and shoot the damn thing?"

"Because shooting didn't work last time," Jamie said. "Remember?"

"Jesus, there isn't an animal in this world that can't be shot to death," Erin said, and went to push away the clutter scattered across her prone body. A sudden and sharp agony made her wince. Her left ring and middle fingers were bent at unnatural angles. "Uh-oh," she said, "I think I've fractured my hand."

"Just be grateful you didn't break it," Jamie said.

Erin sat up, lifting herself on her good arm. "Fractured means broken."

"Does it? I figured it meant, you know, hairline cracks." He looked around at her and raised his eyebrows. "Well, then I reckon you've fractured your nose."

She touched at it, recoiled at the shooting pain.

Megan leaned over to the glove-box and took out a pack of tissues. Offering a bunch, she ordered, "Blow. Don't freak, okay? Expect a mess."

Erin did as she was told. A large amount of blood and mucus came out. It frightened her. Perhaps her nose was nothing but a flattened nub smeared across her face. She said, "How bad is it?"

"Not too bad," Megan said. "The bone isn't showing. We can fix it."

"We?" Erin said. "You mean us? Here and now?"

"No time like the present. Jamie always fixes noses. Horses buck their heads and sometimes your face gets in the way. Otherwise they kick you, or throw you off. Jamie's reset my nose more times than I can count. Shit, he evens fixes his own. And our youngest, Ryan, has had his nose fixed at least three times."

"And Caleb once," Jamie added. "Then again, he hasn't got the feel for horses like the rest of us. He reckons he wants to be a dentist. Can you believe it? That's no way to make a living. Staring into people's filthy gobs all day? Screw that. I'd rather clean out sewers in my Speedos."

Erin started to laugh. This whole situation was ridiculous, surreal. When she found that she couldn't stop laughing, she became afraid. Was she hysterical?

"Take off your glasses," Jamie ordered. "Lean forward between the seats."

"And give me your hand," Megan added. "The one that isn't broken."

She obeyed. Both the Robinsons had light abrasions across their cheeks, most likely from coming in contact with the deployed airbags. Erin stopped giggling as Jamie lightly rested his fingers along both sides of her nose.

"Will it hurt?" she said.

Megan smiled encouragingly. "Squeeze my hand."

"On the count of three," Jamie said. "Are you ready? One!"

And with force, his fingers pressed into her nose and dragged straight down. She felt a sharp, grating pain. Then she could breathe through her nostrils again.

"How's that?" Jamie said, wiping his fingers on more tissues.

Gently, she touched the tip of her nose. It didn't seem to hurt as much. "You went on 'one'," she said, putting her glasses back on. "What happened to the count of three?"

He winked. "Better if you don't know when it's coming."

"I'll splint your hand," Megan said, "as soon as we find the first aid kit."

Forcing open the front passenger door with his shoulder, Jamie said, "Okay, let's try to figure a way out of this shit-fight."

16

They climbed out of the car.

The granite ledge was smooth, wide and almost level, reminding Erin of the concrete slab in a small garage. The drop, however, was three metres to a jumbled field of jagged, sofa-sized rocks that stretched on and on. If the car hadn't stopped when it did.... Just the thought gave Erin vertigo.

The belongings from the roof-rack lay scattered down the craggy gradient: tents, pots, trestle table, food tins, split garbage bags, an unfurled roll of toilet paper. And, oh God, a long way down the slope lay what remained of the deer. Erin gagged. Crushed and mutilated, the stag had burst open, fanning its guts over a wide radius. A handful of glossy black crows had already gathered.

Carrion-eaters.

Erin's thoughts turned to the *Varanus priscus*, to Noel, his two thumbs up....

"Keep away from the brink," Megan said, opening the boot door and fossicking through the clutter in the back of the car. "Go sit in the front passenger seat. I'll be with you in a minute."

Erin did as she was told. Silently, she observed the Robinsons.

Using his hands to shield his eyes from the glare, Jamie surveyed the cliff face above them. Erin looked up, too. The car had fallen 12 metres or so.

"Can we get her back up top?" Megan said.

He scratched at the stubble on his chin.

"What do you reckon?" she continued. "Electric winch?"

"Yeah, maybe. We might have to bust out the hand winch too, crab a little sideways. Dunno. We'll have to see how we go."

"We'll be fine. The incline's not too steep."

"But it's so uneven." He pointed at various spots. "Look at that shit. How are we gonna get the car up and over those outcrops?"

"Easy does it, that's how," Megan said.

He gave a slow smile, chuckled, put an arm about her shoulders and kissed her cheek. "My little Pollyanna, always looking on the bright side."

She tapped him on his behind and turned serious. "Now sort out the mess of gear in the back of the car. I'll help as soon as I fix the doctor's hand. Keep a look out for the Devil dragon. I've got rifles lined up at the tailgate." Megan came around and squatted in front of Erin with the first aid kit. "Give me a look."

Despite the heat, Erin couldn't stop shivering. She held out her left hand. Gently, Megan turned it over this way and that, scrutinising the injured middle and ring fingers. Both of the nail beds had turned purple.

"We don't have to worry about the Devil dragon anymore," Erin said. "Hunger is its primary motivation. It has no reason to come after us. Its brain is too primal for impulses like revenge."

"Well, that's a fucken relief," Jamie said.

"Are my fingers going to be okay?"

"They're dislocated as well as broken," Megan said. "I'll use a splint, and tape your fingers around it. They might swell up some more. Tell me straight away if the tape starts getting tight. We don't want to cut off the circulation. Okay?"

"Yes, okay. Thank you."

Megan set to work.

Erin watched numbly, and contemplated the possibility of concussion. She had hit her head during the crash. Despite this, she didn't have a headache. Was headache a symptom of concussion? She couldn't remember. She tried to focus on the exact and decisive manner in which Megan was splinting her fingers. Much like noses, perhaps fingers tend to get broken frequently at horse stud farms. Erin had never broken a bone in her life. Now she'd broken a few all at once. For some reason, however, the splinting didn't hurt, even though Megan was pulling and straightening the bent fingers to fit against what appeared to be a popsicle stick. Was anaesthesia one of the symptoms of concussion? Erin couldn't remember.

"How come the car's roof didn't cave in?" she said.

Megan glanced up. "Roll cage."

"Uh-huh. What if we can't get the car out?"

Megan gave a lopsided grin. "Let's cross that bridge when we come to it. There you go, all done." She tossed the first aid kit into the back seat and went to Jamie, who was still looking up at the formidable rock face.

Dazed, Erin scrutinised her splinted fingers. They were beginning to throb. Surely, that was a good sign. It meant her nerves remained intact. She ran her good hand beneath her nose. Damn, it came away bloody. She had blood on her shirt too.

"What about the car?" Megan was saying. "Driveable?"

Jamie walked to the bonnet and gazed along the car body, front to back, with one eye screwed shut. Dispiritedly, he shook his head. "The line's out of whack."

"That might be cosmetic," Megan said. "A few bashed-in panels.

"Nah, the whole thing is twisted. The chassis is fucked."

"But can we still drive it?"

"Jeez Louise, how should I know? I'm not a mechanic." He blew out a long breath. "Let's dial it down a notch, and have a drink."

"Good idea."

He retrieved three beer cans and opened each of them at arm's length, his face turned away as they foamed and spat. He handed them out one at a time.

After a few sips, Erin felt revived. Whether it was the water component or the alcohol, she couldn't tell. She said, "I'm curious. How will you get the car out?"

"With a winch," Jamie said.

"Yes, but how?"

"There's an electric winch mounted under the bull bar. I'll roll out the cable, climb up top and hook it around a tree. Then I'll hop back in the car, reel in the cable, give it a bit of throttle every time the slack gets taken up, and Bob's your uncle."

With a gulp of beer, Erin considered the cliff. Some of its rocky ledges hung out into space. A couple of ledges extended far enough to shelter a small crowd from rain, like a pair of granite awnings. Clearly, she wasn't a car expert, but unless the Robinson's four-wheel drive had the capacity to defy gravity, it wasn't going anywhere, with or without an electric winch.

Jamie must have read her expression. "Relax, will you?" he said. "It might take a bit of stuffing about, but we'll get her up top again."

Erin nodded.

"The engine still runs," Megan said. "If we're not leaking anything, we're probably good to go."

"I'll give her a look-see." Jamie crossed to the front of the car and crouched down. Almost immediately, he cried, "Aw, fuck no."

"What?" Megan leapt up from her perch on a rock. "What is it?"

Even through the distortion of the shattered windscreen, Erin could see his distress. He clamped one hand over his eyes as if he couldn't bear the sight, and pointed low to the driver's side. "Check it out."

Megan walked around to the front of the car. Her face turned white. Heart hammering, Erin got up from the passenger seat and joined them both, wondering if she had enough mechanical know-how to discern the problem without having to ask.

Oh, shit.

No questions were necessary.

The front driver's side wheel lay folded beneath the car, neatly turned under like a tuck in a blanket. No one spoke.

Finally, Erin said, "I suppose that's unfixable."

Dear God. Tomorrow was Monday. She was supposed to give a lecture at 9 a.m., a refresher on genetic drift, gene flow, and speciation. Her students were counting on her. Their final exams were scheduled for the following week.... But wait, no, Erin's future wasn't set anymore. The foundation of her life had shifted irreversibly. Nothing would ever be the same again.

Jamie trudged away to sit on a rock and put his face in his hands.

Megan put her fists on her hips and glared at the broken wheel for a few moments. "Well," she said, "we might as well stop for lunch."

Jamie said, "Hey Erin, you sure the Devil dragon won't come sniffing around?"

"Positive. My guess is that it will stay in the vicinity of the campsite. It's got three deer carcasses and umpteen dead pigs to choose from. That smorgasbord will keep it occupied for weeks."

***

The late afternoon sun bore down. The heat reflected off the surrounding granite. It was like sitting in a frying pan. The trio sweated freely. Erin had wished to change into shorts, but the Robinsons insisted that only long pants offered protection against abrasions and bites. And what the hell would Erin know?

Most of their food supply lay strewn below them. The climb down was too steep and treacherous, so for lunch, they made do with whatever items they found in the back of the car: beef jerky, potato chips, tins of baked beans.

Erin ate without enthusiasm. Her whole body ached. The crows kept drawing her gaze. The six or seven birds worried and pecked relentlessly at the stag's corpse, reeling out long, wet cords of flesh. Jamie tossed another empty beer can over his shoulder. The can bounced and echoed its way down the cliff. The crows ignored the distraction. Two of them were busy working their beaks into the stag's abdominal cavity, tugging at something without luck. The others pecked at eyeballs and exposed guts. Nauseated, Erin put down the tin of baked beans and looked away.

"Are you all right?" Megan said. "You're white as a sheet."

Erin shook her head. "I'm about as far from all right as I could possibly get. What are we going to do now? Clearly, we can't stay here."

"Why not?" Jamie said. "It's the best plan. Look, if your car breaks down in the bush, always stay with it. You get rescued that way. If you try to walk back to civilisation, you die from exposure. That's survival one-oh-one."

"Yes, of course. I didn't think of that."

"Now, wait a second," Megan said. "That's only true if you get stranded in the outback. But we're not in the middle of Woop Woop. Town is just fifteen ks away."

"Babe, you're still talking a five or six hour walk. And the doctor's injured. Nah, if we sit tight, Caleb and Ryan will call the cops, and the cops will charter a rescue chopper. No worries. The car sticks out like dog's balls against these rocks. A chopper will find us by first light, I bet."

"Yeah, and the cops will find our rifles, too."

Jamie looked stumped. "Oh, shit yeah."

"Here's my plan: first, return to the campsite and pick up those shell casings."

Erin sputtered out a shocked laugh. "You want to backtrack?"

"People are going to investigate Noel's death. And if those investigators find shell casings, they'll know we were hunting. So yeah, I want to backtrack."

"Have you forgotten the Devil dragon? It will likely be nearby on account of all those animal carcasses you threw off the escarpment."

"Fine. We'll have loaded firearms and plenty of ammo."

Erin gave a bitter laugh. "Oh, such bravado. You crashed the car in your panic to escape. Now you imagine yourself strutting up to the beast on foot?"

Megan tightened her jaw, but went on as if she hadn't heard. "Once we clean up the campsite, we come back here, load the gear and firearms, and hike to town. We cut through the rear of Noel's property to get to our place. That way, no one will spot us. We stash the rifles and call the cops."

"Christ almighty, why are you still worried about getting caught for hunting?" Erin rubbed at her temples. "There are far more important issues at stake here, such as your lives. Returning to the campsite would be insane."

"Why? You told us the Devil dragon was overheated, that it would be asleep in the shade by now."

"Uh, now hold on," Jamie said, "it could be running around like a puppy. Don't forget, a lot of what she's told us about the dinosaur has been complete horseshit."

Erin didn't know whether to be angry or grateful. At least he appeared to be taking her side. She said, "This six-hour walk you want us to do? When we have minimal food and water, and feral animals at every turn? Come on, be reasonable. Jamie's right. We should stay with the car and wait to be rescued."

"That'd suit you, but not us," Megan said. "It's not your livelihood at stake."

"Yes, it is. In fact, my job is already as good as gone. Once the Dean finds out about this expedition, he'll terminate my contract. And without his reference, I doubt I'll teach in any university ever again."

"You don't know that for sure. If we leave the firearms out of our story, maybe this Dean of yours won't be so pissed off."

"Well, yeah, that's true," Jamie said, and began to nod, as if seriously considering Megan's point of view.

Stunned, Erin looked from one Robinson to the other. "What's the punishment for illegal hunting? A fine? I'll pay it for you. How's that? It can't be more than a few thousand dollars. We've discovered the paleontological find of the century, remember? That gives us immunity."

"It might if we had concrete proof," Megan said.

"But we have got proof. What about my footage?"

"Thanks to Photoshop, your footage means shit." Megan's lips formed a tight line. "We can't afford to lose our D-licences."

"Are you mad? We're exhausted, low on supplies."

"If we lose our licences, we lose our income."

Unbelievable: what stubbornness, such sheer bloody-mindedness. How could Erin make this woman see goddamned sense? At last, she said, "Noel is dead."

"Yeah, but we still need to pig-hunt up north."

"Noel is dead."

"We can't pay our bills without pig-hunting."

"Listen to me." Erin leaned forward. "Noel is dead."

Megan recoiled slightly. Her eyes filmed over with unshed tears. Jamie put a reassuring arm around her as she pressed a set of knuckles to her mouth, probably to hide a trembling chin. She composed herself within seconds.

Oh, she's tough, Erin thought.

The Robinsons had been neighbours with Noel Baines for years. They had probably eaten dinner at each other's houses countless times; loaned equipment; helped each other with fence repairs, recalcitrant animals, family tragedies. When Noel's wife had died, Jamie and Megan would have been there for him, offering home-cooked meals. Erin touched her shirt pocket, at the whittled figurines of the crocodile and *Varanus priscus*. She'd known Noel for only a couple of days and she felt stricken. How deeply must his death grieve the Robinsons?

"I loved that old bastard," Megan said. "He was one of my best mates. If I could bring him back, I would. But I'm not going to lose our home and our farm because you're scared of a little hike through the bush. Got it?"

Erin sat back, flummoxed.

Impasse.

Now what?

Jamie said, "Here's another idea. How about we leave the doctor in the car with food and water, and the two of us hike back? We can tell the chopper pilot exactly where to find her."

"That's crazy. We can't leave her alone. It'd be like abandoning a baby."

Erin flushed, humiliated.

Jamie threw up his hands. "Then what do we do?"

"Exactly like I told you. Get the empty shells and all three of us walk home."

No, Erin thought, I've been through enough and I can't go through any more. Her body felt battered, shaky, every inch of skin bruised. She hadn't slept properly since coming to this town three days ago. And a six-hour hike? She wouldn't be able to walk for six goddamned minutes. There had to be another solution.

"What about this?" she asked. "We compromise. You go back and collect the shell casings. I'll wait here. When you return, we wrap your guns and bullets in something waterproof like a tent, and bury them with a marker you'll recognise at a later date. Then we stay by the car and wait for rescue. We tell the police everything, but leave out any references to hunting."

Megan laughed. "That's thousands of bucks' worth of equipment you're talking about. And you think I'm going to bury our cache in the dirt?" She stood up. "Come on, Jamie. Let's go get the shell casings."

So that was it.

Erin had lost the argument.

Dear God, did she have the strength? Could she push herself any further?

Silently, she watched the Robinsons fill their backpacks, load their rifles, check that both walkie-talkies still operated. She felt like crying, partly from exhaustion, partly from frustration.

"Stay inside the car," Jamie said. "We'll be back in about an hour."

Miserably, she nodded. As if fresh from a good night's rest, the Robinsons briskly and carefully scaled the granite cliff face. It took them only a few minutes to reach the top. Jamie leaned over and gave a jaunty wave. Erin waved back, using her unbroken hand. Then she crawled into the back seat and closed the door.

She could hear just two sounds: her own breathing, and the cawing of the crows as they fussed over the dead stag. What if the Robinsons didn't come back? The idea of being alone out here scared her half to death. Oh, but she was so sick of being scared. With determination, she pushed every thought from her mind.

And despite the heat, she immediately fell into a dreamless sleep.

17

Somebody was knocking at her bedroom window. But how? Her flat was on the third floor. Yet there it was again: rat-a-tat-tat. Groggily, Erin opened her eyes. A grinning face stared at her through a broken car window...Jamie Robinson.

Oh, God.

Reality washed over her in a sickening wave. She sat up. As if triggered by the change of position, a throbbing pain started in her nose.

Jamie opened the car door. "It took longer than we thought. You okay?"

"Fine. Did you have any trouble?"

"Nah, sweet. Check it out." He held a large plastic bag filled with brass-coloured tubes of various sizes: the oh-so-goddamned precious shell casings. Nevertheless, the sheer number of casings was impressive. During Noel's attack, how many times had the Robinsons shot at the *Varanus priscus*? More importantly, how many bullets had actually hit the animal? Dozens, surely; perhaps scores....

Erin got out of the car. "Did you see any sign of the Devil dragon?"

"Not a trace," Megan said, unloading her backpack and rifles.

"Could it be dead?"

"How should we know?" Megan said with a tight smile. "You're the expert."

So our professional relationship has come full circle, Erin thought; Megan once again thinks I'm an idiot. Erin sighed. Rolling her shoulders, she tried to loosen her neck muscles. Her body felt stiff and strained from head to toe.

"What about the casings that went over the cliff?" she said. "The ones you dropped in the forest during the chase? You couldn't have collected them all."

Megan sniffed. "True. But city homicide detectives won't go bush. Okay, let's head out tomorrow, early, about four."

"What about the dinosaur?" Jamie said. "It hunts in the dark."

"Big deal. The doctor here reckons it's not hunting us in particular. So what are the odds of meeting up with it again? Zip. It's boars and dogs we've got to worry about, and by four in the morning, they'll have given up the hunt and gone to bed for the day."

"Pigs and dogs are nocturnal?" Erin said in surprise.

"The wild ones can be."

"I still reckon we should hike when it's hot," Jamie said, "just to be sure the dinosaur is asleep. You know, to be on the safe side."

"We can't risk dehydration," Megan said. "There's hardly any water left."

Looking dubious, Jamie scratched at the stubble on his chin. "Well...okay."

"Then it's decided," Megan said. "Now let's pack."

Doing so didn't take long.

There wasn't much left, considering most of their equipment lay scattered down the cliff face. Despite this, it seemed too much for them to carry: three giant rucksacks and three backpacks loaded to seam-bursting capacity, three ammunition bags, and a selection of rifles. Erin's share must be at least 12kgs, about one-quarter of her bodyweight. I will fail again, she thought. Fully-laden, she would attempt a single step and crumple to the ground.

"There's naff-all for tea," Megan said. "A big bag of peanuts and a few chocolate bars."

The setting sun began to leach the colours from the landscape. Everywhere looked rugged and hostile. The breeze picked up. Erin touched the granite wall. It felt lukewarm. Soon, the rocks would be cold. She thought of the *Varanus priscus*. Maybe the lizard was digging its nightly burrow, using its massive front feet as shovels, flicking out dirt to either side. Or maybe it had succumbed to its multiple bullet wounds. The thought gave her an uncomfortable mixture of relief and distress. The next gust of evening wind carried a chill. She put her jacket back on.

Dinner took all of ten minutes to eat.

"Okay, breakfast at four a.m.," Jamie said, setting the alarm on his watch.

***

They slept in the car.

Erin had the back seat to herself. Not that it made any difference. She couldn't sleep, anyway. The Robinsons had reclined their front seats and were snoring soon after: Jamie from a vibrating palate, loud as a wood chipper; and Megan from a deviated septum, judging by the snuffling and whistling noises.

Erin hunkered beneath the sleeping bag and stared up at a window. The stars shone bright and brittle, tinged orange like the points of a thousand soldering irons. She turned over. The back seat was moulded to accommodate three distinct backsides. The lumps and dips were uncomfortable to lie across. She pulled up her legs. The loud snoring went on and on, sometimes in concert, sometimes at odds. How didn't the Robinsons wake each other up?

It felt colder within the cabin as time passed. Erin tried tucking the sleeping bag tighter around her neck, but kept shivering. Her nose hurt, her fingers hurt.

Oh, what she would give to be at home right now.

Life had been dull, yes, but so much better than this. The reverse-cycle air conditioner set to 16 degrees, the soft mattress, satin sheets, goose-down pillow....

She shifted about. On Thursday, the day she had arrived in town, she had promised to call Russ on Sunday night. It was now almost 1 a.m. Monday morning. How might he have reacted to her failure to call? No doubt with worry. Then again, Russ was an advocate of Occam's razor. Like others who believed that the simplest explanation is usually the correct one, he'd assume something innocuous: she had forgotten her promise or else lost her phone. But how would he respond when she did not turn up for work today? Would he wait to hear from her? Report her disappearance to the police?

Erin turned over again. The moulded seats dug into her hips and ribs. The duet of snoring droned on. Eventually, she sank into a fitful doze. She dreamed of Noel's two thumbs up, again and again. Each time, she jerked awake, and would stare out the window at the cold and brilliant stars.

***

"Rise and shine."

Erin opened her eyes. Jamie was smiling at her, leaning over the seat and giving her arm a shake. It was still dark. Groping for her glasses, she mumbled, "What time is it?"

"Time to go."

The Robinsons hopped out of the car. With effort, Erin followed suit. She hung the digital camcorder around her neck. The cold air nipped at her ears and stung her nose. At least the breeze had died down. The sliver of moon shone a weak light on the rock face, turning the granite to silver.

They took turns to pee, nominating the area at the bonnet-end of the car as the urinal. It offered a modicum of privacy as the others waited by the boot, their backs discreetly turned. The Robinsons must be doing this for Erin's benefit, and she appreciated the gesture.

Megan handed out the potato chips. They ate quickly. The water bottle passed around. Erin's mouth felt woolly.

The Robinsons got to work. Megan lashed each small backpack to the top of a rucksack. Jamie took a large hank of rope from the car boot and knotted the rucksacks and ammunition bags into a big bundle. Tying the other end of the rope around his body, Jamie gave the women a cheerful salute and began to scale the cliff face, nimble as a goat. Was he going to drag that deadweight behind him? No, the rope was long, and spooled out plenty of slack. Meanwhile, Megan loaded the rifles into duffle bags.

"Heave ho," Jamie called from the top. "You ready?"

"Yep, no worries." Megan glanced at Erin. "Just stay here. Don't fall off."

Erin sighed.

Jamie ducked out of sight. A few seconds passed. The rope went tight. The bundle of rucksacks inched upward, as if Jamie had the other end of the rope wound around a tree trunk and was reeling it in, hand over hand. Megan followed behind, manoeuvring the rucksacks so that they wouldn't snag on rocky outcrops. Soon, she and the rucksacks disappeared over the top.

Yawning despite her nervousness, Erin huddled into her jacket. Crickets sang from all around. She gazed up at the stars. A fruit bat glided its silent way from one side of the escarpment to the other. It was a quiet, meditative sight. Erin closed her eyes. A scrabbling noise punched her heart into her throat and she spun around.

It was just Megan, climbing back down.

She tied the duffle bags full of rifles to the rope and called, "Heave ho."

The procedure repeated itself. Jamie hauled on the rope from above; Megan eased the passage of the duffle bags over the rocks.

Despite being awake for some half an hour, Erin's eyes still felt puffy. She eased into the front seat and swung the rear-view mirror to take a look.

Dear God!

She had two black eyes and a nose so swollen and bruised that she barely recognised herself. She twisted the mirror this way and that. The plaster on her chin was crusted with dried blood. Her hair hung about her dirty face in lank, greasy strings. Who was this woman? Not the same one who had driven to town in a breezy summer dress and sandals, blow-waved bob, mascara and perfume. Tears rose. If only she could go back in time. If only.... She had sat at the bar in the local pub. Noel Baines had arrived later, standing at the entrance with his hands on his hips, looking about. Erin had got up and lifted a hand, attracting his attention. From the moment they had locked eyes, he was as good as dead. If only she had turned away and waited for him to leave instead of going over and introducing herself, dragging him into this nightmare, sealing his fate—

The sound of Megan negotiating the rock face made Erin hastily wipe at her wet lashes and get out of the car.

Megan climbed down to the ledge and dusted her hands on her jeans. "Ready?"

"I think so."

"Follow my lead," Megan said. "Do exactly as I do. Watch my footholds in particular. With your broken hand, use your thumb and palm only, not any of your fingers, okay? If you get dizzy or feel like you're stuck, let me know. I'll come down and help you. Understand?"

Erin nodded.

Megan faced the rock wall and began to ascend. Swallowing a hard lump of fear, Erin did her best to copy the woman's athletic moves. It was tough going. Maybe Erin was too short, weak or unfit. Maybe she was simply too exhausted. Whatever the case, she had travelled only a few metres before she felt breathless and shaky. She leaned against the cold granite, trembling, her eyes fluttering shut.

"Push through it," Megan said from above. "Don't stop. Just keep moving. Every time you breathe out, move a hand or foot. Get into a rhythm."

Sweat popped over Erin's forehead. She thought of how Dad might be laughing at her right now, and found a shard of determination.

"That's good," Megan said. "You're doing great. We're nearly there."

Erin didn't dare look up to check. Instead, she focused on Megan's sturdy boots, the tread on each sole, the tinkling of loose pebbles and debris. Megan's feet vanished from sight. Erin froze. What had happened?

"Here, I'll help ya."

Jamie's huge paw appeared at Erin's face. She took it with her good hand. As if she weighed nothing at all, he hauled her up while her toes scrambled for purchase on the rock face. Don't let go, she thought in alarm. She could see herself freefalling, being dashed to bits on the outcrops, her guts spilling like those of the stag.

Then her feet were on solid ground. She had made it to the top of the cliff.

Jamie slapped her on the shoulder and said, "You right?"

Feebly, she nodded.

"Here," Megan said, holding out what appeared to be a necklace.

"What is it?"

"Your compass."

She put the chain over Erin's head. The pendant, about the size of a fifty-cent piece, was indeed a compass; a pretty one that featured a black background with elegant silver lettering. Staring at it, Erin turned her body. The needle swung.

"Don't worry, it works," Megan said. She offered a walkie-talkie. "Carry this, too. The range is about one and a half to three kilometres in this terrain. Hang it through a belt loop. If we get separated, press down on this switch with your thumb and give us a hoy. Don't yell. You might attract dogs or boars if you do."

Erin clipped the walkie-talkie to her belt. Jamie helped her with the rucksack. It felt impossibly heavy. Erin's knees wobbled. He fastened the buckles for her at the front, grabbed at the straps and shook the rucksack to straighten it. Erin shook too.

Jamie laughed. "Shit, hey. You're like a little doll, aren't you? Don't worry. We'll carry everything else."

"Except for this." Thrusting the Remington into Erin's hands, Megan said, "It's loaded. Don't touch the safety unless you have to."

The Robinsons put on their rucksacks and slung various rifles over their shoulders. Megan carried one ammunition bag, while Jamie took the other two. Neither appeared fatigued in the slightest. How strong must they be? Erin felt a pang of envy. She'd never met anyone like the Robinsons.

"Okay, this is the plan," Megan said. "Northwest to the fire trail. That should take about three hours. Then northeast until we come to the sealed road. Say, two hours, tops. We follow the road east. If anyone hears a car coming, we all duck into the bush, understand? I don't want us to get sprung with this gear. Then we cut through the back of Noel's place."

"Sounds fine by me."

Erin hesitated. "Northwest, northeast, then east? That sounds like we're executing a big U-turn. Why don't we just head east in the first place?"

"Because we'd hit a gorge. Trust me; you don't want to hike near that. The ground is so rocky it'd take us twice as long to get home." Megan looked at them both. "Ready?"

Jamie nodded. "You go point. I'll take the rear. Erin, you're in the middle."

"And keep your rifle aimed at the sky," Megan said, holding up a warning finger. "I don't want to cop an accidental bullet in the back."

"Yes, of course."

"Okay," Megan said. "Let's move out, single file."

***

After about the first hour, the monotony of the landscape began to play tricks on Erin's weary brain. Was she trudging on a hidden treadmill, getting nowhere? It was like one of those dreams where you run along a corridor, yet the faraway door never gets closer. Every now and then, she stumbled. That's when she realised she had been walking for the past few seconds with her eyes closed. Was it possible to fall asleep while standing up? Apparently, yes. Before long, she'd lost count of the number of micro-naps she found herself having.

Sunrise had escaped her notice too. One minute, the endless parade of gums and straggly bushes were shades of black and white; the next, she realised the world appeared in full colour. Vivid browns, reds, greens, yellows. And the chatter of hundreds of birds had risen up from all around. She recognised a few: the warbling of magpies, the screeching of cockatoos, and the melodic whistling of crimson rosellas. But those other peeps, squeaks, hoots, bell-like tones, squawks? She wanted to ask the Robinsons, but it seemed that talking was not permitted on this hike, and especially not about something as mundane as birds. At home, she had a CD of birdsong that sounded very similar, except it featured the occasional flourish on the piano and flute. She listened to it while soaking in the tub with a glass of wine....

She stumbled again.

Her eyes snapped open.

Shit.

A double-shot of a good, oily espresso was what she needed. Now the repetition of trees resembled a computer screensaver, one of the old kinds where you hurtle endlessly through streaming stars, as if in hyperspace. Oh, she was tired. So tired, she could collapse face-first into the dirt and sleep forever....

"Hold up, babe," Jamie said. "She's falling behind."

Uh-oh, Erin thought. I'm to be chastised again.

Megan, about five metres in front, started to turn around. In the next moment, something in the bush caught her attention. She startled, raised her SKK to her hip and fired. Like a train hitting a car stalled on the tracks, the *Varanus priscus* charged with incredible speed across their path and was gone, along with Megan.

Erin's heart stopped.

The path ahead lay empty.

Megan was *gone*.

But where?

Jamie gave an anguished bellow. Running off into the bush after the whipping tail of the lizard, he began shooting. Erin hurried after him. But how could she offer supporting fire? Jamie was between her and the *Varanus priscus*. If she risked a shot on the run, she might hit Jamie.

Puffing, huffing, the rucksack wrenching and yanking at her shoulders, the weight of it buckling her knees, Erin shambled after Jamie's dwindling form.

God almighty, the lizard was an incredible sight.

Even though it was about 10 metres or so ahead of Jamie— who was about the same distance from Erin—the beast still appeared massive. The muscled body undulated from side to side with every step, the tail held off the ground in the manner of a Komodo dragon at full speed. Yes, it was the same lizard. She could tell by its banded tail tip of luminous yellow and green scales. Beautiful. If only she had a spare hand to lift the camcorder that hung about her neck. And those legs, as thick as an elephant's, that swung out and over with each step; those feet moving in sweeping, lateral arcs. Lithe, the beast dodged and weaved around trees with unerring accuracy. It brought to mind the darting flight of a bird through close-knit branches. Who would have thought that *Varanus priscus* could move with such grace? The title came to her instantly: *Locomotor performance and spatial awareness in the modern-day* V. priscus.... The stutter of gunfire broke into her thoughts.

Jamie stopped to dump his rucksack, swap out the magazine in his SKK. When he started running again, unencumbered, sprinting flat-out this time, Erin knew she could never keep up. Trees had already enclosed the *Varanus priscus*. Soon, Jamie would be hidden from sight, too.

18

Erin pulled in a huge lungful of air. "Jamie," she screamed. "Wait."

Oh shit, she was doing exactly what Megan had warned her against: yelling. She grappled with the walkie-talkie, yanked it from her belt and thumbed the button.

"Jamie," she said, in a gasping stage-whisper. "Jamie, hang on."

No answer.

And now she couldn't see him anymore.

She stopped, gazed about, and strained her ears. The far off staccato of gunfire sounded. She was wide awake now, as if plunged into an ice bath. Her heart thumped hard inside her throat. Time to make a decision.... Do something, anything. Okay, she would go back and try to find Megan.

She turned and ran.

The poor woman must have been thrown clear somewhere nearby.

"Megan?" she said as loud as she dared. "Can you hear me?"

Erin couldn't remember if there was a first aid kit in her rucksack. Probably, yes. But Megan's injuries would have to be a crushed ribcage and pelvis, just for starters. What kind of first aid kit had items suitable for such life-threatening damage?

A satellite phone.... Why the hell didn't the Robinsons have a satellite phone?

She ran on and on. Everywhere looked the same.

Slowing to a walk, she said, "Megan? Where are you?"

There was nothing but the cheerful sound of birds, the occasional burst of distant gunfire. Erin looked about carefully.

Megan might be unconscious or too wounded to call out. It had happened so fast. Those scant, shocking moments played out in Erin's mind: Megan lifting the rifle and beginning to fire; the racing hulk of the *Varanus priscus* hurtling like a runaway train, its foaming jaws agape. Oh God, those open jaws. The realisation washed over Erin in a flood of nausea. The *Varanus priscus* hadn't knocked Megan flying into the scrub. It had taken her.

Woozy, Erin leaned the rucksack against a tree.

Dead.

Megan was dead. There could be no other explanation.

Erin shuddered. *Killed right before my eyes.*

Killed right before Jamie's eyes too....

The repeated knock of the Remington against the buckles of her rucksack made Erin realise that her hands were quaking. She gritted her teeth. *Don't go into shock.* She had to get a grip. She had to figure out what to do next.

But, Jesus, why had the *Varanus priscus* come after them?

Presumably, it was injured, having been shot multiple times by the Robinsons as it killed Noel. Wounded animals tend not to travel. Wasn't that true? Yes, of course. Besides, the escarpment by their old campsite offered dozens of pig corpses, enough food to last a couple of weeks, which meant there could be just one reason why the *Varanus priscus* had followed them—revenge.

She dismissed the idea as soon as it came to her.

Revenge? What an insane supposition. Russ Walker-Smith would be scornful of such an attempt to anthropomorphise, of all things, a goddamned lizard. They didn't have emotions as such, only instinctual drives. The Komodo dragon even eats its own young. That's about as emotionless as a species could get. No, the *Varanus priscus* couldn't possibly be feeling something as complicated as vengeance.

Unless....

One time, at a herpetology function, Erin had been seated next to a man who owned a variety of reptilian pets. Around the restaurant table, he had told an amusing anecdote about his Savannah monitor. Apparently, one of his friends had accidentally stepped on her tail, and ever after, the Sav had responded to the friend with a threat display. Everyone at the table had laughed, including Erin. Privately, however, she'd doubted the story's veracity. Pet owners are notorious for anthropomorphising their pet's actions. The reptilian limbic system offers basic instincts like fear, aggression and sex drive, but complex emotions? Forget it. Reptiles can't hold a grudge.

But what else would explain the behaviour of the *Varanus priscus*?

Erin took a steadying breath. Forget about its motivations for now. She had to decide what to do next. Obviously, her only course of action would be to catch up to Jamie and help him kill the beast. She lifted the walkie-talkie and thumbed the button.

"Jamie? Can you hear me?"

No reply.

"If you can't speak, press the button a few times."

Still nothing.

"Jamie? Are you there? Please respond."

Her heart began to beat faster. She clipped the walkie-talkie onto her belt and gazed around. The forest looked the same. She hadn't checked her compass before charging after Jamie. How could she follow him? She had no idea in which direction he had gone. A slow crawl of panic clutched at her throat.

She was lost.

Lost....

She clenched her teeth, harder this time. Stop the hysterics and *think*. Use rational, deductive reasoning for once. So they had been travelling in a north-westerly direction. The *Varanus priscus* had charged from the southwest. She consulted her compass, turned toward the northeast. Now what? Closing her eyes, she replayed the memory of Jamie running after the monster. And then it came to her.

Empty shell casings.

Casings would be Jamie's breadcrumb trail.

She walked forward, scanning the ground systematically. The leaf litter was grey and brown, a perfect camouflage for the brass-coloured casings, but surely, the sunlight would glint off their metallic surfaces.

Five minutes went by, ten minutes, twenty. She had to keep wiping the sweat from beneath her eyes to stop her glasses from fogging. Come on, she thought, just a single shell casing would do. Just one was all she needed.

There!

With a gasp, she shuffled over.

The casing shone like gold. A metre further on was another casing, and then another. She had found Jamie's trail. She limped along, keeping her eyes on the ground ahead, feeling her confidence grow with every step. In all likelihood, the shell casings would lie in a straight line. Being an apex predator, the *Varanus priscus* would not run in the bob-and-weave pattern typical of prey animals. As long as there were no obstacles in its path, it should run directly to its destination, which might be...where? Erin had no idea. But she'd worry about that later. Right now, she had to catch up to Jamie.

She saw an empty SKK magazine. After running a few steps past it, she hesitated. Jamie's words came to her: *We dropped them on the chase, and picked 'em up on the way back.* But this time, there may not be a way back. She picked up the magazine, put it in a jacket pocket, and continued on.

Something lay ahead, through the trees.

Erin clutched at the Remington, slowed down to a shuffle.

It was Jamie's rucksack. Dashing over, she slung her rifle and struggled down onto one knee. She didn't have the strength to carry this second rucksack, but she could raid it for supplies. Water bottles, chocolate bars, peanuts...she put these into her jacket pockets.

And then she found one hell of a knife.

She drew it from the leather scabbard. This was one of Jamie's hunting knives, one of two that he had used to dress the deer they had shot at the creek. About 20cm long with half that being steel blade, the tip featured a nasty hook. *For gutting,* Jamie had said, as he'd pushed the knife into the deer. *See how the hook catches the hide?* Sheathing the knife, Erin tucked it into her belt.

A rustling nearby threw her off balance. She landed on her back. Kicking her legs in the manner of a flipped tortoise, she grappled at the Remington. A wallaby stared at her. Relieved and annoyed, Erin stopped flailing.

"Oh, you stupid little shit," she murmured. "I nearly shot you."

The wallaby bounded away.

Now all Erin had to do was get up. She rolled one way, then the other. No good. Taking off the rucksack was an option, but could she put it on again? In the end, using the Remington as a crutch, she managed to get to one knee. Panting, she closed her eyes, the sweat running from her hairline. She was spent. For a tantalising moment, she imagined simply giving in and lying down to sleep.

With a burst of determined effort, she wrenched herself to her feet. She tottered a little. The rucksack had shifted. She tried jiggling the straps as Jamie had done, but with no success. Okay, fine. She would walk lopsided. She grabbed the walkie-talkie.

"Jamie? If you can hear me, I'm following you."

No answer.

"I'll catch up soon."

Again, nothing.

It occurred to her that she hadn't heard gunfire in a long while. Perhaps Jamie had killed the *Varanus priscus*, and was heading back to join her, his walkie-talkie lost or smashed in the chase. Yes, that was the explanation. It had to be.

She set off again at a slow, shambling walk. The straps of the rucksack dug into her collarbones. She contemplated hanging her thumbs inside the straps to redistribute the load, but how would she keep the Remington ready to fire?

A stray thought meandered through her mind....

I'm going to die out here.

She took a chocolate bar from her pocket and ate it without pleasure. No, she wouldn't die. Maybe she wasn't a country girl, but she had plenty of theoretical knowledge. And she'd wrangled a crocodile, hadn't she?

And once, a very big one. While still earning her doctorate, she had picked up work at a family-run animal park that included a number of reptiles, among them a three-metre saltwater crocodile. The reptile had outgrown its pen. The family had made a purpose-built enclosure for it on the other side of the park, the only problem being the animal's transport. The owner, a plump woman with permanently flushed cheeks, asked if Erin would help with the move, and considering Erin's educated status, would she mind taking charge of the head?

The old childhood memory had surfaced: Dad allowing that man to hold the croc by its snout, the croc flinging sideways to split the man's face from nose to chin. The blood, so much blood....

"Well?" the plump woman had said. "You gonna wrangle the head or what?"

Up until that point, Erin had only touched a grown salty under supervision. But she knew an awful lot about them. For instance, salties have the strongest bite of any animal alive, with over 16,000 newtons of force as compared to the human bite of some 900 newtons. This fact had given Erin pause, as she had contemplated the possibility of losing an arm in a single bite. Yet one can clamp a salty's jaws with a rubber band. She agreed to wrangle the head.

The zookeepers hauled the crocodile out of its pond with a rope lassoed around its upper jaw. The crocodile spun over and over in its characteristic death roll. When it landed on its feet and stopped for a moment, as if drawing breath, the zookeepers, including the ruddy-faced owner, leapt onto its back, pinning the animal to the ground. From over the fence, one of the owner's children handed Erin an empty hessian sack, yelling, "Chuck it over the mongrel's eyes". And she did, throwing herself down straight after it. She gripped the jaws in her bare hands. The jaws felt surprisingly warm, like a pebbled poolside on a summer's day. She wound the duct tape around the jaws, once, twice, three times. People clapped. She had looked up and noticed for the first time an audience on the other side of the fence—not just staff members, but visitors to the animal park. She recalled a child holding a balloon, a fat and bearded man taking photographs. *Watch me*, she had thought with fierce pride, imagining her dad's face in the crowd.

Properly applied, theoretical knowledge is as good as practical know-how.

Yes, it is.

Yes, it is.

She could do this.

Erin continued to tramp through the bush, following the trail of shell casings. Occasionally, with difficulty, she stopped to pick up an empty magazine. Soon, she had nowhere to put them. Oh, to hell with this. Propping the weight of her rucksack against a tree, panting and grunting, she unclipped it and shrugged the straps from her shoulders. As the rucksack fell to the ground, she felt light enough to fly. What the hell was in that thing, bowling balls? As it turned out, spare clothes, toiletries, hammer, air pump, water filter, lantern, rain gear, binoculars, ammunition for the Remington—all items seemed necessary. Next, she untied the backpack and checked inside. First aid kit, insect repellent, water bottles, snacks, her photography equipment....

What could she afford to leave behind? She had to lighten the load somehow. Damn it. She took a long drink of warm water. There were three bottles left. She would have to conserve the supply.

Trying the walkie-talkie again, she whispered, "Jamie?"

Nothing.

It was time to make tough decisions. She kept the food, water, first aid kit, toiletries and photography equipment, and put them in the backpack. In her jacket pockets and belt, she stored the Remington ammunition, SKK magazines, and sheathed knife.

She slipped her arms into the backpack straps. Oh, so much lighter. She went to leave. With a stab of anxiety, she glanced back at the rucksack leaned against a trunk. Please God, don't let her come to regret leaving any of that other stuff behind. On impulse, she unzipped the rucksack and took the hammer. A considerable weapon, it had enough weight to break bone. She hung the hammer through her belt. Perhaps she and Jamie would pick up the rucksack on their way back.

She kept walking.

Time passed. The sun began to heat up the earth. She unzipped her jacket. After a while, sweat beaded and trickled. She recognised her exhaustion in the slow drag of each baby step, in the micro-sleeps that made her bump into trees or pitch against shrubs. When was the last time she had sighted a shell casing? Her boot stubbed against something hard. Opening her eyes, she saw the rock for a split-second before she sprawled over it. Falling, she put out both hands. A jarring pain shot through her broken fingers. Yet taking the weight off her feet still felt good. Her blisters must have developed blisters.

She got to her knees and checked her watch. Just on 8 a.m. She had been wandering in this godforsaken bush for hours. Where the hell was Jamie?

Forgoing the walkie-talkie, she dropped her head back onto her shoulders and screamed, "Jamie!"

Her voice echoed back.

No response.

A skittering noise amongst the leaf litter jolted her to her feet, Remington at the ready. It was just a bird; some whatever-kind of bird with green feathers, who gives a shit. Frantically, the bird took off into the sky. Erin wiped the back of her hand across her forehead. The skin-on-skin contact felt gritty. She couldn't remember what it felt like to be clean. Disheartened, she glanced around.

And saw an ammunition bag.

Hurrying over, she picked it up by its strap. Retreating to the rock, she sat down and opened the bag. Inside were many different boxes. The yellow ones drew her attention, since she knew they contained the cartridges for the SKK. She fumbled the empty magazines out of her pockets. Could she reload the magazines? As it turned out, yes, she could. It wasn't too difficult. The cartridges only fitted one way. Her broken fingers slowed her down, but in half an hour, she had reloaded all five mags, save for the last cartridge or two in each—the problem being the springs were too tight, and her hands too pained and weak. Yet Jamie would be pleased with her efforts, she was sure of that. She stashed the mags in her pockets and stood up.

Shit, the mags were heavy.

For a few seconds, she contemplated abandoning the ammunition bag, yet decided against it. Reluctantly, she put the strap over her head so that it lay across one shoulder. She took a step, wobbled, and sat down on the rock again.

Eyes closed, she grabbed the walkie-talkie and brought it up to her lips. "Jamie, for God's sake, please say something. I need to hear your voice."

She took her thumb off the button.

Nothing came back.

Heaving herself to her feet, she kept going. Occasionally, she checked her compass. Now she was moving in an easterly direction. Didn't Megan warn that a gorge lay this way? Erin kept her eyes on the ground, stepping from one spent shell casing to another.

Until the trail stopped.

No more casings. Halting, she raised the rifle, gazed about. Unseen birds squawked and chirped.

Clutching the walkie-talkie, she whispered, "Jamie? Are you there?"

Of course, there was no answer. For a time, Erin didn't know what to do. Then she remembered that the *Varanus priscus* would take the beeline unless physically prevented by an obstacle. She checked her compass. Just a tad off north toward the east, the needle about four minutes past the hour if this were a regular watch. Shit. Comparing a compass to a watch? Really? She had no idea what she was doing.

Doggedly, Erin continued on. The bizarre sensation of walking on a treadmill recurred. I'm falling asleep, she thought, and soon I'll fall down.

Something caught her eye.

At first, she assumed it to be a lone rock thrusting out of the ground, a white talcum stone about a metre high. But the only rocks she'd seen so far had been granite. She stopped. It didn't look right. The shape was too soft, too organic. Adrenaline coursed lazily through her veins. She flipped off the Remington's safety and cautiously advanced.

What the hell was it?

The closer she got, the faster her blood whipped around her body. The object wasn't made of stone. No, the contours suggested a set jelly, a kind of aspic. Then the smell hit her, acrid and sharp. She flinched. A reminder, like a little warning bell, went off in the back of her mind. Even so, she had to get closer to the mound, closer still, before she could positively identify it. Flies buzzed and flitted. She knew. She knew already. But she had to be sure. She inched nearer. Items were suspended in a type of glue. Oh no, Jesus, a hat?

Yes, a bush hat. She recognised it, misshapen and crushed....

A belt, holster...six-shooter revolver.

Was that a single boot?

An iliac fossa, sacrum, coccyx....

Erin stopped. Her blood drained away as if a plug had been pulled. White paste, the thick and stinking white paste enveloping it all—this was a gastric pellet from the *Varanus priscus*. It had vomited the products that it couldn't digest.

And those products were all that was left of Noel.

19

Erin stared at Noel's remains. She saw again his two thumbs up, those unhinged jaws emerging from the trees directly over his head. Faint, she closed her eyes. The world seemed to tilt beneath her feet. When she opened her eyes, she scanned the leaf litter for a suitable stick. She found one soon enough. Working quickly, she snapped off the twigs from the stick, releasing the fragrance of eucalypt: a camphorous mixture of pine, mint, and honey.

No, I can't do it.

Pausing for an instant—oh, dear Christ—she thrust the stick into the gastric pellet and slashed from side to side, breaking apart the jelly-like mound. Eons ago, yet somehow only a few days ago, she had done the same to the gastric pellet containing what was left of Noel's heifer.

Be careful, Dr. Harris.... Hell's bells....

No, she was a scientist, not just a grief-stricken friend. She had to focus. Steeling herself, she inspected the contents of the pellet. Apart from the indigestible items she had already identified, she discovered a belt buckle, what appeared to be a cardiac stent from a coronary angioplasty, a dental plate with two artificial bicuspids. Noel's tight smile came to mind.

Can I climb over your fence?

I don't know, Dr. Harris. Can you?

She pushed the memory aside. The paste broke open in wet clots like an undercooked cake, hot from the oven. The incongruous analogy made her gag. She turned away. Dear God, the stink reached down her throat and tried to pull out the meagre contents of her stomach. She couldn't afford to vomit. The risk of dehydration was too high. If only she had a handkerchief to place over her nose.

She exhaled, centred herself, went back to the broken pellet and fossicked with the stick. And there it was: blowfly eggs. Yellowish-white, balled like clumps of sticky rice, the *Calliphoridae* eggs included a number of hatched maggots. Erin was not an entomologist, but this stage of insect infestation suggested that the gastric pellet must be at least 12 to 24 hours old, which meant....

The *Varanus priscus* had not regurgitated this pellet during Jamie's pursuit.

Most likely, the *Varanus priscus* had regurgitated sometime last evening.

This posed a frightening hypothesis: the *Varanus priscus* used this particular trail on a regular basis. But why? What lay at the end of this trail? Not a self-dug burrow, not a naturally-occurring cavity, not a hollow beneath overhanging vegetation; these sleeping places were opportunistic. No, something familiar to the *Varanus priscus* lay at the end of this path, something important. What could it be? Erin scrambled to think. A reliable water source? A deer crossing?

She lifted the camcorder from around her neck and took a few seconds of footage, murmuring, "Here is what's left of Noel Baines."

If only some inspired words might come to her, a meaningful eulogy, but she couldn't think of anything to say. Next, she took the still camera from her backpack and snapped a separate photograph of every item belonging to Noel that the *Varanus priscus* had failed to digest. The sight of the crumpled hat made her sob.

No, she must be strong.

Turning from the gastric pellet, she took the walkie-talkie from her belt.

"Jamie?" she whispered. "Please answer me."

She waited.

No reply.

Cold fingers of dread crept up her spine. Occam's razor explained Jamie's radio silence. But no, Erin would not go there.

She refused to contemplate that terrible possibility. Instead, she clipped the walkie-talkie to her belt, consulted her compass, grabbed the Remington in both hands, and advanced.

Dr. Harris, this is our expedition, yours and mine, not yours alone. I'm coming with you. It'll be a team of four: us and the Robinsons. And I'm paying. I won't take any arguing, you get me?

Tears stung her eyes. If only she could mark the site of Noel's remains so that a search party could retrieve them. His family would at least have something to bury. However, she had no way of knowing the latitude and longitude. On impulse, hoping against hope, she took out her mobile phone. No signal. How typical of this whole expedition. Her father used to complain all the time: *If I didn't have bad luck, I'd have no luck at all.* You and me both, she thought grimly.

She halted for a drink of water. A stirring through the leaf litter made her almost choke. Capping the bottle, she tucked it into a pocket and lifted the Remington to hip-height. It would just be a bird, a wallaby.

She froze.

The boar saw her at the same time and stopped moving too.

At a distance of a few metres, they stared, motionless, sizing each other up.

The animal was about the size of a Rottweiler, with three times the muscle. The tusks in the lower jaw jutted out, long and yellow. Erin shifted her gaze all around. She couldn't see any other pigs. Maybe this was a lone boar. Slowly, very slowly, she began to lift the Remington.

The boar tensed.

The sight of its grey, bristled fur balling up at the shoulders kicked Erin's heart into a crazy gallop. The boar was preparing itself. And Erin had yet to load the rifle. The slide and clack of the bolt would no doubt startle the animal, compel it to attack. Why hadn't she thought to load the rifle earlier? Perhaps she could retreat instead. One gentle step at a time.... If she retreated, would the boar stand down? She put one foot behind her.

The boar took a couple of steps forward. Its small, beady eyes glared steadily.

She would have to kill it. She would load, aim, and shoot, all in a piece. If she executed the procedures correctly, the boar would be dead before it could gore her legs. The weight of the rifle pained her broken fingers. She took hold of the bolt in her right hand. The boar lowered its snout. Snarling, it released low, snuffling grunts.

Now or never.

With a cry, she pulled the bolt. The boar shied at the sudden noise.

Erin squinted down the scope. Her finger stuttered against the trigger. The animal swung its head out of her scope. Panicked, she looked up from the rifle. Had she missed her chance? Was the animal closing on her already? But no; the boar, huffing and growling, was plodding away into the bush at a trot, its shaggy tail held straight out. Soon it was gone from sight.

Relief took the strength from Erin's body. She leaned her forearm against a tree and rested her face in the crook of her elbow, catching her breath. After a while, she opened her eyes. That's when she noticed that the rifle, held loosely by her side, happened to be aiming straight down at her foot, with the safety off and a bullet in the chamber. Jesus Christ. Wouldn't that be the icing on the goddamned cake? A self-inflicted gunshot wound. She stood up and took hold of the Remington in both hands, making sure it was pointed harmlessly to one side.

She had to be more careful, more proactive.

With the rifle at chest-height, she did a 360-degree sweep. Nothing. She consulted her compass and started walking. Her knees felt like jelly. Every five steps, she would stop, turn in a circle, and scan the surrounding bush. For reasons unknown, this particular *Varanus priscus* liked to use this trail. But a *Varanus priscus* wouldn't clumsily give away its position like the boar had done, shambling through leaf litter and causing a racket. No, the lizard would stalk her quietly from behind. Erin had to be on guard. She had to assume danger at every moment.

She inhaled sharply.

Dead ahead, just through the trees: another ammunition bag.

She hurried over. How many ammunition bags had Jamie carried? Two, while Megan had toted the third. Erin checked inside: full of boxes. Standing up, she hauled the strap over her shoulder. Now she had two ammunition bags, one on each hip, loaded up like a pack mule.

But why had Jamie left the bag behind?

She couldn't think of an explanation, except perhaps the dumping of ballast to help him run faster. However, that didn't make sense. Without ammunition, how would he propose to kill the beast that had killed his wife?

A few metres farther on, a frightening sight: Jamie's SKK.

It lay on the ground, seemingly intact.

Erin paused, loath to approach it. What if the strap was sheared through, as if by razor-sharp teeth? What if blood—or worse—covered the rifle? She glanced around in all directions. No sign of him anywhere. Birds called from hidden places. Flies and bees droned. White cabbage moths darted. A skink sat perfectly still on a sandy rock, basking. She thought of the *Varanus priscus* doing the same.

"Jamie?" she said as loudly as she dared. "Where are you?" She grabbed the walkie-talkie. "Answer me. Can you hear me?"

No response.

She advanced on the SKK. She couldn't see blood on it. Kneeling, she picked it up and checked if it was loaded. Both the chamber and magazine were empty. Okay, a possible scenario began to take shape. When the SKK had run dry, Jamie, too impatient to stop and reload, had abandoned the rifle and continued on, choosing instead to use another of the rifles he carried on his back.

Erin flipped the safety switch on the Remington and hung the rifle over her shoulder. Then she reloaded and cocked the SKK. Now she could fire 30 bullets in a row. It made her feel a little better. Consulting her compass, she marched forward.

One step, two, three, four, and five.... She stopped, did a slow circle, staring between the trees for any sign of movement, for any colouration that looked out of place. She counted out another five steps, performed her sweep....

Could Jamie be dead?

No.

No, he couldn't be.

She continued walking, scanning the ground in search of shell casings. Now was not the time to speculate on gruesome possibilities. Jamie was alive until proven otherwise. The hot sun leaned down on her. She wanted to remove her jacket, but it contained most of the SKK magazines.

Everywhere looked the same.

She checked her compass periodically, did her 360-degree sweep at every fifth step. Fatigue crept over her. She contemplated eating a chocolate bar. Wouldn't that make her thirsty? She didn't have much water left. If she stumbled across a creek, would its water be safe to drink? She had no idea.

...Three, four, five.... Sweep.

Her feet dragged. She had to lift them higher. Jesus, her feet hurt.

...Three, four, five.... Sweep.

Perhaps she'd eat something anyway. She needed the energy.

...Three, four, five.... Sweep.

Why would the Robinsons pack salty foods like roasted peanuts? How stupid.

...Three, four, five.... Sweep.

Salt increased thirst. What if a trip to the bush turned to shit and you had to hike with limited drinking water and the saltiest foods in the whole world?

...Three, four—

What is that?

Erin pulled up, suddenly wide awake and frightened. A boot; it looked like a boot. She took a couple of wary steps closer. Yes, there it lay; definitely a boot, some eight metres ahead, peeking out from behind a stand of trees and shrubs. Resting on its heel and drooped sideways at about a forty-five-degree angle, its posture suggested that a foot was still inside it, that the foot was still attached to a person, and that the person was lying on his back, as still as death. No, don't contemplate death.

Grabbing the walkie-talkie, Erin said, "Jamie? Is that you?"

"Jamie? Is that you?"

Her own words came back to her a moment later, tinny and shrill.

She went cold.

To double-check, she whispered into the walkie-talkie, "Jamie Robinson."

"Jamie Robinson."

Her own voice, yes, sounding a few metres away, emanating from the walkie-talkie clipped to Jamie's belt. She had found him. Maybe he was unconscious.

No, not unconscious. Stop pretending.

He was dead.

And Erin had killed him.

Her ambition, run amok, had killed them all. Noel, Megan, Jamie—all dead because of her lust for a scientific breakthrough....

But that wasn't exactly true, now was it?

She flushed with a hot, burning shame. No, her desire to find *Varanus priscus*, to prove to the world that it still lived, had had nothing to do with science, the pursuit of truth and knowledge. She'd wanted fame, fortune. More than that—immortality. To be lauded, her name spoken in the same breath as Richard Dawkins, Alfred Russel Wallace, even Charles Darwin.

What pathetic arrogance.

I can't share this discovery with anybody, she had said to Russ during her drunken phone conversation with him from her hotel room. *It has to be called Harris's dragon, okay? Remember that: Harris's dragon.*

What galling vanity. She pushed aside the momentary vision of her father's sneer. The *Harris's dragon* was how she'd imagined her posterity lasting throughout the ages. Oh God, she felt sick just to think of it. The contents of her stomach roiled. She heaved, retching up a scant amount of watery vomit.

She wiped at her chin and stared at Jamie's single boot.

Three people had died horribly because of her inferiority complex, her Daddy Issues, her conceit that she ought to live forever. A tightening sensation began to crush her chest. Good, let this be a heart attack. She deserved to die out here.

A skittering in the leaf litter made her jump. She raised the SKK and aimed it straight at a frightened rabbit. The animal bounded away in an instant. Erin lowered the rifle and let out a ragged breath. What a poser. So she wasn't ready to die after all.

Stop feeling sorry for yourself, she thought. And stop the histrionics. Go check on Jamie. If he wasn't dead, he would need all the help she could offer.

She advanced toward the boot.

Whatever happened, she had to stay calm. She had seen some awful, disgusting sights in her time. A reticulated python, stressed by clumsy handling, regurgitating three semi-digested birds in a row. The soupy remains of a dog cut from the stomach of a saltie captured and brutally killed with machetes after terrorising a community up north. The bizarre effects of the Ebola-like "inclusion body disease" that makes an infected snake literally tie itself into spine-cracking knots. There was no need to be afraid. No matter what physical state Jamie was in, Erin could handle it.

Now she could see both his legs below the knees. The rest of him remained hidden behind trees and brush. She paused, heart thumping. Quickly, she performed a sweep of the area. No sign of any other living thing. She looked down again at the two motionless legs.

"Jamie?" she whispered.

She forced herself to take a few more steps.

The full length of both his legs appeared unharmed, his jeans without a single spot of blood. Getting closer, she saw his belt, the walkie-talkie, the revolver in its holster. She peeked a little more around the tree trunk. His flannelette shirt was half-tucked into his belt. No sign of blood. The odds that he was simply unconscious were getting better. With a deep gulp of air, she came out from behind the trees and stood between his splayed legs. His body ended just beneath the armpits. Instead of arms, shoulders, neck and head, Erin found herself gazing upon a gory slop of organs and tattered flesh.

A giddy swoon passed through her. She fought it off. Scanning the ground nearby, she searched for the top half of his body. It was nowhere to be found. The *Varanus priscus* must have bitten Jamie clean through and swallowed the mouthful.

She stared at the corpse for a long time.

This is my doing.

She lifted the camcorder from around her neck and thumbed the button.

"Here is what's left of Jamie Robinson," she whispered hoarsely.

Stumbling against the nearest tree, she tried her best not to faint. It took a few moments to regain control of her senses.

She looked back down at Jamie.

"I'm so sorry," she whispered.

At some point, the *Varanus priscus*, tired of being pursued and shot, had turned around and attacked Jamie. Where were his other rifles? Apart from the SKK, which Erin now carried, he'd had at least two more hanging from his shoulders. Did the lizard eat them too? Yes, that was the most likely scenario. And in a few hours, the *Varanus priscus* would heave out a gastric pellet that included Jamie's firearms, the compass that hung around his neck, his wristwatch, any dental fillings....

Erin briefly closed her eyes, gagged on the bile in her throat.

Working quickly, she squatted down and unclipped the knife sheath from Jamie's belt. She pulled out the blade for a moment to appraise the notched serrations. They resembled a row of teeth from a great white shark; no, from a *Varanus priscus*. Next, she unclipped the holster. It fastened with a heavy press-stud. She opened it and took out the revolver. It was a kind of gun she recognised from old movies. Cocking the gun would involve drawing back the hammer. Was it loaded? She found the release button high on the butt. The cylinder rolled out. Yes, it appeared full to the naked eye: six cartridges. She pressed the cylinder back into the body of the revolver until it clicked into place. Holstering the gun, she clipped it to her own belt, along with the sheathed knife. She stood up.

So, she had an SKK, a Remington and a handgun, all loaded, with two ammunition bags for back-up, plus two hunting knives and a hammer.

Okay, fine. Now what?

Well, for starters, she was headed in the wrong direction. Megan had said to go northwest toward the fire-trail. Erin lifted the compass. Sooner or later, her mobile phone would get a signal. She'd check periodically, and then call for help. She turned to the northwest and took the SKK into both hands. Only then did she see something unusual out of the corner of her eye.

20

The huge mound of soil, leaves and twigs had been next to her all along, close enough to touch. Erin hadn't noticed, too transfixed by Jamie's corpse. If this was a natural hillock, then she was a goddamned Martian. She roved her gaze over the titanic pile of dirt. It looked like the nest of a saltwater crocodile. Yet wild salties weren't found in southeastern Australia. Tentatively, Erin approached.

The mound was some two metres high and six metres wide, situated within a natural clearing. The lack of canopy permitted the warmth of direct sunlight, a factor desired by mothers of all reptiles.

No, it couldn't be....

Leave, she thought. For the love of Christ, *go*. But her whole life had led her to this revelation, to this history-remaking discovery. How could she run away?

Slinging the rifle over one shoulder, she dug both hands frantically through the dirt, ignoring the pain in her broken fingers. She felt the object before she saw it. Warm, smooth and leathery.... Her leg muscles tightened involuntarily as if preparing to sprint. Erin braced herself. With slow, gentle brushes of her fingertips, she unearthed the object and pulled it from the soil.

It appeared to be an egg.

She palpated the object: intact, off-white, the size and shape of a football, weighing about a kilogram. She squeezed it experimentally between her palms. From within the leathery shell, something nudged at her in return. Erin gave a startled cry.

The object didn't just look like an egg....

It *was* a goddamned egg.

And not just one; a Komodo dragon could lay 20 or more in a single clutch. Erin gaped at the nest in trepidation. Then she inspected the egg, careful not to move it too quickly for fear that the embryo might detach from the egg wall and die. Should she open the egg to make sure of the contents? Just one little cut.... She put one hand onto the hilt of a knife. She could slice through the shell, check that the foetus inside was indeed a *Varanus priscus*....

But what else could it be?

The shivering began in her ankles and travelled up her body until she shook all over. She fought the urge to flee. With great discipline, she calmed herself, forced herself to think logically, rationally. She had to move from one known fact to the other, as if crossing a fast and tumultuous river on stepping stones.

So the *Varanus priscus* favoured this trail as a regular route to its nest. That accounted for the presence of the gastric pellet containing Noel's remains. Sometime yesterday, most likely in the evening, the lizard had regurgitated the pellet on its way back to the nest via this particular trail. She held up the egg to the light.

The faintest of shadows stirred.

The sight hooked her breath. Movement butted against her palms. Dear God, she could feel the developing foetus through the tough, mobile shell.

Tears blurred her vision.

How glorious.

Evolution at its finest and most ingenious....

Erin gave a shocked laugh as tears spilled down her cheeks.

Right here, in her hands, was the greatest paleontological find of the century.

For a few more seconds, she stared at the egg in awe. Then she pressed it to her cheek like a treasured pet. The tiny monster shifted within; a gentle, lazy scrabble of jaws and claws. Yes, she could feel it. Every movement galvanised her heart. Erin and the prehistoric foetus were separated by the thinnest veneer, a layer of calcium carbonate crystals arranged over a protein matrix. The thought made her short-winded. Might the foetus have an egg tooth? Yes, more than likely. When the time came, the infant would slice through the shell using its egg tooth like a blade. Once free, the egg tooth would fall away, redundant.

Hastily, Erin shucked the SKK, Remington and ammunition bags in order to take off her backpack and unzip it.

"You're coming home with me," she said to the egg.

She put it carefully into her backpack and closed the zipper all the way. When she put on the backpack, the weight of the egg...was it pressing against her spine? Or was she imagining things? Unexpectedly, she felt the tug of maternal instinct. I will protect you, she thought, against any and all threats. I will oversee your development from a newborn to a prepubescent, into adolescence and adulthood. I will be there, always, constantly.

She imagined a specialised zoo enclosure.

Tempered glass and steel....

A massive structure built to order....

The enclosure would mimic natural environs, a terrarium on a grand scale, including running water and enough space for the lizard to dig its own sleeping burrow every night. Scientists and members of the public from every corner of the globe would flock to see the baby *Harris's dragon*. Its developmental milestones studied in mind-boggling depth. Thousands, perhaps millions of photographs documenting its every moment: each meal, gastric pellet, bowel motion. Of course, Erin would have already quit her job at the university to care for the lizard and give daily addresses to rapt audiences. Wait, she'd need to engage a stylist, make-up artist, hairdresser; a personal assistant to field the many calls, texts and emails from a fascinated world.

And a hawker, yes. Resplendent in a worsted wool three-piece suit, handsome and charismatic, a hawker to warm the crowd with his hypnotic voice.... Striding the stage, back and forth, a discreet microphone at his lips....

Ladies and gentlemen, boys and girls: prepare yourselves for the sight of a lifetime. In just a few minutes, a wondrous vision will be revealed to you. An animal unseen by human eyes for thousands of years. A vicious, predatory animal; its mother took the lives of three brave Australians. Only one member of the expedition lived to tell the awful tale. And to relate this awful tale of her perilous journey, please put your hands together and give a warm welcome to a scientist who needs no introduction, Dr. Erin Harris, renowned evolutionary biologist....

The applause is deafening. The faces in those rows and rows of steeply tiered seats are shining, beaming, transfixed.... Erin takes the stage, offers a gently waving hand and bows at the waist. The intensity of applause doubles and triples....

Erin half-lifted a grimy hand to the trees. The action broke her reverie.

Idiot.

Oh, for the love of Christ, was she losing her goddamned mind?

She would take three more eggs to increase the odds of getting one viable female. A single female Komodo dragon could produce a clutch of eggs all by herself via parthenogenesis, so why not the *Varanus priscus*?

The capability of the female Komodo dragon to reproduce without a male—that is, asexually—was quite a recent discovery. Some ten years ago, when a female Komodo at a London zoo had laid eggs despite not being with a male for two years, herpetologists had classified the births as superfecundation, the ability of a female to store sperm for fertilisation at a later and more convenient time. But about a year hence, again in England, another captive Komodo laid a clutch. This time, however, it was a virgin birth. The female had never even seen a male of her own species. Out of the clutch, seven of the eggs hatched. All hatchlings were male. Collectively, herpetologists were dumbfounded. Finally, an American zoo, via genetic testing of its own virgin Komodo and her hatchlings, scientifically documented the female's ability to reproduce asexually.

Erin contemplated the probabilities.

The *Varanus priscus* must have the sex-determination of ZW chromosomes, just like the Komodo dragon. In parthenogenesis, the Komodo female gives each egg a single chromosome, either Z or W. The W-chromosome, which produces a female, always dies. The Z-chromosome, however, doubles itself within the egg and the ZZ duplication results in a male. The male hatchling tends not to suffer genetic deficits. A lone female can be isolated geographically yet still reproduce sexually via coupling with her parthenogenetic sons. And unlike the mammalian sex-determination of XY chromosomes, inbreeding amongst ZW reptiles doesn't present immediate problems.

She had the title for her treatise already: *Reproductive plasticity including parthenogenesis in the modern-day* V. priscus....

She dug out three more eggs, placed them carefully in her backpack.

Shouldering the rifles and ammunition bags, she grabbed the camcorder and began filming. She sidestepped around the mound, intending to show every angle.

"This is the nest of *Varanus priscus*," she said. "If it's anything like that of the Komodo dragon, it will contain an average of eighteen eggs. The Komodo often commandeers the mound of a megapode, or mound-building bird, but this appears to be the work of the *Varanus priscus* herself. The huge claw-marks within the soil, here and here in particular, support my hypothesis. The *Varanus priscus* probably nests more like a crocodile than a Komodo dragon, for reasons unknown."

Erin swapped the camcorder to her left hand, wincing in pain from her broken fingers. While continuing to film, she thrust her right hand into the soil and dug around. Within moments, her efforts had exposed two eggs. Tenderly, she brushed away the remaining dirt. The eggs, laid symmetrically side by side, were leaned together and touching, as if posed for a sentimental family portrait.

"There," she said, panting. "Two examples, incubation period unknown. Each one about thirty centimetres in length, a near-perfect prolate spheroid, cream-coloured—"

Tripping over something, she glanced down.

And stifling a scream, stumbled backward, let go of the camcorder.

Dear God.

Shattered into pieces.... that's how Megan looked. She had all of her parts—head, torso, limbs—but each separated from the other; the gaps bridged with blood and ripped flesh, abuzz with flies. The strength left Erin's legs. She knelt down and put a hand on the cooling body. The half-open eyes, dusted with soil, gazed at infinity. Even in death, Megan gripped the stock of her SKK. During the attack by wild pigs, she had seemed like an Amazon, a warrior, unafraid and unbowed. Erin scanned the ground near the body. Where were Megan's rucksack, backpack, other rifles, ammunition bag? No trace. Perhaps the items had been shorn from the body in stages and dropped in the bush as the running *Varanus priscus* had gripped her within its razor-sharp teeth.

Self-loathing washed over Erin. She had imagined her own grand and lauded future while both the Robinsons lay dead at her feet, defiled by insects.

If anyone should be dead, it should be me.

Tears welled. "I'll find my way back here," she said, wiping at her running nose. "I won't let you and Jamie rot in this place. You'll have proper burials with headstones. I'll pay for it. You'll have orchids and music and eulogies. I'll give Noel a funeral too, with all the trimmings. And money, I'll give money to your dependants—"

The growl cut Erin's words as definitively as a knife to the windpipe.

She sat upright.

Had she imagined that sound?

No, there it was again—a slow, rumbling growl.

Adrenaline ran through her body in sheets, like pelting rain. Biting at her lips to stop them from trembling, Erin picked up Megan's SKK and draped the strap over her shoulder. Then she stood up. As soon as the wooziness abated, she swept the area with Jamie's fully-loaded SKK. On the other side of the giant mound was the banded tail, its alternate stripes of yellow and green scales luminescent and shining. Erin broke into a cold sweat. It all made sense now.

Ghastly, perfect sense.

Of course, the *Varanus priscus* would be hovering nearby; it was the expectant mother. And the Robinsons must be food. The *Varanus priscus* had brought the corpses of Jamie and Megan to the nest as food for the hatchlings. No other species of reptile behaved this way, but what other explanation could there be? As soon as Erin had seen the nest, she should have retreated. Now it was too late. She would die, and horribly. Clutching the SKK, she thumbed off the safety. The growl sounded again.

She peeked out from behind the nest.

As if exhausted, the *Varanus priscus* had its belly and head flat on the ground. Could it be sleeping? Or was the lizard suffering, perhaps even dying? To get a better view of its head, Erin went around behind the nest and peeked from the other side.

To her surprise, the *Varanus priscus* had its lips closed over its fangs. Like the flews of a dog, the flexible upper lip had unfurled to cover the long, dagger-like teeth. Of course, no land animal exposed its open mouth perpetually to the elements. A dimple in the infra-nasal depression suggested where the forked tongue could extend and retract through the dental diastema. Yet there was no sign of the tongue. The beast hadn't smelled her because its olfactory organ—located on the forked tongue—was fully retracted inside its sheath. Erin may as well be invisible. Similar to the Komodo, *Varanus priscus* must respond mainly to scent rather than sound or sight.

A decision had to be made. Run? Or shoot?

Neither. She was invisible. Just a few seconds of footage....

She tiptoed back to the other side of the nest and lifted the camcorder. The bands on the tail looked even brighter and richer through the lens. She began filming. The faint murmur of the camcorder...would the lizard hear it? But no, Erin had already blundered around the site, talking out loud, even crying and wailing, for God's sake. If the beast hadn't heard all of that commotion, it wouldn't hear the soft whir of the camcorder's motor.

"Ladies and gentlemen," she whispered, "I present *Varanus priscus*."

A surge of pride put strength into her limbs. The discovery of the century...the *Harris's dragon*...the cover of National Geographic magazine....

Wow, there were bullet wounds.

Plenty of them.

Erin pressed the zoom button for a better look. Yes, the tail had at least 16 bullet holes. Flies swarmed each one. Yet there was very little blood. How far had the bullets penetrated? She had no way of telling. Chipping and scuff marks on the scales suggested that many more bullets had been deflected. Jesus, how thick was the hide? Erin leaned out from behind the nest to see more of the beast. Then she took a step, and gasped in surprise and appreciation. The back leg of the *Varanus priscus* lay straight out from the body, its foot rolled over to expose the thick padding of its sole. Oh, she could see the underside of its foot.

Erin moved out from behind the nest and inched closer.

The huge sole was roughly oval-shaped. Like the Komodo dragon, the toes were arranged in descending length from medial to lateral. The hallux grew out from the sole on an angle, akin to a thumb; again, like the Komodo. Intriguing. The foot and toe pads appeared scaled. She zoomed in. Yes, very small, tightly clustered, symmetrical rows of non-overlapping scales. The curved claws sent a shiver through her. They were sharp enough to disembowel prey. But how beautiful; their bands dark grey and parallel, each claw a scimitar of black onyx. She imagined them clean, buffed and polished. They would feel so smooth....

It occurred to her that the *Varanus priscus* hadn't made any further sounds.

Erin stopped filming, looked at the animal with her own eyes.

No movement whatsoever. No signs of respiration. It was completely still, as if carved from stone—or wood. A pang of grief, or perhaps guilt, squeezed Erin's lungs and choked out a sob. She touched at her pocket, felt the outline of the two whittled figurines. Noel, I'll make it up to you, she thought. I'll make you famous with these baby *Varanus priscus* I'm carrying. Their enclosure will be called *The Noel Baines Terrarium*. I will financially care for your daughter, Kylie, I promise....

Erin wiped away tears and started filming again.

The tough hide was riddled with bullet holes. Flies, gnats and other insects swarmed everywhere. Oh, but the girth of the beast was nothing short of astonishing. She kept the camera steady, roamed it, spotted the front leg splayed and rolled like the back leg. The sole of the front foot was also scaled, as expected. The foot itself was smaller, however, its toes more slender. And yet the *Varanus priscus* would, like the Komodo, dig or disembowel using only its front feet. Interesting.... She filmed the massive shoulder joint, the muscled hump at the base of the neck, the jaw, the ear hole, and then she stopped. Now she could smell the beast; an acrid, sour odour that included notes of decay, dust and shit.... A panicked flutter started up in the pit of her stomach. She lowered the camcorder.

Oh, Jesus. The relative safety of the nest lay far behind. Mesmerised, Erin had walked out into the open and alongside the beast. She was standing so very near, as if admiring a parked car from the footpath. Involuntarily, her elbows tightened against her sides. The camcorder had tricked her, made it seem like watching TV.

But there was something else; that hypnotic pull the animal had over her.

She stared at the beast's ribs, belly, at the sagging folds of hide for any hint of respiration. Nothing. It did appear that the *Varanus priscus* was either dying or dead. Or holding its breath? The Komodo can hold its breath for long periods of time, such as when swimming underwater. On the other hand, perhaps this inactivity was a stress reaction; a captured saltwater croc, if incorrectly handled, can become overwhelmed and fall into a trance-like state of hibernation wherein it lies motionless for days, reducing its heart rate to a few beats per minute, hardly needing air. Whatever the case, the *Varanus priscus* seemed incapacitated.

She could film its entire head if she took just a few more steps.

The nose was so close. It would be beautiful, so beautiful.

Three...maybe four steps away....

The lizard was dead; it had to be dead.

She lifted the camcorder.

The luminescent yellow and green colouring of the scales took on a vivid sheen through the lens. How strange that the colouration wasn't red, which is the typical colouration of the female Komodo, if any occurs. Erin sidestepped again. She could see the closed eyelid, thick and crusted with scales, the entire orbit protruding from the skull in a pleasing shape, reminiscent of a conch shell. This was the lizard's eye on the right-hand side. A brief walk around its snout would show the bullet hole beneath its left eye, the wound that Erin had made with the Remington as the

Varanus priscus had attacked Noel. Her bullet would be lodged somewhere in the sinus cavity.

Well, she'd come this far, hadn't she?

Heart drubbing into her throat, Erin took a couple more paces, filming now with the camcorder held at shoulder height, staring hard for any signs of life. Not a trace; she was safe. She would finish her recording of the lizard, retreat, and hike to the fire-trail.

The eyelid quivered.

Or did it?

Erin froze. Seconds passed.

There, oh fuck, it quivered again.

The lid opened. Then the cartilaginous plate retracted. The hazel eye with its bright green collarette gazed about for a moment, and found Erin.

21

They looked at each other for a long time. Neither of them moved.

Erin felt pinned, giddy; falling through an abyss.

The melon-sized eye of the *Varanus priscus* had an intent and penetrating stare. The cornea shone with a high gloss. The pupil was the darkest shade of black she'd ever seen. And the iris wasn't hazel after all, as she had first thought, but a rich and nutty russet, which perfectly contrasted the green of the collarette. The eye was more beautiful than any gemstone. Then the very tips of the lizard's forked tongue protruded.

Erin's body tightened like a fist.

The passage of the tongue in and out through the diastema made a slippery, whisking sound. With a rustling of leaf litter and a grunt through flaring nostrils, the *Varanus priscus* lifted its head a few inches, and swung it toward Erin.

Oh no.

Oh, God.

But wait, don't panic, she told herself; the lizard was severely injured. The Robinsons had knocked the fight out of it. And so had Erin—on the lower rim of the left orbital bone was her bullet hole, the giant eye above it bloodshot, the lids purpled and swollen. And besides, Erin had three loaded rifles, a handgun. She could kill it right now. *Shoot.* Did she want to die like the others? Shoot, for Christ's sake. She dropped the camcorder on its strap—had she been filming this whole fucking time?—and groped for an SKK. Whether it was Jamie's or Megan's, she couldn't tell. The rifle felt alien. Where was the trigger? She patted along the stock and barrel. Her broken fingers flared in pain.

The tongue snaked out again. It glistened, the tissue obscenely pink, membranous and delicate. The forked tip quivered. Slaver drooled from the jaws. Then, with a slurp, the tongue retracted into its sheathed pipe. Erin whimpered. *It tastes me.* She was simply a deer or goat, a meal of hot blood, organs and meat....

The beast exhaled in a growl. Dank, rotten breath fanned over Erin's face, stirred through her hair. She muffled a shriek. Her leg muscles unlocked. She took a few jerky steps backward. The *Varanus priscus* twitched its head, alert and watchful. Its tongue lashed about. Sinews flexed beneath the hide in its feet.

Avoid sudden movements, Erin thought. If you make a sudden movement near a Komodo, it might attack you. But, oh shit, this wasn't a Komodo. This was a strange, primeval, unfathomable monster with behaviours all of its own. Erin's education and experience told her nothing, nothing; nothing could save her....

"Stay," she found herself whispering as if to a dog, while her teeth chattered. "Please stay. I'm leaving now. See? I'm leaving. Stay. Just stay."

The monster hefted its bulk onto all four feet.

"No," Erin cried.

Its upper lip curled to unveil long, yellowed fangs. The leathery throat blew in and out. Its mouth yawned open. Strings of saliva, thick and white, sticky as glue, stretched between the jaws. Erin let out a full-bodied scream that echoed around the park in shockwaves. Her finger found the SKK trigger guard and, sweet mercy, the trigger itself. She squeezed and squeezed and squeezed and didn't let go.

The SKK stuttered a volley of bullets.

The noise pained her ears. But the bullets struck home. The *Varanus priscus* reared its head, flinching, bloodied holes rupturing across its snout. But an instant later, the SKK bucked and wrenched upward, spraying at the sky. *Recoil....* Erin remembered the theoretical lesson from Jamie and Megan: one must grip this rifle tight, as if it were a fire-hose opened full bore, or else lose control. Erin struggled to correct her aim. The SKK fought against her, and clicked empty.

Empty?

Her finger pulled helplessly at the trigger.

Out of ammunition already? But only seconds had elapsed.

She yanked at the magazine, which wouldn't detach. The *Varanus priscus* narrowed its eyes and hissed. The grating sibilance raised every hair on Erin's body.

Frightened beyond measure, she turned and fled.

And ran at a speed like never before. She became more than herself, more than human. The rifles, backpack and ammunition bags weightless, her blistered and bleeding feet fitted with wings, her heart and lungs powerful enough to take her to the ends of the earth. The ground whipped beneath her in a blur. The surrounding forest passed by without incident. The *Varanus priscus* and its nest would soon be far away. That hiss and throat flutter—mere threat. I'm flying, she thought, dazed, relieved. I'm hurtling like a goddamned missile.

...And yet....

The shuffling of huge feet kicking through leaf litter sounded behind her.

Erin's stomach heaved and fell.

The *Varanus priscus* was following her.

Panic tasted like copper. She found herself wailing, mindlessly, on every exhalation. Would the monster chomp her in half? Swallow her whole and alive? Oh God, she feared Noel's fate the most: suffocation within the crushing pleats of that massive throat, dissolution head-first in stomach acid. A stitch threatened to double her over. The superhuman feeling was wearing off. Oh Jesus, she was slowing down, gasping with burning lungs. The solution: halt, turn and shoot. But in those few wasted seconds, the monster would be upon her. Already, she could hear it coming up fast behind, smashing through boughs, trampling shrubs. It let out a snarl, so very close. Would it catch her with its teeth? Hamstring her with its outstretched claws? Erin screamed in terror. Go faster. She had to go faster.

And then the answer came bright and clear: *zigzag*.

Predators, especially lizards, move quickest in a straight line. Prey animals, such as mammals, gain the advantage on the turns. Erin cut left. She heard the clumsy footsteps of the monster behind her momentarily lose their rhythm. She sprinted on and on, and then cut right. The fumbling of the heavy footsteps encouraged her. Left, right, left, right....

And as she sped, leaping over obstacles, ducking branches, streaking sideways past trees, the noise of the monster's ungainly waddling seemed to come from farther and farther away. She risked a glance back. The mouth was open, teeth bared, throat a cavernous mass of red, wet, rumpled folds. Pumping her arms, Erin increased her stride. The stitch between her ribs felt like a stabbing blade. Straining, she pushed to increase the pace. The *Varanus priscus* would soon reach exhaustion. It was badly— perhaps mortally—injured. At any minute, it'd lose interest or energy, stop the chase, and return to its nest.

Any minute now...any minute....

Zigzag right, left, right....

The pounding steps sounded ever more distant. Another glance; yes, the monster was falling back. Erin laughed, sobbed. Her collarbones and spine ached from the pack, bags and rifles. Hanging from its strap, the camcorder bounced a rhythmic beat of bruises across her chest. Keep going, keep going.... Her tattered feet slipped inside her boots. Push harder.... And now her nose started bleeding again. Damn. She blew her nose into her hand, flung the haemic mucus into the bush. Please God, don't let the smell incite the *Varanus priscus*. She glanced back again. That massive head was almost lost through the trees. Zigzag left, right, left....

Without warning, Erin burst into a clearing.

She lost her momentum for a second.

Long ago, a ribbon of fire must have blitzed through here, razing the forest to nothing but grassy stubble and dirt. A mangy cat startled and flashed away into the scrub. Erin fought down a jag of hysteria. The nearest cover lay straight ahead, perhaps 80 metres distant. Over flat and empty ground, zigzagging would do no good.

Panting, sprinting in a burst of frantic speed, tasting blood in her mouth....

I'm going to die.

The monster crashed through the forest behind her, growling and hissing. Erin locked her gaze on the faraway line of trees and ran hard. The *Varanus priscus* reached the clearing. She knew because its footsteps pounded on flat earth, with no scattering of leaf litter, no splintering of branches. Could she smell its fetid breath? Erin's scalp crept, anticipating the bite. Chomped or swallowed alive....

No, fuck that.

She would shoot herself.

The rifles jounced against her with every step. She snatched up the Remington, cocked it. Leaping over ferns, a fleeting memory of Russ Walker-Smith zipped through her mind: last year's Christmas party; his indulgent smile upon opening a bottle of Cabernet Sauvignon, his dimples, cleft chin. Goodbye Russ. She thought of the lectern in LT5, its smooth wooden edges, the nick that her right thumbnail always found as she addressed her students. Those keen, young faces.... Their exams coming up next week.... And her books; oh God, her books, and her unfinished paper.... Did she believe in heaven? In any afterlife? She didn't know.

She lifted the Remington.

But instead of putting the barrel to her chin, on impulse, she hoisted it over her shoulder and shot backwards without looking. The explosion burst her eardrum in a sharp and sudden pain. Even so, she heard the tread behind her falter. *I hit it.* Trotting now, floundering, she reloaded and fired again over the same shoulder. A ringing tinnitus started up in her head. Hit or miss? Deafened, she couldn't tell. Why was the lizard pursuing her? Why? She couldn't think of an answer.

The line of trees engulfed her.

The forest was thicker here on the other side of the clearing; the trees and shrubs packed tight and close, side by side, the leaves greener and more abundant. Twigs slashed at her on every step. The density of the vegetation would slow the *Varanus priscus*, perhaps bar its entry altogether. Could she hear its pursuit? No, she couldn't hear anything. Her ears still rang with a loud, high-pitched and muffled buzz.

The ground sloped away without warning.

Erin fell, jarring both hands into the dirt. The splint between her broken fingers snapped, and the bones grated against each other. The hurt galvanised her. She struggled upright. Mud plastered her trousers. One of the rifles had slid off her shoulder. She yanked at its strap as she regained her footing. Where was the monster? She didn't know. Her ears were ringing. She ran on, downhill, slipping and sliding, grabbing onto branches as she stumbled to prevent another fall. The steep angle of the terrain threatened to topple her again. She turned her head, couldn't see the monster. Was she safe? Had it given up the chase?

The ground beneath her disappeared altogether.

She dropped through the air. Leafy switches cut across her face. Her knee hit something sharp and blazed in agony. A shock of cold water took her breath and closed over her head. It took a moment to figure out what had happened.

She must have fallen into a river.

The current tumbled her along. The weight of the equipment held her under. A rifle tore away. Erin's feet scrabbled for purchase on the riverbed and found stones. With a mighty push, she managed to clear her face from the water. She took a deep, gasping breath, lost her footing again, and went under. Grabbing the strap of one ammunition bag, she pulled it over her head and let it go. She bobbed higher in the water. Kicking at the riverbed, she broke the surface again. Now she could float a little. She rolled onto her back and looked about. The river was wide, brown and fast-flowing. Debris swirled around her. Along the bank, there was no sign of the *Varanus priscus*.

No sign at all.

The monster just wasn't there.

Unbelievable, Erin thought in dazed wonder.

I survived.

Had she really outrun it? Yes, but more than that; she had *outsmarted* it.

And the monster would never find her now. In all likelihood, it had been thwarted by the densely packed forest, unable to force its way through. Or, even better, it was dead. That second shot from the Remington could have hit the bitch right between the eyes. Erin sobbed out a laugh.

The current powered her along. Fatigued, she went limp, trying to catch her breath and slow her hammering heart. It felt good to wash the grit from her face.

Oh no, *shit*, the submerged camcorder.

Was it ruined? With a cry of dismay, she lifted it by its strap from the water. But to what end? Defeated, she let it go again. The camcorder plunked with a forlorn little splash. But all wasn't lost. Computer specialists might be able to salvage the footage. It could be as simple as wetting the discs and drives with methylated spirits and allowing them to dry out. She'd read somewhere that using a solvent could evaporate all traces of—

Erin's head glanced off something in the water, something hard that exploded a brief dazzle of stars in her vision and ripped out a clump of hair. Christ, a big embedded rock. There would be more of them. Alarmed, she fought the current to turn onto her belly, to face forward. If she could spot the rocks in time, she might be able to avoid them. But she was unable to flip over. The combined weight of the backpack, ammunition bag and rifles made it impossible. She struggled to put her feet on the riverbed. Her boots slipped through silty mud. Another boulder flashed by her. She had to somehow turn over or else risk getting her skull bashed in. She couldn't ditch the rifles and ammunition. And not the backpack either, not with the treasured *Varanus priscus* eggs inside. Frustrated, Erin screamed through gritted teeth. Why couldn't she catch an even break? This was Dad's doing. Somehow, her bad luck must be his fault, his revenge, his hatred from beyond the grave.... *You'll never be better than me....*

And then she saw it.

Her bowels gave a lurch.

In the distance, the monster's giant snout had emerged from the trees.

Taking a gulp of air, Erin ducked, keeping only her eyes above water.

Would the *Varanus priscus* spot her? Probably not.... Erin's wet brown hair must be camouflaged by the colour and turbulence of the water, by the multitudes of twigs and eddying leaves. And she was travelling so fast in the current. She'd hold her breath for a while longer; wait to be carried out of visual range or around a bend. Her elbow hit a rock. Pain made her involuntarily suck a breath. The river crammed into her mouth, choking her. She came up for air, spluttering and coughing. But the monster wouldn't hear. The tumultuous drub of the river would make sure of that. The *Varanus priscus* dwindled farther into the distance as the river bore Erin away at speed. The monster, its snout peaking from the trees, was nearly gone from sight. Against the bright blue of the sky, almost in silhouette, the monster raised its head. Its delicate tongue spooled out and worked the air.

A fresh wave of terror surged through Erin's veins.

The *Varanus priscus* would smell her.

All varanid lizards are good swimmers.

Erin snatched a breath and pulled her head completely underwater.

Her foot snagged on the riverbed. She kicked away just in time. Thank God, she didn't lose a boot. She opened her eyes. The murky water had a visibility of about one metre. A shoal of tiny fish darted past. Her eyes began to sting. One of her burdens, the ammunition bag, grazed past a rock. Her scalp tightened in terrible anticipation. Sooner or later, her skull would dash against a boulder. It was only a matter of time. She put her arm behind her head in an attempt to protect herself. She needed to surface, to turn over. What was the *Varanus priscus* doing? Erin couldn't risk a peek. Oh, she'd been underwater for so long.

Her heart pounded. Her lungs ached.

Hold on, she had to keep holding on....

Ten more seconds passed, fifteen....

No, she had to come up for air.

Gently, she allowed her face to break the surface. She drew in long breaths. Her eyes darted about. Where was the *Varanus priscus*? Not seeing it felt worse than seeing it. She kept scanning the riverbank. The river must have swept her well out of sight by now. She was safe. It was gone. The monster was gone.

And yet....

Her gut told her different.

She took a deep breath and lowered her head until just her eyes were showing. A tingle of adrenaline started up in her limbs. Trees and shrubs flashed by on the banks, standing shoulder-to-shoulder. The *Varanus priscus* couldn't possibly push its way through such dense vegetation. Yes, the lizard was terrifically strong, but not strong enough to knock over scores of fully-grown eucalypts and paperbarks. The *Varanus priscus* was not tracking her progress. She was safe. Why couldn't she believe it? The feeling of dread was probably a hangover from the chase. Relax, she told herself, again and again, even as her guts churned. Relax. Come on now, she had to focus on turning over. She had to face forward before she smashed her skull. If she gathered the rifles and ammunition bag into her arms, the combined weight would counteract the backpack, and allow her to flip onto her front.

Plunging her face underwater, she opened her eyes to see which two out of the three rifles remained. She had the Remington and an SKK. Bad luck—two SKKs would have been the better deal. She lifted her face clear. Groping underwater, she clutched both barrels in one hand, and hauled the ammunition bag to her chest with the other arm. The current fought against her.

A realisation occurred: her mobile phone was completely wet and dead.

Shit.

Forget ever obtaining a signal and calling for help. She would have to hike her way to the fire-trail—if she even could find it. And in a skittering of panic, she let go of the rifle barrels and frantically clutched for the compass that should be hanging around her neck. Oh, dear God, thank you, it was still there, safe on its necklace. She gripped it in her fist. This small deliverance evoked a pricking of tears. All was not lost. She would turn over, travel face-first in this river for a time, negotiating the rocks, and then climb out and start hiking to town. She let go of the compass pendant and gathered the rifles to her chest once more.

Something in the water caught her attention.

No, it couldn't be true.

The *Varanus priscus* was in the river, a few hundred metres away and closing.

Moving faster than the current, streaking past the bobbing detritus, the colossal head lifted clear of the water, the tail lashing from side to side. Like most lizards, including the Komodo dragon, it would be pressing its limbs flat alongside its body—a living, streamlined torpedo. Its tongue stabbed at the air. The delicate forks quivered.

The *Varanus priscus* had found her, was gaining on her.

In half a minute, it would catch her.

22

Erin took a breath and ducked under. Thrashing her feet, she kicked against the river's stony bed, rolled, and let the weight of the rifles and ammunition bag turn her onto her stomach. She let go. The rifles and bag trailed along beneath her. Outstretching her arms, squinting through the cloudy water, she prayed for a boulder.

And found one.

It was big, half a metre to her left. Erin lunged. She caught the boulder with her injured hand. She clenched her teeth against the pain. The current threatened to tear her away. With strength borne from desperation, she managed to lock both arms around the boulder and hold on tight. The boulder grated, coarse and grainy, against her cheek. Now she had to wait and watch. God, she needed to breathe. But she had to stay down. If she came up for air, the lizard would smell her.

Little silvery fish cruised along in the current. Suddenly, dozens shot forward in a great spurt, swimming and scattering at top speed. Erin braced herself.

The lizard came into view.

So close that the scales shone bright and clear through the water, so close that Erin could have reached out and touched its glittering flank. The lizard glided past in seconds, front and back feet flat against the body, hips swinging. Despite her horror, Erin felt an awestruck, thrilled admiration. Then the undulating tail caused a tidal surge that almost dislodged her from her hiding spot. She clutched at the boulder. With a whip of its tail, the *Varanus priscus* was gone, lost from sight in the murky brown water.

Erin waited, waited, her lungs convulsing. When black dots swirled in her vision, she tipped back her head and lifted just her face to the surface. Panting, puffing, she filled her lungs and ducked under again.

What should she do?

She had to figure a plan.

But that depended on the *Varanus priscus*. Lizard tongues can pick up scent molecules in water as well as in air. But it had been holding its head out of the river, thank Christ; it wouldn't smell her no matter how fast it worked its tongue. So how would the lizard react now that it couldn't detect her? Would it keep swimming? Dunk its head and try "tasting" the water? Double back along the river or the riverbank? Abandon the chase altogether? Erin had no way of guessing. This lizard behaved like no other.

She stole another breath.

One thing was certain: she couldn't cling like a barnacle to this rock forever. Her best option was to climb out—onto the other bank, not the bank from which she had fallen—then head into the forest and run upriver. She had to get some distance between herself and the *Varanus priscus*. At least falling into water had done her a favour. The unscheduled wash had likely flushed away the odour chemicals in her clothes, namely apocrine gland secretions, skin bacteria and sebaceous oils. She would be more difficult to smell. And if the wind was blowing at her back, well, the lizard might not smell her at all.

She took another breath, ducked under, psyched herself to swim toward the opposite bank, and froze. Terror crept out from somewhere in her guts and spread in a hot, jangly flush throughout her body. She tightened her grip on the boulder.

I can't do it.

She bobbed her head above water, gasping, and looked downriver. No sign of the *Varanus priscus*. She plunged back under. Get out, she told herself. Let go of this goddamned boulder and swim to the bank. Yet the idea of it made her tremble.

The monster would smell her and turn around.

Her throat ached with the need to cry.

No, she had to push those feelings down. She had to be determined, strong....

You'll never be better than me.... Dad holding out a snake by its head...it's a Stephen's banded snake; she recognises the colourations. He laughs. *I bet you're scared stiff, right? No, I'm not. But if it bites you, it'll kill you. No, it won't, Dad, its venom isn't strong enough.* His face darkening, he thrusts the snake's head with its twisting, open mouth at her, as if wishing to sink its dripping fangs into her face. And Erin, a stubborn and defiant little girl, refuses to flinch, will not flinch....

Erin released her grip on the boulder. The current pushed her along a little way. She half-walked and half-swam to the bank. The earth was soft and crumbly. Lunging, she gripped at exposed tree roots. Hand over hand, she hauled herself out, wincing; goddamn these broken fingers. She felt heavy, sodden. The straps of the ammunition bag and rifles cut into her flesh. Muscles quivering, she dropped her head for a moment, panting. Then with a final push, she was on solid ground again.

And running.

The compass pendant danced on its chain. She didn't bother to check her direction. The fire-trail was northwest, yes, but for now, she simply had to get as far away from the *Varanus priscus* as possible. The river started to bend. And then it kept on bending. Soon, Erin would be running the circumference of a circle. Where the hell would she end up? Oh, she was lost, hopelessly lost in this forest of mirrors, but running was all that mattered, all she had left.

The heat of the afternoon sun began to steam her wet clothes. The raw, aching tendons of her thighs and calves slowed her pace. Both feet felt mashed as if pounded by mallets. The rifles smacked against her with every step.

Oh Jesus, the rifles.

Would they still work after being submerged in the river?

She stopped, her heart in her throat, and reloaded the Remington, swapped out the magazine in the SKK for a fresh one, and inspected the handgun. All firearms waterlogged, flecked with grit and mud, inside and out. Dear God, would they work or not? The only way to tell would be to shoot. But she was certain the

Varanus priscus, that intelligent bitch, would recognise the sound and double back to continue the chase. Another possible outcome, just as awful: what if test-firing proved the rifles and handgun to be inoperable? Erin would be defenceless. But no, wait, the knives, the hammer...oh, come on, what use would they be? She had to keep running.

She pushed herself harder.

Air grated in and out of her dry throat.

Hurry up and run, run, run....

The thick vegetation forced her to stay close to the bank. Every now and then, she glanced back at the river, expecting to see the *Varanus priscus* powering through its waters. She was too tired anymore to lift her arms and deflect passing twigs. Leafy switches whipped by. Her face soon felt crosshatched with hundreds of tiny cuts. On, and on, faster, try to go faster.... But she was stumbling now, almost shambling. She ought to stop for water. If she wasn't careful, dehydration would fog her brain. Okay, she would stop...but not just yet.

The riverbank became loose and sandy, forcing her into the forest. A kangaroo bounded away. Cockatoos screeched from their hidden places in the trees and took flight. Thank Christ; some of Erin's hearing must have returned. Come to think of it, the high-pitched buzzing had almost disappeared. She swiped at the lenses of her fogged, muddy spectacles. The cracks in the right-hand lens weren't too bad; she could still see well enough. Sunlight flashed in patches through the canopy. She was getting sunburned. When had she lost her Legionnaire hat? She couldn't remember.

After a long time, staggering now, she had to stop for a drink. Luckily, the water bottles were sealed and not polluted from the river. The *Varanus priscus* eggs appeared unharmed. She patted them before zipping the backpack closed. Leaning on a tree, allowing the trunk to support her weight, Erin gulped at the bottle until it was empty.

At first, she mistook the faraway rasping sound for the screech of a cockatoo.

Then she dropped the bottle and sprinted.

Madly, wildly, sobbing with each breath. Branches clawed at her and ripped out strands of hair. The ground was treacherously uneven. She had to focus on each step to prevent twisting an ankle. The rasping growl sounded louder. How had the *Varanus priscus* found her? And why in God's name was it still chasing her? What kind of fucking lizard had a brain sophisticated enough to want revenge? Maybe it sensed its eggs. Could it smell the eggs she had stolen?

Erin had to cut deeper into the forest. The closely packed trees and bushes would slow the monster. How near was it? As she ran, the vegetation thinned. The ground became more rugged and gravelly. Oh no, this was bad. An alarm went off in the back of her mind. What had Megan said about hiking to town? That they shouldn't go east because of a gorge.... *Trust me; you don't want to hike near that. The ground is so rocky it'd take us twice as long to get home.*

Erin grabbed the compass pendant.

She was headed east, straight toward the gorge.

The Komodo dragon was well-suited for travel over every terrain, from beaches to tropical forests to mountain ridges. Presumably, *Varanus priscus* would be just as adaptable. The rocky ground near a gorge would present no problem. Despite its massive size, the *Varanus priscus* would scamper amongst the crags as nimbly as a skink. She thought back to the monster's first appearance above the escarpment, how Noel and the Robinsons had rushed over with rifles only a minute later and found no trace of the beast. It had already flashed away over the rocks.

I'm going to die.

No, she could devise an escape plan. What if she found a ditch and buried herself under dirt? But the ground felt as hard as concrete beneath her boots. She blundered over a half-buried stone and fell against a tree. Her nose started bleeding again. Her ragged breath ripped in and out of her throat. Behind her, the startled calls and peeps of frightened birds taking flight made her heart thrum against her ribs. What if she found a pile of dung and smothered herself in it? Large varanid lizards, including the Komodo, typically shy away from excrement. But where would she find a goddamned pile of dung? She heard the distant sound of splintering branches. The Komodo dragon was an ambush hunter, yes, but it would charge, heedless of any noise it might make, once it felt sure of the kill. Therefore, the *Varanus priscus* must feel sure. A thin wail moaned out of her.

She kept running as fast as she could. The vegetation became sparser. The *Varanus priscus* would charge straight through. Guttural hissing raised the hair on her neck. Erin was amongst a dog pack before the danger even registered.

Her steps faltered. She looked about.

The dogs were a shabby bunch of mongrels, thin and muscled, numbering 20 or more: red-coated, black, black and white, kelpie-mixes. They tensed and stared at her for a moment, sizing her up, and closed in, snarling, noses and flews pulled back to show their fangs. *Are you kidding me?* Enough, by Christ...she'd had enough.

Furious, she grabbed the SKK.

The rifle barrel tried to rear up, but she held it tight to her shoulder and swung it in a half-circle in front of her. Oh yes, she'd caught a break at last, a break that actually counted—the SKK worked, it really worked, despite the water and mud. Dogs flipped and yelped and spurted blood in geysers. Some fled. She shot just enough to make a clear passage ahead and then she ran on, ears ringing.

Pain lanced her hamstring. She tottered, almost lost her footing under the weight of a dog that pulled at her, its teeth in her trouser leg, tearing at her skin. The dog wrenched and shook her onto one knee. The SKK was too long to manoeuvre. If the other dogs regrouped, they would pull her down and start eating her alive—until the *Varanus priscus* came along to finish the job.

Spurred, she grabbed the hammer from her belt and smashed its claws into the dog's skull. Fatally wounded, the dog fell away. Erin got to her feet. The bite-wound sent pain down the length of her left leg. Shuffling sideways to keep one eye on the terrain ahead, she prepared to shoot any dogs if they followed, would use only one cartridge at a time to conserve ammunition. As it turned out, there was no need.

The dogs startled and turned. Something else had their attention. They barked in earnest. Erin understood.

The *Varanus priscus* charged into the fray, its snout a mess of tattered bullet holes and gory tissue, its mouth open and drooling with slag. The dogs attacked as a group, out of fear or aggression, Erin had no way of telling. The lizard picked up a dog and chomped it in half. The corpse fell to the ground in pieces, spraying blood and dropping loops of intestines.

This seemed to incense the remaining dogs.

Fast and agile, they bit at the lizard and kept darting away. They barked constantly, loudly. The *Varanus priscus* lumbered about, slow to react, as if confused by the pandemonium. Then its scissoring jaws snapped up another dog. Erin unloaded the SKK, aiming for the lizard's eyes. Fresh bullet holes erupted. The lizard shook its head as if sneezing. When the rifle clicked empty, Erin ran. The fight raged behind her in barks and roars. The dogs didn't stand a chance.

And neither did Erin.

Yet because of the dogs, she had a few precious moments of grace. Now what? She looked about, saw only trees. The answer came to her.

She had to climb.

Juvenile Komodo dragons could climb trees, but adults were too heavy. In the pursuit of prey that had scaled a tree, an adult Komodo could only walk its front feet up the trunk as far as it could reach, while its back legs and tail remained on the ground. This *Varanus priscus* would be no different. She had been wrong on several counts, but this was a matter of physics. Erin made a quick calculation: if the beast was 10 metres, with its tail making up about half that length, Erin would need to climb an absolute bare minimum of four metres, taking into account the angle of the lizard's body as it leaned against the tree.

Four metres: about two and a half times her own height.

Erin hadn't climbed a tree since childhood. And the surrounding eucalypts didn't appear to sprout any low branches. She shuffled on. Her injured hamstring made her limp badly. Where the hell was a suitable tree? The fight between the *Varanus priscus* and the dogs continued behind her, but the dogs were yipping and yelping, frightened out of their wits. Soon, the fight would be over.

I'm going to die.

No, here was salvation.

A paperbark, its main trunk split into two separate trunks like a tuning fork, the split close to the ground. The twisted branches led up, up and up, high into a delicate canopy of leaves and spindly bottle-brush flowers growing from the very tips of its branchlets. Erin ran to the tree.

The close-knit boughs allowed easy handholds. She didn't have to look down to place her feet, just kick around until each boot landed. Moths fluttered amongst the layers of brown and grey bark. Above her stretched a complex web of branches and green leaves, white blossoms murmuring with drowsy honeybees, glimpses of sky. It felt as if she were ascending a ladder to heaven. Perhaps that's what she was doing.

God, her hamstring must be bleeding profusely. Damn that dog. The trouser leg felt plastered to her skin. Nothing would draw the monster like the scent of fresh blood. Faster—she had to pick up the pace.

But the straps of the rifles and ammunition bag kept snagging. Mostly, she wrenched herself free. Whenever that didn't work, she stopped and untangled the strap manually. A couple of lorikeets chittered and flew away. The branches were becoming more and more interwoven. The bulky backpack forced her to turn and twist as she climbed. Maybe she ought to shuck it, drop it, but no, the fall would damage the eggs, dislodge and kill the foetuses.

Straining every muscle, lungs burning, Erin pushed on. Flies gathered at the perspiration streaming down her face. There was no time to wave them away. A huntsman spider, as big as her hand, reared out from beneath a flap of bark, showing its fangs. Ordinarily, she would have baulked. Instead, she pulped it with one punch of her fist and kept going. On and on she climbed. The branches started to sway and bend under her weight. Then one of them broke in her hand.

Jesus, no.... She glanced down.

Was she far enough from the ground? Did it look four metres away?

The *Varanus priscus* bolted at the paperbark as if to run straight through it. Erin screamed. Lowering its head, the lizard butted the trunk with great force. The tree jolted. Erin hung on tight. Hissing, the lizard backed up. Erin scanned the canopy. Was there any possible route higher? Her exploratory handholds broke a branch, then another, another.

Oh, this was it. She was stuck, could ascend no further.

23

The lizard butted the tree a second time. The shockwave dislodged Erin's feet. With a cry, she pulled up her legs and thrashed to find new footholds. Boughs creaked beneath her weight. Fear bit like a trapped rat inside her chest. The monster's growl was so low that Erin didn't hear it so much as experience it; a dreadful, rumbling resonance that quivered her heart, lungs and abdominal organs.

She looked down and quailed.

The *Varanus priscus* was gazing up at her.

They locked eyes. The monster's luminous green irises shone as bright as polished apples. Wetly, the tongue whisked in and out. The sub-audible growl sounded once more, blowing out the folds of the lizard's neck. One clawed front foot pressed itself against the trunk, followed by the other. The tree shuddered, its blossoms rattling overhead.

The lizard was coming for her.

Panic jolted Erin into action. Tightening one arm around a branch, she swapped out the empty SKK magazine for a fresh one, and pulled back the rod.

Shoot.

Shoot the goddamned thing.

Erin squeezed the trigger, over and over.

The bullets ripped across the snout. The lizard continued to walk its front feet up the trunk. Then its mouth fell open with the speed of a trap door. The unnatural sight coursed a shiver down Erin's spine. Behind the teeth, the red and wrinkled tissue led to a central dark slit, a black hole of unimaginable horror. Erin blanched. Noel's two thumbs up, his muffled screams against the folds of that throat as the muscles massaged him towards the stomach full of acid.... In an emotional release that tore out a shriek, Erin shot the SKK at the oesophagus. Convulsively, the monster gagged, swallowed and retched.

The SKK clicked empty. Erin fumbled at the full magazines in her jacket pockets. In her haste, she dropped one. It bounced away. Damn it. She checked her pockets and found two loaded magazines. Her heart lurched.

Only two magazines left?

Hastily, she fitted one and drew the bolt.

With a speed that belied its size, the *Varanus priscus* pounded both front feet up the trunk and lunged. It extended its jaws, snatching and ripping at the air. Erin pulled up her legs. Hot, stinking breath fanned over her like steam.

I'm going to die.

Reflexively, she emptied the whole magazine into the monster's skull before realising her folly. Its gigantic bones were dense, the injuries survivable. But bullets into the open mouth...if the beast would just open its mouth again, she could fire into the wall of its nasopharynx and smash into brain tissue. No animal could survive catastrophic brain damage.

"Come on," she whispered, fitting the last magazine. "Come and get me, bitch."

But it was as if the monster understood Erin's intentions.

Quiet now, it leaned against the trunk, breathing gently, as if resigned to waiting. The muscles in its hide smoothed out and relaxed. Some predators, such as lions, sit patiently beneath a tree until the prey gives up from thirst or hunger. Was this the situation here? If so, Erin would push back with bullets, force the lizard to attack. She needed the target of its open mouth. Seconds passed. In the pause, she noticed her ringing, buzzing tinnitus. What had happened to her earmuffs? Lost somewhere in the park, she supposed, like her hat. Lost like her old self, who had driven to town four days ago in a summer dress and sandals, with styled hair, coral lipstick. I've aged a lifetime out here, Erin thought, and took hold of the Remington.

Aiming at the eye of the *Varanus priscus*, she pulled the trigger.

The bullet hole exploded on its brow.

The *Varanus priscus* lifted its ragged, bloodied head.

"That's it, come on," Erin whispered, dangling a leg. "I'm right here."

A sibilant hiss released a raft of stinking breath. Erin aimed for its eye again. The shot punched another hole in its brow. Still, the monster would not attempt a bite.

Damn the bitch.

Erin swapped out the Remington's magazine. The *Varanus priscus* hadn't moved. Or had it? Suspicious now, Erin watched. And, oh yes, the lizard was moving all right, but subtly. It was hunching, tensing, its unblinking gaze never leaving Erin's face. What the hell...? Then its tail began to curl and bunch.

Oh no.

In a rush of awful comprehension, Erin knew what was about to happen. She let go of the Remington and clutched the SKK. Thirty bullets remained. She would have to make them count, every last one. A saltwater crocodile, regardless of size and weight, can thrash its tail in water with enough power to propel its entire body, back feet and all, into the air. The *Varanus priscus* was preparing for the same manoeuvre, but on land. Using the considerable muscle in its tail, it would spring up through the branches and catch hold of Erin's legs. In just a few moments, she would be dead.

It sprang.

Jaws agape, the mouth flew up at her. Erin fired the SKK. The bullets tore through the monster's palate. For a heart-stopping moment, Erin's lower legs were inside the yawning mouth. If the *Varanus priscus* should close its jaws, she would be caught. The lizard snapped too late. Dropping onto its back legs and tail, it roared. Erin had never heard anything so eerie, so harrowing.

Bellowing, rearing its head on its massive neck, the lizard took one front foot off the tree as if preparing to climb down. Instead, it barrelled up through the branches again, the exhalation from its open mouth as hot as a northerly wind. Its teeth grazed her boots. Erin aimed at the soft palate, the nasopharynx beneath. Bullet holes opened up, wet and bloody. The *Varanus priscus* landed on its tail and back legs, gnashing the air.

Oh, for the love of Jesus, why was it still alive?

There could be only one explanation: she was shooting at the wrong place. Her bullets must be hitting too far forward in the snout to damage brain tissue.

The SKK clicked empty.

That was it. No more magazines for the SKK, no time to refill the empties.

Snarling, the monster pushed on its back toes and lurched, its open mouth and throat a wide and red tunnel. Erin screamed in frustration. Then she took the hammer from her belt and flung it into the maw. The lizard swallowed and gagged.

"Why won't you die?" Erin yelled, and hurled in Jamie's knife, the serrated one with the nasty gutting hook on its tip.

The lizard's throat convulsed.

Erin remembered the revolver. Taking it from the holster on her belt, she thumbed off the safety, pulled back the hammer, and fired at the oesophagus until the gun clicked empty a few seconds later. The monster kept lunging, snapping at her with its wide jaws. How? In God's name, how was this lizard still alive?

"Eat these, too, you fucker," she screamed, and threw in the other hunting knife and the walkie-talkie.

This time, the monster seemed to inhale instead of swallow. Its breathing immediately became irregular, laboured. It shook its head, snuffled, retched, and began to walk its front legs down the trunk.

Erin felt a small jag of hope.

Was this the end? Was the lizard about to die?

Inside the ammunition bag were boxes of cartridges for the revolver. The only problem was that each cartridge had to be inserted into the cylinder one at a time. For the love of Christ...one, two, three, four (she dropped one), five (dropped another), and oh, yes, *six*. She clicked the cylinder into place, drew back the hammer, aimed at the monster, and hesitated.

Moving slowly, deliberately, gasping and grumbling all the while and slavering long ropes of bloodied saliva, the *Varanus priscus* adjusted its position. Erin watched in fascinated horror. What the hell was it doing? The tail snaked against the rocky ground and found purchase. The back feet went up on their toes, pressing the claws into the dirt. The front feet moved closer together on the trunk. Muscles bunched along the length of the lizard's body. The paperbark started to creak. Branches shivered. Erin shook her head in disbelief.

That bitch planned to push over the goddamned tree.

The trunk made a cracking sound.

Erin holstered the revolver and cocked the Remington. "Hey," she yelled, and shot the back of the monster's neck. "Hey, look at me."

The *Varanus priscus* hesitated, raised its head and fixed its unblinking stare at her. Its long, slow hiss sounded demonic. The tongue slurped and whipped.

Erin squinted down the Remington's scope.

Found the lime-green collarette of the already damaged, bloodshot eye.

Put the crosshairs of the scope on the centre of that pitch-black pupil.

Breathed calmly in and out—once, twice—to quell the shakes, as Jamie had instructed her so long ago.

And squeezed the trigger.

The eyeball erupted in a shower of gelatinous tissue. The head jerked back. The front feet slid off the trunk. Limp, as if boneless, the lizard fell sideways to the ground and didn't move.

Erin watched and waited.

Could this be a trick?

Komodo dragons never play dead. As Erin knew by now, however, the *Varanus priscus* was a different creature. She had to stay alert. The lizard appeared to be deceased. How could Erin be sure? With the Remington, she sighted the cloaca, the lizard's combined excretory and sex organ, a sensitive area with plenty of nerve endings. Erin squeezed off a shot. The bullet tore into the cloaca. No response. It took a few seconds for Erin to process that information.

She lowered the rifle. Could it be true?

Apparently, yes. The battle was over and she had won.

She had killed the monster.

Sagging, she hung her head and wept. Every pain in her body—too many to count—flared into her awareness. She felt more dead than alive. Scrabbling with the backpack, she took out a bottle of water and drank it dry within a minute. She threw the empty bottle through the branches and managed to hit the lizard with it.

"Hah," she murmured. "Go fuck yourself."

She put her head back and rested. The cawing of crows woke her. Groggy, she looked down. About a dozen crows were already clustering around the lizard, poking their beaks into the bullet holes and pulling out ribbons of flesh through the hide.

Erin lifted the camcorder from around her neck. Wiping off as much grit as she could with her torn fingers, she pressed the button. Nothing; the camcorder was broken. She had no way to document the demise of the *Varanus priscus*.

Oh, wait, yes she did.

Gingerly, wincing with every movement, Erin descended from the paperbark. Her limbs shook uncontrollably. A few times, she thought she might fall. When she reached the ground at last, the crows reacted to her presence, grizzling, flapping away to the other side of the giant corpse. Erin ignored them.

The *Varanus priscus* was an incredible sight.

Excitement pumped a fresh flood of energy around Erin's body. She knelt. Reaching out, she ran both hands across the pebbled, leathery hide of the lizard's back leg and foot. It felt electrifying. The claws were as smooth as she had expected, as sheened as polished marble. She touched a finger to the very tip of one claw, which drew a bead of blood. Impressive. She wiped the blood on her trousers and patted at her pockets for the Swiss Army knife. Instead, she found the whittled figurines that Noel had made: the wooden crocodile and the *Varanus priscus*. She regarded them, her chin starting to tremble.

No, she wouldn't throw the figurines away, as previously planned.

She would keep them on display in her home so that she would always remember what had happened out here; always feel her guilt, her shame and grief. Tears flowed without restraint. She cried for Noel, for Jamie and Megan, for their families. Very quickly, her sobs began to sound hysterical.

No, that wouldn't do.

Breath hitching and hiccupping, Erin fought to regain control. Don't lose it now, she thought, you're not safe yet. If she wanted a mental breakdown, she could damn well have one as soon she reached town. With the dirty sleeve of her jacket, she scrubbed away the tears, snot and blood. She took a breath, held it. *I am in charge of my faculties*. She exhaled slowly.

Her head felt clearer.

Putting the figurines away, she groped through other pockets until she found the Swiss Army knife. She selected the longest blade, stood up and walked the length of the corpse. The crows scattered and complained, then fluttered back down to continue feasting. Erin paid them no mind. She cared only for the *Varanus priscus*.

By Christ, this animal was gargantuan.

And exquisite too, yes, so exquisite....

At her feet lay the miraculous vision.

Harris's dragon.

When she reached the head, she paused to admire the colouration of the remaining eye. If she'd had a working camcorder...well, that couldn't be helped. Squatting, Erin began to cut out the eyeball. The tissue around the orbital bone turned out to be surprisingly soft and easy to slice, but the optical nerve required determined sawing. Finally, she hefted the eyeball in one hand. It felt heavy for its size, like a ripe cantaloupe. A mottling of petechial haemorrhaging had ruined the appearance of the sclera. The collarette, however, still shone a fluorescent and verdant green.

She prised off a handful of osteoderms, solid as stones, from the dorsal hide. Next, requiring persistent work, she severed the outermost toe on a front foot. She packed the trio of souvenirs, these irrefutable items of proof, into her backpack alongside the eggs. When she returned to civilisation, all books on palaeontology would have at least one chapter rewritten. A slim but important subject in reptilian evolutionary biology would be turned upside-down. She itched to take her place in history. Even so, she stayed with the *Harris's dragon* for a long, peaceful time. Dreams don't often come true. She wanted to savour the moment.

The scales of the lizard's belly shone iridescent. She stroked her hands across the soft, cooling hide, and pressed her face against it. How smooth.... Like pearls, she thought, a blanket of polished pearls. Just how much would someone pay for a handbag or wallet made of this silky, prehistoric hide? Ten million dollars? Fifty million? One hundred million? If she had the strength, she would saw out a section. But she didn't have the strength. Just breathing felt too much, almost beyond her physical capacity. The desire to sleep alongside the *Varanus priscus* was overwhelming. Erin forced herself to sit up.

The crows kept feeding. Blowflies twitched around the bullet wounds. Soon, the smell of decay would bring other, more dangerous carrion eaters such as dogs and pigs. For her own safety, Erin needed to leave.

She reloaded her firearms, picked up the dropped SKK magazine, refilled the empty magazines from the ammunition bag, and put them in her pockets. She stood up, using the Remington as a crutch. God, her body ached. Time to go....

Instead, she paused.

She gazed at the *Harris's dragon* with a pricking of fresh tears.

"I'll return to find you," she said. "I'll display your skeleton at the Melbourne Museum. You'll be flown all over the world from one museum to the other. You're going to live forever. And so am I."

She ran her hand along the broad tail from root to tip. The pads of her fingers would never forget the coarse feel of it. With a sigh, she consulted her compass and started trudging northwest. Everything would be fine. She had water, some food. She had ammunition and knew how to shoot. It might take the rest of the day and night, but she would reach the fire-trail, follow it to the main road, and walk back to town. Her heart squeezed. Back to the civilised world....

Time passed. The straps of the backpack bit into her shoulders. Erin smiled. The eggs weighed her down, much like quad foetuses must weigh down a pregnant woman. These are my babies, she thought. I've dragged myself through heaven, earth and hell, and these precious eggs belong to me. Her mind wandered to the terrarium she would have custom-built. The hundreds of tiered seats, the hawker....

Ladies and gentlemen, boys and girls; prepare yourselves for the sight of a....

And then she heard it.

The distant roar echoed around the park and froze her to the spot.

Could it have been an auditory hallucination? With impaired hearing, anything was possible, surely, and she was so fatigued, her nerves stretched to breaking point—

The roar sounded again, choking off her breath like a pair of hands.

No mistake.

That was a *Varanus priscus*.

So, there was another gigantic lizard nearby.

Oh, Jesus....

Upon discovering the nest, she should have realised that the mate couldn't be too far away. Why hadn't she kept this danger in mind? Because everything had happened so fast: the shock of Jamie's half-eaten corpse, Megan's broken remains, the discovery of the nest, the terrifying flight from the mother lizard.... She hadn't had time to think straight.

Dizzy, Erin leaned over, hands on her knees, panting, nauseated.

Another throaty roar sent a jolt of panic through her nervous system.

That was the Big Daddy, she felt sure. The scent of its dead partner had just reached it on the breeze. Erin broke into a run.

Please God, don't let the fire-trail be too far away.

And don't let the lizard smell these stolen eggs.

END

ACKNOWLEDGEMENTS

There is scant information on the actual *Varanus priscus*, so I created my own version of the lizard. However, I wanted it to be as realistic as possible within the novel's fantasy framework. I'm grateful to four experts who offered their time to check my manuscript for technical accuracy.

Tim Bannister advised me on matters relating to firearms and hunting. As the CEO of the Sporting Shooters' Association of Australia, Tim has represented this association at the United Nations, and has acted as a councillor to various governments on firearms policing and customs laws. He has also worked as a photographer, journalist and editor on various newspapers, magazines and books, some of which were about shooting and sustainable, ethical hunting.

The following three herpetologists advised me on aspects of reptilian biology and behaviour, scientific matters, and Dr. Erin Harris's vocation.

Nick Clemann leads the Threatened Fauna Program at the Victorian Government's Arthur Rylah Institute for Environmental Research, and is an honorary researcher with Museum Victoria. His specialty is the conservation management of reptiles and amphibians, and the management of human–snake conflict.

Dustin Welbourne is an evolutionary bio-geographer. Much of his research has focused on reptiles. He has a background in science communication, and has worked in the philosophy of science arena with a focus on ecological and biological philosophy.

Ray Draper is an Environmental Consultant working with Flora and Fauna. He has 40 years' experience as a herpetologist, with part of that time serving as President of the Victorian Herpetologist Society.

Thanks Tim, Nick, Dustin and Ray for your input and suggestions.

Please note: any technical errors with regards to hunting or herpetology are mine.

ABOUT THE AUTHOR

Deborah Sheldon is a professional writer from Melbourne, Australia. Her short fiction has appeared in many well-regarded journals such as Quadrant, Island, Midnight Echo and Aurealis. Her work can also be found in various anthologies.

Her latest releases include the crime-noir novellas, "Dark Waters" and "Ronnie and Rita", and the crime-themed collection, "Mayhem: selected stories". Upcoming titles include the horror collection, "Perfect Little Stitches and other stories", and the contemporary crime novel, "Garland Cove Heist".

Other credits include television scripts such as "Neighbours", magazine feature articles, stage plays, non-fiction books (Reed Books, Random House Australia), and award-winning medical writing.

Visit Deb at http://deborahsheldon.wordpress.com

CHECK OUT OTHER GREAT DINOSAUR THRILLERS

WRITTEN IN STONE
by David Rhodes

Charles Dawson is trapped 100 million years in the past. Trying to survive from day to day in a world of dinosaurs he devises a plan to change his fate. As he begins to write messages in the soft mud of a nearby stream, he can only hope they will be found by someone who can stop his time travel. Professor Ron Fontana and Professor Ray Taggit, scientists with opposing views, each discover the fossilized messages. While attempting to save Charles, Professor Fontana, his daughter Lauren and their friend Danny are forced to join Taggit and his group of mercenaries. Taggit does not intend to rescue Charles Dawson, but to force Dawson to travel back in time to gather samples for Taggit's fame and fortune. As the two groups jump through time they find they must work together to make it back alive as this fast-paced thriller climaxes at the very moment the age of dinosaurs is ending.

HARD TIME
by Alex Laybourne

Rookie officer Peter Malone and his heavily armed team are sent on a deadly mission to extract a dangerous criminal from a classified prison world. A Kruger Correctional facility where only the hardest, most vicious criminals are sent to fend for themselves, never to return.

But when the team come face to face with ancient beasts from a lost world, their mission is changed. The new objective: Survive.

CHECK OUT OTHER GREAT DINOSAUR THRILLERS

SPINOSAURUS
by Hugo Navikov

Brett Russell is a hunter of the rarest game. His targets are cryptids, animals denied by science. But they are well known by those living on the edges of civilization, where monsters attack and devour their animals and children and lay ruin to their shantytowns.

When a shadowy organization sends Brett to the Congo in search of the legendary dinosaur cryptid Kasai Rex, he will face much more than a terrifying monster from the past.

Spinosaurus is a dinosaur thriller packed with intrigue, action and giant prehistoric predators.

LAND OF DEATH
by Eric S Brown & Alex Laybourne

A group of American soldiers, fleeing an organized attack on their base camp in the Middle East, encounter a storm unlike anything they've seen before. When the storm subsides, they wake up to find themselves no longer in the desert and perhaps not even on Earth. The jungle they've been deposited in is a place ruled by prehistoric creatures long extinct. Each day is a struggle to survive as their ammo begins to run low and virtually everything they encounter, in this land they've been hurled into, is a deadly threat.

CHECK OUT OTHER GREAT DINOSAUR THRILLERS

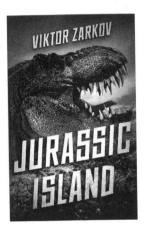

JURASSIC ISLAND
by Viktor Zarkov

Guided by satellite photos and modern technology a ragtag group of survivalists and scientists travel to an uncharted island in the remote South Indian Ocean. Things go to hell in a hurry once the team reaches the island and the massive megalodon that attacked their boats is only the beginning of their desperate fight for survival.

Nothing could have prepared billionaire explorer Joseph Thornton and washed up archaeologist Christopher "Colt" McKinnon for the terrifying prehistoric creatures that wait for them on JURASSIC ISLAND!

K-REX
by L.Z. Hunter

Deep within the Congo jungle, Circuitz Mining employs mercenaries as security for its Coltan mining site. Armed with assault rifles and decades of experience, nothing should go wrong. However, the dangers within the jungle stretch beyond venomous snakes and poisonous spiders. There is more to fear than guerrillas and vicious animals. Undetected, something lurks under the expansive treetop canopy . . .

Something ancient.

Something dangerous.

Kasai Rex!

38403995R00145

Made in the USA
Middletown, DE
17 December 2016